Finding Alice

By Rebecca Carlyle

ISBN: 978-0-578-71384-7

Published in 2020 by Ink and Quill Publications.

Cover design by Chelsea O'Sullivan.
Photo by Aaron Wagoner Photography.

This is a work of fiction. All of the characters, organizations, and events portrayed in this novel are either products of the author's imagination or are used fictitiously.

This book is dedicated to the friends and family who never stopped believing in my ability to finish this novel.

Prologue

The cold air had permeated her bones years ago when she had first woken up on the hard ground. She didn't even feel it anymore. She lay on the floor of her cement prison and thought about her last day of freedom. It was something she thought about often. Why hadn't she caught on sooner? Why hadn't she stayed at the party? Maybe it wouldn't have mattered anyway. Maybe all roads led to this eventually. Everybody dies at some point, so why not here and why not now? Considering how long she'd been here though, she knew she wasn't going to die soon. She needed to find a way to do it herself. There was no way she would let that bastard get off one last time. She didn't want to see the look on His face, the one that told her it was all a game.

She had been over it a million times, even running her hands along the walls; goosebumps flying up her arms as her fingertips felt every groove in the cement that surrounded her. The room was nearly empty. The walls and floor were smooth cement and the metal door let no light inside. She couldn't even see her hand in front of her face. In the corner furthest from the door was a bucket with her own waste that was switched out once a day in the small sliding panel at the base of the metal door. Food was slid in through the sliding door on a plastic cafeteria platter. This platter never contained utensils—only food that she could eat by hand. A thin, basic mattress lay pushed up against a wall without a box spring to hold it up. There weren't even sheets on the mattress or any light fixtures. The room only had one entrance and exit, which meant that escape was essentially impossible.

Frustrated, she smashed both her fists on the ground and shrieked from the pain. At least it was better than feeling numb. She cradled her hands in her lap and rocked back and forth, loving the sensation of her blood pumping through her veins. She craved more. She wanted to feel things that she knew she would never get to. She wanted to feel the sun warming her skin as she lay on the beach and read her school books, to smell the salty ocean air and feel the sand between her toes. She missed the wind on her face as she ran on the soccer field in practice. She wanted to be short of breath from hiking with her little brother through the back roads, kicking up dust from the gravel. She wanted much more than that; she wanted to be free.

2017, Day 1

The moon barely lit up the street; the clouds obscured too much coverage. The neighborhood was quiet except for the pack of high school boys ahead of her, probably heading to the same house as she was. The boys glanced back at her every now and then and a burst of laughter would erupt from the small group.

Melissa tried to ignore them, but this wasn't something she was used to doing. She didn't get out much. Even though it was a Saturday night and perfectly acceptable, her Ma had been surprised when she had asked to go out tonight. Melissa didn't have many friends, she usually just stayed home with her younger brother. It had been a last-minute decision to go to this party even though it was all anybody could talk about at school. She would have rather stayed curled up reading in her refurbished armchair with Danny reading his comic books on her bed. Instead, she found herself dressed up and walking to the party that the rest of the girls from her cheer squad were going to tonight.

The cold evening air enveloped her bare shoulders as a result of forgetting to grab a jacket in her rush to get out of the house. She shivered aggressively and sped up her pace. The boys up ahead turned around the corner and she was alone on the dim street, only she didn't feel alone. She whipped around, looking for someone, anyone, to explain this feeling and the goosebumps on her neck. No one was there. She turned the same corner as the boys had and she watched them approach a pale blue house with black trim. They didn't knock, they just let themselves in and immediately started talking with whoever was on the other side of the door. The door shut and there was silence again, the party was nothing more than a murmur. Could she just walk up and let herself in as well? Was that allowed? Her footsteps echoed, bouncing off the parked cars and reverberating back to her as she drew closer. She could feel herself slowing down with hesitation with each cookie-cutter house she passed. She always wished to live in this neighborhood. All the houses were well maintained, the lawns were freshly trimmed and the front walkways were lined with colorful flowers.

Tonight was different; she didn't want to be there. She didn't even like most of these people and she knew that they didn't like her. She turned to walk away and retrace her steps back home, but couldn't get her feet to move. She couldn't get herself to move at all. Something inside her head told her she couldn't go back. Fear pulsed through her veins for a moment as the rational part of her brain tried to tell her that she was being silly. She merely stood in the middle of the sidewalk, facing away from the house, staring at what she knew was the BMW of a boy in her homeroom and chewing her lip as she tried to make a decision. This clearly wasn't going to be a group of people she talked with regularly. She wouldn't have fun, but would the look on Kate's face be worth it? Maybe. It would be satisfying, even if it was only for a moment. When was the last time she had done something for herself?

She rubbed vigorously at the raised hairs on her arms and looked around again. It still felt like someone was out there, watching her. She couldn't tell if her goosebumps were from the cold or the fear. She nervously turned back to the house and forced herself to walk towards it. If anything she needed to get away from this feeling of being watched. At the door, she froze for a second, then grasped the doorknob with a surge of urgency and pushed inside the house, past the surprised faces that stared at her as she made her way into the crowd. The confused looks directed at her mingled with her own doubts. She hadn't been invited here tonight and there was still time to turn around and leave. If she left now though nothing would change.

There were so many bodies cramming the hallway, she felt immediately hot and suppressed. She didn't like having to squeeze through, her body rubbing against others. She was out of place here. Feelings of cowardice and disappointment would follow her around and haunt her if she left. With that in mind, she scanned the faces for the one she wanted. Almost immediately someone latched onto her arm and drew her attention away from her search.

"What are you doing here?"

"Hey, Cameron."

"Seriously. Kate isn't gonna like that you're here."

"I know."

His brilliant blue eyes bore into her own. "What are you wearing?"

"If you're asking, then I think you know." She glanced down at her outfit and forced herself to stop fidgeting with the hem of the black vest.

"Are you trying to start a fight?"

She thought about it for a minute. "Yeah, maybe I am."

She set her jaw defiantly, yanked her arm from his grasp, and stalked away from him before he could say anything more to change her mind. This was a mistake. She shouldn't have come. Before she knew it she was in the kitchen and there was Kate, with the ever-present Mia at her side. It took a moment for Kate to understand what she was seeing as her eyes swept Melissa up and down, taking in the outfit. First confusion, then fury twisted her pretty features. Melissa couldn't help it, she smiled at the reaction. Then Kate started to yell and curse.

"You fucking freak! What the hell do you think you're doing?" Kate screamed as Mia tried pulling her backward out of the room, frantically telling her to calm down.

Melissa just stood and soaked in the pleasure that was flooding her. Time seemed to slow down so she could savor it. She took in the expressions of shock on whispering groups nearby, she vaguely recognized them from school. She watched as a girl in a letterman's jacket slipped on the spilled beer cup on the floor where Kate had dropped it. The music blasting so loud that she couldn't hear the shriek as she went down. It was Lauren; she was on the cheer squad. Melissa tried not to laugh. And then time caught up with her again. She was being jostled around by people pushing past her to get the fridge. Others took baby steps away from her, trying to remain unassociated. Then Cameron was grabbing her arm again.

"You should leave. Before she comes back."

"I know. I just…want to relish this feeling for a moment."

He smirked, "A small victory for sure."

"I think I want a celebratory beer." She surprised herself with her own words.

"Have you ever had one?"

"No. But I want to try one."

He laughed, "Here, just finish mine. I'll grab a new one for myself."

A half-empty cup was thrust into her hands and he was off to get himself a new one. She watched as he got a clean cup and used the keg to fill it up. He knew what he was doing, he wasn't new to this like she was. He came back to her, which she wasn't quite expecting, but it was nice to not feel so alone. She wanted to share her victory with someone. She was frighteningly aware of how close

he was standing. She took a sip to distract herself. It was

warm and sour on her tongue. Once she had managed to

swallow, it felt like someone had drawn inside her throat

with chalk.

"Oh god. People drink this?"

He chuckled. "I promise it gets better."

She didn't believe him, but she took another sip and

tried not to make a face this time.

"Let's get you into a different room. We don't want

her coming back and starting a fight. You were lucky Mia

was around."

She obliged and let him lead her into a crowded

game room. A pool table in the middle of the room had a

few girls in tight jeans leaning on it while a few guys she

recognized from the basketball team tried to play. A

dartboard on the opposing wall had a guy with saggy pants

and red-rimmed eyes aiming for it. A bookshelf in the

corner contained board games and cards. This was where

the hub of noise was coming from. A circle of people she

knew and had never spoken a word to sat on the white

carpet playing some sort of drinking version of Jenga.

Everyone here was laughing at something that had just happened.

Cameron took her to sit on the grey leather couch nearby that faced the group and watched the game progress for a while. Eventually, her cup was drained and she wasn't quite sure how she managed to finish the warm, light brown liquid. She didn't know why she was smiling, she just was. Her cheeks felt tingly and she was positive they were pink. She laughed with the others at jokes and relaxed into the couch, her jeans sliding easily on the leather. Cameron had his arm around her and she was snuggled into the crook of his arm where he had pulled her down. She had never been this close to a boy. His body heat warmed her petite frame and she found herself enjoying this more than she thought she would. He glanced down at her cup.

"You're empty. Do you want another?"

She just looked up at him and blinked. No, she didn't want another. She knew what she wanted, and it wasn't another drink. She started to move closer and lifted her chin.

"Shots!" someone from the doorway yelled.

Everyone swiveled their heads to see. Brandon held up a bottle of tequila. He sat himself down in the circle and started passing it around with the small stash of plastic shot glasses he produced from the pockets of his blue hoodie that proudly proclaimed "Seahawks" across the chest.

"Have you ever had a shot?" asked Cameron.

"Nope."

"You want to try one?"

"Why the hell not?" Who was she tonight?

He laughed and poured two shots for them when the bottle reached them up on the couch. She held the small cup in hand and examined it. It was bright pink and had "#GirlsNight" in white letters wrapping around it. She glanced at Cameron's. His was neon purple, with something just as stupid and girly written on it. They waited until everyone in the circle had a glass of their own. Brandon held his glass up, flipping his auburn bangs out of his face. Everyone else mimicked him, holding up their tiny cups, Melissa's own arm was slow to follow.

"To…" He paused theatrically and winked at the girl next to him, "good times." He threw the shot back in one fluid movement.

She looked around and watched everyone else do it before copying them. She spluttered and forced herself to swallow it. It burned all the way down her throat. She coughed once it was all down and she was sure it wouldn't come back out. She looked at the empty pink glass she held between her thumb, middle finger, and ring finger and cringed. Cameron tried and failed to hold back his laughter.

"You alright there?"

"I think so. That was disgusting. Why does it burn like that?"

He squeezed her shoulders closer to him with the arm that was wrapped around her. She let her head fall back to rest on his bicep so that she could look up at him. She immediately forgot about the taste in her mouth and enjoyed the tingling sensation that trickled down her throat and warmed her belly.

"I should go home…" she trailed off.

"But?"

"I'm cozy here." She grinned at him and snuggled closer. He squeezed her shoulder with the hand that rested there in what she hoped was an affectionate way.

Tonight was turning out better than she thought it would. Kate was mad, so that was an accomplishment. Melissa's cheeks were flushed pink and now she really couldn't stop smiling. She glanced around the room, her eyes lingering on the faces of everyone in the circle. There was a girl with adorable freckles and light red hair who was perched with her back leaning against the couch. Melissa had never heard her laugh before. There was Elliot who sat across the circle from her next to Brandon. Elliot was another basketball player that she had never spoken to. He looked at ease leaning back on one hand and waving his other hand in the air to emphasize a story he was telling. Melissa had always wanted to know what it would be like to be apart of this social group. This would be a moment to remember.

She let her head fall to the side, so her cheek was on Cameron's shoulder. She was inching her face closer to his, thinking that she was being subtle. A few people in the circle were looking at her a little weird.

Brandon leaned to his right and whispered to Elliot, "That's not Kate is it?"

Elliot shook his head. "Nah. Pretty sure that's Melissa."

"Seriously? Since when does she ever come out?"

Melissa pushed herself up from the couch and out of Cameron's arms. It was time for her to take her leave. She checked her phone for the time. An hour and a half had somehow slipped by. Instantly Danny was on her mind and her forehead creased with worry. Cameron followed her to the front door.

"Are you okay to walk by yourself? It's dark out." He looked genuinely concerned.

She felt a little wobbly so she leaned her back against the wall next to the door. "Yeah… I think I'm okay. It's not that far of a walk."

He slipped a hand into the curve of her spine and pulled her close, he supported some of her weight so she wouldn't lose her balance. He put his other hand on the back of her head and held it to his chest. She listened to the rhythm of his breathing with her eyes closed. This was beginning to be a lot for her to take in. Her eyes roamed around the room, trying to get her brain to stop running at a hundred miles an hour. There was a small table pushed against one wall that had framed family photos and a dish where people were stashing their car keys. Between the door and the table was a pile of shoes and purses. Melissa's gaze fell on a familiar purse and black leather jacket that was placed carefully beside the pile. Of course Kate was too special to toss her own things in with everyone else's. She pushed away from Cameron and picked up the jacket, examining it.

"That's Kate's jacket."

"Yeah, I know." She tried it on. Of course they were the same size.

"You should really take that off."

She raised an eyebrow at him. "And why's that? Her parents are rich. They'll just buy her a new one tomorrow."

He didn't say anything. She zipped it up and then looked at him. He looked uncomfortable, shifting weight anxiously. Maybe she was taking this a step too far, but she couldn't stop herself. She was a different girl tonight and she was enjoying it. She wrapped a hand around his neck, curling a few fingers into his sand-colored hair, and pulled his face down so that she could kiss him. Her nose brushed against his as their lips met. She didn't know what she was doing, but instinct seemed to take over. He tasted like the beer she had drunk earlier. Reluctantly, Melissa pulled away. He looked as dazed as she felt. Then she took off without a word, out into the street with her new jacket, knowing that tomorrow everything would go back to normal. But hopefully not.

2017, Day 3

Emily Anderson pulled into the last parking space in the small lot. The dark clouds were dumping everything they held. She shivered with goosebumps racing up and down her arms. The file on her passenger seat mocked her. *You can't solve me.* It was probably true, but she just couldn't let go of her compulsion to keep trying. She picked up the file and held it underneath her black, ratty sweatshirt so it wouldn't get waterlogged. She opened the car door and was at once assaulted by the sideways rain and by the wind that tried to rip her coat off her shoulders. She struggled to make a dash to the front entrance of her nightly addiction. The bell above the door clanged as she opened it, announcing her arrival to the meager amount of patrons that were scattered throughout the room. No one looked in her direction and not a single conversation paused. This was where people went when they wanted to have private conversations or when they wanted to be left alone. Everyone who spent time here regularly respected this and never drew attention to anyone else who was seated here.

"Hello there, suga," called Beatrice. "Your booth in the back is open. Coffee, dearie?"

Anderson took her coat off and hung it up on the rack by the front door to dry. "Yes please, Bea," she called back before clomping in her galoshes to the farthest of the vinyl booths from the front door. No one looked at her as she passed by. She took a hard right at the end of the aisle and slid into the sheltered alcove that had walls on each side with only a small opening to slip in by. She was completely sheltered here, tucked away from the rest of the world and affording her the privacy she desperately sought. The familiar posters shined at her from behind their clear laminations. John Wayne, Marilyn Monroe, and Frankie Avalon were her nightly companions.

Anderson could hear the old floorboards creaking from Bea's footsteps before the cup of hot coffee was placed on the table in front of her. It was nice to know that no one would ever be able to sneak up on her here. Bea pulled out her notepad from the pocket of her red and white checkered apron although she knew she wouldn't need it.

"Your usual, suga?" she asked, smacking her gum loudly, attracting attention to the neon pink lipstick that was painted onto her face.

If it had been anyone else Anderson would have found this habit annoying but instead, it was satisfyingly familiar. She leaned over the menu for a moment, flipping through the five pages restlessly.

"I'll have the two bacon, two eggs, and hash browns."

"Sounds delish. Scrambled, hun?"

Anderson nodded as she tucked the menu behind the ketchup and mustard holder next to the wall.

"Be out in a dash," Bea winked her huge, overly painted lashes at Anderson and sauntered off with a swagger in her hips.

Anderson thumbed through all the colorful sugar packets before settling on Splenda like she always did. She swirled the sugar and half-n-half into the coffee, feeling the steam warming her face and bringing pink to her cheeks. Her goosebumps started to fade as the warmth spread to the rest of her body and she sunk into her booth. The walls creaked achingly as a big gust of wind hit the building. She could hear it whistling through the small holes in the walls and she wondered how much longer the building would remain standing. The diner had always reminded her of a shack.

Without even realizing it, she had placed the file on the table next to her mug and flipped it open to the first page. She was running on automatic and her muscle memory took over her actions. She let out a big breath and took a sip of her mediocre coffee before plunging in and reading the all too familiar words on the pages in front of her.

On the very first page was a picture of her sister. It was like looking at a ghost. The two girls had never looked like each other. While Jamie had been blonde and bubbly and outgoing, Emily had always been quiet and studious. As she read the words in the report for the thousandth time, not a muscle in her face moved. Her eyes analytically scanned the pages, searching for anything she may have missed previously. Anderson's younger sister had gone to a party, and Anderson was supposed to pick her up when she was ready to leave, that was the only reason why Jamie was allowed to go. When Jamie had called she had woken up an already slumbering Anderson. She remembered being groggy and irritated when she had answered and told Jamie to walk home before hanging up, rolling over, and promptly going back to sleep. At the time, she had figured the party was only a few blocks away anyway. According to the police report, Jamie had said goodbye to everyone, hugging them affectionately and saying that she would see them all the next day.

Anderson paused, sucking in a big breath and holding it for a moment. Jamie had always been a happy, extroverted person, unlike Anderson and their younger brother Caleb. Jamie got pleasure out of talking to people and making others smile. It wasn't surprising that she made an effort to say goodbye to absolutely everyone. Anderson let her breath blow out in a big gust. She smoothed out the page in front of her before continuing.

A few minutes after Jamie had left the party, her friends could hear her screams from a few blocks away. The screams even woke up Anderson. She had been terrified waking to them, her whole body reacting in a spasm and getting tangled up in the sheets. She had scrambled out of her bed in a ratty old band t-shirt and boxer shorts and quickly thrown on her slippers on her way to the car. She almost ran into her alert dad and confused brother in the hallway.

They searched the neighborhood, even running into Jamie's friends who had gone to see where the screams were coming from. Nothing had turned up. The police couldn't even pinpoint the block she had been on when she disappeared. Days later they had found her cell phone while canvassing the forest that bordered the edge of the neighborhood. Miller's Forest. Even as an adult, Anderson avoided going near there if she could. There were old stories about that place. Everyone avoided it like the plague. Supposedly there was a scenic pond in the middle, but no one ever ventured past the borders. There was just something unnatural about the place. It was abnormally quiet without any wildlife in the vicinity.

She was spiraling. She pulled her thoughts away from Miller's Forest and refocused her thoughts on the police report. Jamie's cell phone was found in the field leading up to Miller's Forest. The screen was cracked and the police weren't able to lift any fingerprints off the phone that weren't her own. Besides Jamie's screams, there was really nothing to go on. No timeline, no bread crumbs to follow, and they couldn't even trace where she was when she had been taken. The only concrete evidence was the screams, the phone, and the fact that she was gone.

Anderson sat back and rubbed her hands down her face, trying to get rid of the exhaustion. The low light of the alcove cast a shadow over the posters that surrounded her and the wind rattled the nails in the walls. She flipped through the pages until she came to the map of the neighborhood she had drawn by hand. She had drawn lines in a yellow highlighter of possible routes Jamie could've taken from the party house to their childhood home. Then with black ink, she had drawn lines in the routes that were least likely. These were determined by her memory of houses and alleyways that creeped Jamie out. After this, only two routes left were the only two possibilities. The problem was deciding which of the two Jamie actually took.

Floorboards creaked nearby and she looked up to watch Bea turn the corner into her alcove. "That old map again? Hun, ya need a hobby," Bea placed Anderson's usual on the little space of clear table that was left, her long fingernails clicking on the tabletop.

"Like what? This is my hobby."

"That is not a hobby. I dunno what you cops are interested in. Pilates? But hun, ya need a boyfriend. Yer way too high strung. Ya need t'get out summa that energy!"

Anderson smiled at Bea, "I don't have time to date even if I wanted to. Anyway, I'm not ready to start dating again. Charlie and I just split."

Bea shook her head, her badly-done perm bouncing, and clucked in disappointment, "It's never too soon to get back out there."

Year Unknown, Day 1

She awoke to the stench of stale air. Confusion clouded her mind and she couldn't get her thoughts straightened out. She felt the whole room spinning around her. Room? What room? She forced herself to sit up to find that she was sitting on a yellow and brown stained mattress. The springs creaked as she sat up. The walls, the floor, and the ceiling were all concrete. The only door in the room was metal and there was just a sliver of light creeping in through the bottom. The metal door had a square sliding section at the bottom, but there was no handle to it. Besides the flickering light above her, there was nothing else. She laid back down and curled up into a ball on the mattress. How did she get here? She started to inspect herself, looking at her arms for bruises and scratches, anything. She seemed to be unharmed except for a small bump on her head. She was still in her clothes from the night before, a blue sequined mini skirt, a white long-sleeved t-shirt, and her black Chucks. She felt her hair with a hand, still stiff from all the hairspray she had used last night. She combed her fingers through it, breaking the stiff areas apart. Once this was done, she really had nothing else to think about to distract herself from what was obvious. Eventually, she gave in to the tears and they poured onto the mattress, soaking the fabric and her hair. She could feel her eyeliner trickling down her face, staining her cheeks with blue sparkly streaks.

Time was something that she lost track of. It could have been hours that she laid there staring at the wall. Her eyes were swollen and red by the time she sat up. It was a stupid thought, but maybe the door was unlocked. Unsteadily, she wobbled to the metal door and tried the knob. It didn't even rattle. She sank to the floor and sat on the cold cement. She remained still for a very long time, her thighs turning red from the cold where her skirt wasn't covering them. Eventually, she pulled a bobby pin from her hair and worked to straighten it out. She rubbed the rounded end on the floor until the sharp metal end poked out. It took her a long time. Or so she thought. She really wasn't sure how long it took. Her fingers were raw and red with blood and her back and legs were stiff from sitting in the same position for so long. She faced the wall and carved a number one into the floor next to it, barely feeling the metal cut deeper into her fingertips. There was nothing to clean her fingers on but herself or the mattress. So she didn't. Instead, she dripped red splotches to the floor as she wobbled back to the bed where she laid down to cry again.

2017, Day 4

Anderson had just sat down at her desk and turned on her computer when her partner Luke walked up. "Bad day to be late." He practically sang it. He took too much joy in the fact that he was always at the station before her. It didn't matter what time she came in, he was always here.

"Oh?" she asked wearily. Her eyes hurt from her late night and she couldn't help but feel a little disheveled.

"Lieutenant is in a bad mood this morning. He just had an argument with someone and it looked pretty heated. I think it's the time of year of budget cuts again." He sat at his desk just opposite hers but didn't look down at the file in front of him. He lowered his voice for his next statement. "I know you made a copy."

She stared at him. He couldn't know. She had just been paired with him a few weeks ago because his old partner had retired. She didn't think he paid that much attention to her. Only last week he was still asking her to get him tea because he didn't drink coffee. Some sort of hippie bullshit he believed in.

"It's okay, I won't say anything. Just be careful. Lieutenant won't be as easy on you if he finds out. You know very well we can't work cases we're related to."

"Does he know?" She couldn't stop herself, and now she had just confirmed to him that she had made a copy.

"He hasn't mentioned it, so I would assume not."

"Anderson. Office. Now." Lieutenant Manny Sanchez snapped from his office doorway so abruptly that both Anderson and Luke jumped a little.

Anderson ran her fingers through her short, brown hair before pushing herself back from the desk. Luke made a quiet comment about her suit being wrinkled before she walked to the Lieutenant's office. She stopped in front of the doorway and took a deep breath. Getting called to his office was never good. She glanced back at Luke, he motioned for her to brush out her pants. She obliged him and brushed the wrinkles from her pantsuit before stepping inside. She didn't dare sit down without being asked, he hated that.

"How's the Caldwell case going? Any new leads?" Lieutenant asked.

This was a lead up to something. She knew it.

"Nothing new, sir."

He slid a hand over his face in frustration. "How long has it been now?"

"Four days."

"That's no good. What happened to your record-breaking amount of closes?"

"Sir?" She didn't even try to work that out.

"Closes? Last year you set a new record, it was quite impressive."

"Right. Sorry, sir."

"So. Tell me again. How's your case?"

She sighed. "I don't know. I just can't seem to find a lead. This girl, Kate Caldwell, just vanished. We just keep hitting dead ends."

"It's a damn shame."

She shifted her weight and tried to figure out if she should take the bait. "Why is that, sir?"

"We're just short of our close rate and we're being handed budget cuts. Your division will have quite a few unless we can get our close rate up and soon."

She blew out a breath she didn't even know she had been holding.

"I had been counting on you to make that solve so you could move on to another case, you were so reliable last year. I was counting on you to close the Caldwell case. Closing such an important case would've shown everyone why your team is instrumental to the station. I guess it was rookie's luck though."

She stood there waiting for his legendary temper to get the best of him. Instead, he leaned back in his plush chair and crossed his arms. "It's really not your fault. I know sometimes cases like the Caldwell's just go cold. But there are plenty of new ones that come in every day. Now go back out there and get me a solve. And get some sleep Anderson, you look like shit."

Anderson's partner gave her a weird look as she plopped down in her chair. "How bad was it?" Luke asked. She couldn't help but notice that his suit was freshly ironed, not a wrinkle anywhere, the exact opposite of her own suit. His brown hair had been gelled into submission and sat in a perfect side sweep above his ordinary brown eyes. His lean body was resting on the edge of her desk casually.

"Sanchez wants me to switch my focus to another case."

"And?"

"And what?" she snapped.

"Are we going to follow orders?"

"Why are you asking me?"

"Well, he did call you into his office, not me."

"Since when do I ever follow orders? I didn't get all those closes last year because I kept my toes in line."

Luke shot a grin at her, "That's what I wanted to hear. So what's next? Where do you want to start?"

"Well. We have zero leads. We've talked to the family members and her closest friends a hundred times. It seems there are no holes anywhere."

"Talk me through her timeline. Maybe that will help us figure out what to do next." Luke folded his arms in front of his chest. She hated it when he was so condescending. She understood he was trying to teach her and be her mentor or some shit, but it was annoying.

"Well, she got out of school at three pm and went straight to cheerleading practice. Everybody remembers seeing her there. After practice, she went to a study group at the coffee shop downtown, The Ugly Mug. She was there until seven pm when she took the bus home."

"She was with her best friend, Mia, the whole time, right?"

"Right, so she was never alone. They took an hour at her house to get ready for the party and walked down the street five blocks to get there. They arrived at the party at nine pm. Everyone at the party remembers her being there because she was extremely intoxicated. Flirted with a few guys but didn't disappear with anyone. Mia kept a close eye on her and also kept the boys an arm's reach away the whole night."

"I still think those girls spent too much time together."

"I see your point, but they were best friends and Mia was the designated sober friend that night which means that would have been her job for the evening."

"Yeah but, they go to school together, they study together, they take the bus together, they did cheerleading together. I get wanting to spend a lot of time with your best friend, but they even had all the same classes. That's a little strange," explained Luke.

"Let's stick a thumbtack in that idea and come back to it. It may be worth thinking about if nothing else seems off."

Luke raised his hands in defeat for the moment and let her continue with the timeline.

"When Kate Caldwell was finally to the point of stumbling over her own feet, Mia decided to walk her home. Some of the guys didn't want to let the girls walk alone, which normally is a smart idea. However, two blocks away from the party, Caldwell falls behind a little and it takes half a block for anyone to notice. By then, she's gone."

Luke rubbed his chin with a hand, "You're sure one of the guys didn't fall back with her? Take her somewhere special? I mean, she was drunk enough that she could've fallen and hit her head on something. The sidewalk, maybe."

"No. We didn't find any blood splatter when we canvassed the area."

He nodded, offering nothing new to the table.

"We need to think outside the box. All the cases I worked on last year and even the ones this year were so cut and dry. The answer was obvious. This...this is something different. I can feel it."

"How often do you really get handed one of those cases? I think we just missed something that's right under our noses."

Anderson rubbed the already forming headache with her forefinger and thumb. Luke had worked on the police force for ten years longer than she had, but her solve rate percentage was similar to his. This was the first time he had tried to treat her as an equal on a case and she knew she was right about this. She appreciated the newfound balance to their partnership, but she needed to push this feeling.

"Look. I know you and I have different opinions on this. I just have this feeling that this is different. Just let me think about it a little more. In the meantime, call The Ugly Mug and find out who was working there on November 6th and if they can place Caldwell in the shop during the time her friends said. We need to start expanding the people we talk to and confirm that what the friends say is true. If this doesn't give us anything new to work from then we'll take a look at the relationship between Kate and Mia."

Luke nodded and shoved himself up off the corner of her desk that he had been perched on. "I'll give you a call when I know who the employee is so you can join me for questioning. I know you always have more to ask than I do."

After Luke had left the station, she picked up her desk phone and dialed the Caldwell residence.

"Hello?"

"Hi. This is Detective Emily Anderson."

"Oh hello, detective. Is there anything new?"

"No. But I was wondering if I could just confirm a few things with you?"

"Of course. Marcus and I are at home. Please feel free to come by."

"Thank you. I'm leaving the station right now," she glanced at her watch, "I'll be there at 9:45."

Anderson snatched her jacket off the back of her chair and headed for the big double doors.

"Anderson!" Sanchez again.

She stopped in her tracks, and baited her breath, waiting to be yelled at.

"Have you picked up that case yet?"

"I haven't, sir."

"If you insist on following the Caldwell case through, then you need to pick another to work at the same time. Now."

The sound of Sanchez's office door slamming shut made her wince and a few other detectives and officers glanced in her direction. They all knew what his wrath felt like when it came down on them. Anderson squeezed her eyes shut to release her stress before stopping by the front desk.

"Hey, Millicent. Sanchez says there's a case waiting for me up here."

The dark-haired receptionist looked up at her through her glasses. She looked tired, bags under her eyes magnified by the lenses. She reached over to a stack of files and plucked one off the top. Millicent slid the file towards Anderson with one finger and then went back to her computer. The glow of the light made her pale skin look sickly.

2017, Day 4

The front steps leading up to the high school were swarmed with students. It was a beehive of activity and with its queen missing, the worker bees didn't know what to do. The lines of the usual friend groups were blurred for once with everyone whispering about Kate's disappearance. Missing girls didn't happen very often in this small town. There were some old stories about Miller's Forest, but those were just stories. People always saw events like this being reported on the news, it just never actually happened in this town. Even though it had happened a few days ago, it was still the biggest news around.

Melissa could feel eyes watching her from every direction. They probably thought she finally snapped and killed Kate. The crowd parted slightly, making room for her as she passed by. It wasn't easy to ignore them as she made her way to her locker. Once she had it open and had pulled out the books she needed, she leaned forward so her face was hidden in her locker. She closed her eyes and forced herself to take a few deep breaths. Everything would be okay. The cops would find Kate. She'll come home alive and happy and everyone will stop staring at her. Kate will be the center of attention again, just the way everyone liked it.

She pulled her head back out and shut her locker. Almost immediately her eyes locked onto Cameron down the hallway. He hadn't seen her yet, and she didn't want to see his reaction. She turned in the opposite direction even though it was the wrong way to her classroom and hurried away. In her haste, she almost ran directly into a ladder. She barely glanced at the maintenance worker who was changing a lightbulb. Once she had avoided collision with the ladder she tried to make herself as small as possible and hoped that Cameron hadn't caught sight of her. After taking her detour and finding her classroom, she laid out her notebook, textbook, and pens as she usually did. When this was done she slouched into her chair and pulled the hood of her pullover jacket up, shielding her face from others. They could look all they wanted, but she didn't want to see them staring. Her left leg bounced anxiously. She glanced nervously at the girl to her left. Sarah was clearly annoyed with the leg bouncing, but the look on her face made Melissa cringe inwardly. Sarah didn't want to say anything to her about it because she didn't want to be associated with her. Great. That's how low her social status was now. People couldn't even ask her to knock off her annoying habits. She focused really hard on getting her leg to stop moving and let her hood fall further over her face. At least she could escape all this with a memory of one good night. She hoped Cameron didn't think poorly of her.

2017, Day 4

Anderson tossed the file onto the passenger seat before cutting the engine of her car. The neighborhood was a quiet one. A classic suburb. The Caldwell house was a white two-story home with a big lawn out front and a white picket fence bordering the property. This was a world that detectives didn't fit into. She ran through the questions she wanted to ask in her head before climbing out of her plain beige car. The door clicked behind her and her shoes made smacking sounds on the cement walkway up to the bright red front door. She rang the doorbell and could hear the chimes ringing throughout the house. She straightened her suit jacket when she heard footsteps approaching, it was too late for the wrinkles.

Mr. Caldwell opened the door and greeted her with a firm grimace. Anderson guessed he was still getting used to this. She offered him a feeble smile.

"Let me get the missus before you say anything."

He retreated into the depths of the expansive house leaving her alone in the foyer. Her eyes roamed the room and took in the overly ornate framed mirror to her left. It looked heavy as if it was weighing the wall down. Underneath the frame was a small table that was supposed to look vintage but was clearly bought brand new. It held a family photo that had the same kind of frame as the mirror above it, clearly custom made to match. Straight ahead of Anderson was a side view of the staircase to the second floor. Against the wall was a grandfather clock that loudly ticked off the time, informing her how long she had been waiting. Eventually, Mr. Caldwell reappeared with the woman Anderson had spoken to on the phone. She looked frailer than last time— as if any bad news would snap her in half. The woman tried to smile at Anderson like she was still trying to stay strong.

"Please, sit." Mr. Caldwell gestured to the sitting room furnished with stiff-looking loveseats and thin curtains blowing from the light breeze that drifted in through the open windows. Pictures of Kate smiling brightly from elegant thin frames were everywhere, mocking Anderson. *Come get me*, she could almost hear it. It was a challenge. She forced herself to sit on the edge of a stiff seat.

"As I said on the telephone, there's nothing new, but I wanted to check a few things just in case I missed something. Could be anything. Even something small could be crucial to finding your daughter. Do you mind?"

The couple nodded their heads. "Proceed," prompted the husband.

"I want to make sure that I am working off of a correct timeline. Your daughter got out of cheerleading practice at four? And went straight to her study group at the Ugly Mug?"

They nodded.

"Her best friend, Mia, rode the bus home with her afterward?"

Again, they nodded.

"They got home at seven fifteen and went up to Kate's room where they got ready for the party and left at about eight forty-five to arrive at the party at nine?"

Another nod.

"Was it normal for Mia to be around so much?"

"Yes. They were best friends. They did everything together. Mia was constantly spending the night," the wife said quietly.

"Am I missing anything at all?"

"I'm pretty sure that's it," said Mr. Caldwell haltingly, as if he were thinking.

"Actually... Oh, what's her name... Melissa, that's it. Melissa came over at seven-thirty," Mrs. Caldwell interjected.

"Who's Melissa?" Anderson pulled her notebook and pen out of her pants pocket and flipped to the first page.

"She's on the cheerleading squad."

"So she was close to your daughter and Mia? I'm surprised I haven't heard her mentioned before."

"No. She wasn't around much. She's from the poor part of town and Kate only knows her from cheer."

"Did Melissa go to the party with them?"

"I don't know if she went. But if she did, it wasn't with my Kate and Mia. She was only here for a short time. She went upstairs to Kate's room and fifteen minutes later she came rushing down, slamming doors behind her."

Anderson nodded and she quickly tried to write all this down. "Did you find this odd at all?"

"Not really. Those two were always in a disagreement about something. Always yelling at each other."

"Do you know what their argument was about?"

"No. Not that day. I was trying to stay out of it. You know teenagers, there's always drama of some sort. I assumed it was about a boy," Mrs. Caldwell said matter-of-factly and folded her hands into her lap.

"Is there anything else you noticed about that day or the days preceding?"

"Nothing unusual."

"Do you have any photos of Melissa that I could take a look at?"

"Yes, actually she's in photos with the squad. Marcus, do you mind fetching the photo box?"

Mr. Caldwell left the room. Anderson could hear his footsteps all the way up the stairs and back down again. Mrs. Caldwell readjusted her skirt awkwardly to lay across her knees without any wrinkles. Anderson knew she was just avoiding making eye contact.

"Kate kept all her photos of the squad in a box under her bed," he explained as he re-entered the room. He opened the white shoe box and dug through the contents for a while before pulling out a posed team photo. Anderson spotted Kate right away. Team captain, front and center.

"Which one is Melissa?"

He pointed to a girl in the back row with blonde hair and icy blue eyes. If Anderson hadn't known any better she would have pegged them as being twins. They looked about the same height with even the same build. She glanced up at the Caldwell's with bewilderment in her eyes.

"They look alike, don't they," commented Mrs. Caldwell.

"It's certainly startling," Anderson placed the photo back in the box, "Do you have an address or phone number for Melissa? And a last name?"

"Yes, Melissa Jameson. It's in Kate's cell phone that we gave you when she first..." Mrs. Caldwell trailed off into quiet sobs. Her husband pulled her into his arms protectively.

"I'm sorry, I know this is hard. Any little thing could help. Thank you for your cooperation. I'll let you know if this leads anywhere."

Anderson pushed herself off the uncomfortable love seat and made her way to the entrance hall. Her hand was already on the doorknob when Mr. Caldwell stopped her.

"Detective?"

She turned to face him reluctantly.

"I'm not naive about these things. I want you to be honest with me. What are the chances of finding and bringing home my little girl?" His face was stone-still, expecting the worst.

"Sir. I'm not giving up." Anderson awkwardly shifted her weight.

"The chances, detective."

"I'm sorry. After forty-eight hours our chances get slimmer every day..."

"Next time you come here I want good news. My wife can't keep going through this. We've told you all we know." He seemed more impatient than he did angry.

She gave him a curt nod, aware that she would probably never have good news to tell the Caldwell's. She said goodbye and stepped out on the front porch. She got her phone out of her pocket and speed-dialed Luke.

"What's the word?" he says.

"Possible lead. Any luck on your end?"

"I got lucky, didn't have to track him down. The barista on duty was the one that was working the shift while Kate was there. Says there's always a few creeps, but none that were watching our vic."

"Damn. Meet me at the station."

"So what's this possible lead you mentioned on the phone?" Luke asked as he approached Anderson's desk.

She looked up from the case file Millicent had handed her earlier. She had been giving it a precursory glance while waiting for Luke. This new case seemed to be a pretty clear cut, basic hit and run with a witness and all. "There was a piece missing from our timeline. Mrs. Caldwell says that a girl by the name of Melissa Jameson came over and was pretty upset when she left a few minutes later."

"Mrs. Caldwell? I thought she gave her statement at the beginning of the case?"

"Well. I checked on that, reviewing the interviews at the beginning. Mrs. Caldwell was so upset that she didn't say much. Mr. Caldwell did most of the talking. But that isn't even the best part. Check this out." She pulled up the squad photo on the school website. "Okay, you see Kate here in the front? Now look at Melissa," Anderson tapped the screen, indicating where Melissa was to Luke.

"Freaky. Was one of them adopted?" asked Luke with the same bewilderment Anderson had initially.

"Nope. Checked on that too. Just an odd coincidence."

"So we need to talk to Melissa. Find out what she was so upset about."

"Hold up," Anderson waved the new case file in his face, "Sanchez wanted us to pick up a different case because this one is going, quote-unquote, nowhere. Millicent gave me this hit and run after you went downtown earlier. I took a look at it. I'm pretty sure it was a drunk driver. There was a witness that caught part of the license plate number. So we need to run that and see what comes up."

"I can do that. You go talk to Melissa."

"Are you sure?"

"Anderson, I know you. You want to close the Caldwell case, so go. I've got this. You owe me though."

She gave him a quick nod, snatching her keys off the desk on her way out of the station. She left Luke standing at her desk reviewing the new case, double-checking her notes.

Melissa Jameson's house wasn't that far from where the party had been. It was in the part of the neighborhood where rentals outnumbered owned homes. Yards were unkempt and paint was chipping from the harsh rain they had been enduring that winter. Anderson climbed the uneven wooden steps to the front door. The deck underneath her feet creaked the whole way. This could not in any way be safe for residents. She was distracted from her thoughts when a window screeched open.

"Who are you?" a croaky voice yelled.

"Detective Anderson. I have some questions for Melissa Jameson."

"Come 'round through the side yard. That deck there is unsafe." The voice had a distinct Irish accent.

The window slammed shut. Astounded, it took Anderson a moment to move off the deck. The side yard was overgrown, but there was a thin path leading towards the back of the house. Weeds pulled at her clothes as she pushed her way through the plants. Abruptly, the path stopped and her way was blocked with bushes. Glancing around she saw the door was hidden in the shade of a tree and it was wide open. She knocked on the door frame.

"Come on in," croaked that same voice.

Cautiously, she peeked into the room. A middle-aged woman was slumped on a lumpy couch watching the television. She had an ashtray on the table next to her with a still-burning cigarette in it. She was overweight and wore baggy clothes that hid most of her shape. Her hair was scraggly, thinning, and stopped just short of her shoulders. Anderson pulled her badge out of her pocket and held it up so the woman could see it.

She coughed into her arm, "Well, come sit down."

Anderson shoved her badge away again and slowly walked into the room, weaving between all the trash that littered the floor. The hardwood wailed at her in response, it wasn't much better than the front deck. She wiped crumbs off the seat before sitting on the very edge, wincing inwardly that she even had to sit in this pigsty.

"Well. What did that no-good daughter of mine do now?"

"I'm sorry?" shocked, Anderson stared at this woman. "I'm here because a classmate of hers is missing and I just received information that Melissa saw her shortly before she disappeared."

"Are you accusin' 'er of somethin'?"

"No. I just want to know what happened."

"She should be home shortly. Cheerleading practice is almost over. Would you like some pop?"

"No, erm...thank you. Is Melissa's father at work?"

"Him? We ain't seen him in years."

They sat in silence for a while and the woman stared at the television screen, ignoring Anderson's presence. Awkwardly, they waited like this until the sounds of bushes being pushed around could be heard from outside. Expectantly, Anderson faced the doorway. A girl almost identical to Kate came sauntering into the room in her powder blue cheerleading outfit. Her blonde hair was pulled back into a harsh ponytail. Her sneakers were covered in grass stains but had perfect white bows sitting on top. She had a strained backpack slung over one shoulder that looked as if it was on its last legs. Beside her was a younger boy with clothes that didn't fit him properly. He clutched at Melissa's hand and was excitedly telling her about his day. He stopped when he saw the stranger in his home.

"Ma, who's this?" asked Melissa, clearly trying to dominate and take charge of the situation.

Anderson introduced herself before the croaky voice could assault her ears again. She pulled her badge out of her pocket to show Melissa. Unlike her mother, the girl actually took a moment to look at it.

"Why are you here?" asked Melissa.

"Because you're a no-good," coughed her mother.

"Actually. I wanted to talk to you about Kate Caldwell's disappearance."

"Why don't we go to my room? Ma doesn't need to be distracted from the telly." She turned to the boy and crouched down to be at his eye level. "I want you to go to your room for a little bit. If you finish your math homework by the time I'm done talking to this nice detective then I'll make you some mac and cheese. OK?"

"Mac and cheese!!" he excitedly ran out of the room, backpack bouncing on his shoulders.

Anderson followed Melissa down the same hallway where strips of wallpaper were half torn down and the carpet was a dirty brown where it should have been white. It was obvious which door belonged to Melissa and which was the boys. Melissa's was freshly painted pale green and had an oval sign hanging by a ribbon that said her name in precise cursive writing. His was plain white with chipping paint. There was a childish sign made from construction paper that said his name and was taped from the corners to the door. Melissa pushed her door open and flipped on the light switch. An off white shaded lamp in the corner turned on. It was like Anderson had stepped into a Pottery Barn Teen catalog. It wasn't that the items were expensive or ordered from Pottery Barn. It was the fact that everything had its specific place. Everything was put away, not even a pen lay out of place. The desk had been an old model, probably got it from Goodwill, but it had been fixed up, sanded, and restained. In the corner opposite the door was a ceiling-high bookshelf that contained mostly CDs, school books, and college test prep books. There was an armchair that looked as if it had been recently stuffed and sewed up with a velvet cover that was a patchwork of jewel tones.

"Sorry about Ma. We don't have visitors very often."

"You did all this yourself, didn't you?" asked Anderson.

"Yeah. Ma won't do it, so I have to. I can't really focus anywhere else in the house."

"I wish I had been that industrious when I was your age."

"Go ahead and sit," Melissa nodded at the patchwork armchair while she got comfy on her bed, dropping her backpack to the floor. Anderson apprehensively sank into the armchair. Cozy, much better than that couch.

"Melissa, I recently acquired knowledge that you went to Kate's house before the party last Saturday. Can you tell me about that?"

"There's really not much to tell," she shrugged, "I won't try to hide that Kate and I never really got along. I went over there to talk to her about practice."

There was a slight pause and Anderson could see Melissa's hesitation. "Cheerleading practice?" she prompted.

"Yeah..."

"And how did that go?"

"Well, I tried to ask her why I'm always a catcher. I should be a flyer. I've been practicing really hard in my own time. But she wouldn't listen. Said she's captain, she calls the shots. If I don't like it then I could quit. There's no way I can quit. It's the only thing that keeps me sane, besides Danny. I mean, can you imagine being here all the time?" Melissa paused again and her eyes flitted to Anderson and then back to the emerald area rug on her floor.

"And what happened next?" Anderson prompted again.

"I told her that one day, being popular wouldn't cut it anymore. She yelled at me to get out. So I left."

Melissa was no longer cozy on her bed, she was now sitting on the edge of the mattress, her feet planted flat on the ground with her gaze directed at her shoelaces. Her fingers were curled into the comforter. She was leaning forward as if she wanted to hug her knees to her chest. She was clearly still emotional from this confrontation.

"I bet you were angry."

"I was at the time. When I got home I decided to go to the stupid party. I wasn't originally going to go. That's not really my scene. But I thought I could embarrass her somehow."

"Did you?"

Melissa blinked at Anderson in confusion. "Did I what?"

"Embarrass her."

"Oh. Sorta. I wore the same outfit as her. She absolutely hates that. Sometimes she makes girls at school who wear the same shirt or jacket go home and change. One time she made Mia miss her Algebra exam because she was wearing the same shoes and..."

"How did you know what she was going to wear?" Anderson interrupted.

"When I went to her house she was getting ready for the party. She was already dressed so I saw her outfit, but she was still doing her hair and makeup."

"What did she do when you showed up with the same outfit?"

"Oh, right," Melissa shifted her weight backward and leaned back on her palms. "She got really drunk and tried to ignore me pretty much. At first, she was yelling at me in front of everyone, but Mia pulled her into a different room and I guess calmed her down."

"How long did you stay at the party?"

"Not long. Just long enough to see her reaction, then I went home. Like I said before, it's not really my scene."

"Can you give an approximate time that you left?"

Melissa's eyes narrowed. "Am I a suspect or something?"

"I just need to know every detail so I can formulate her timeline correctly. With missing pieces, it's hard to figure out what happened. That and you may have seen something nobody else saw since they were all drinking that night and you weren't."

Melissa nodded, but her eyes told Anderson that she didn't believe her. She knew she was a suspect.

"Okay then... I left here at nine. I stayed for about an hour...so ten. And got home at ten-fifteen."

"Can your mom verify that?"

"Have you seen Ma? No. She was already asleep. She hits the gin pretty early in the evening." Melissa's face turned slightly red as she realized what she had just said and then she ducked her head to stare at her shoelaces again.

Anderson leaned forward, closer to Melissa, trying to get her to look at her. "You know. You're not the only kid to ever grow up in a situation like this. It's nothing to be ashamed about."

Melissa finally met Anderson's eyes. "You know what's crazy? Sometimes I daydream that Kate and I got mixed up in the hospital and that one day I'd get to switch places with her and actually have a family that wants me around." The anxiety in her eyes was clear. "But then I think of Danny. I couldn't leave him here without me."

"You've done a good job here. Your room is really nice and you've developed some skills that are rare for your generation. I remember high school, none of my friends knew how to sew or fix up furniture. And your brother clearly loves you."

An awkward silence descended, only the TV could be heard faintly through the thin walls.

"Is that it, Detective? I have a lot of homework I need to get to."

"Yes, that's all." Anderson pushed herself up out of the plush armchair and got to the door before she turned back to Melissa. "Actually, two more things. What's your GPA?"

"4.2," beamed Melissa.

"What happened to the squad after Kate disappeared?"

"Mia is the captain now. She's a lot better. She actually notices the talents of the girls. I'm a flyer now."

Anderson smiled and nodded at her before heading back down the hallway to the front room where Melissa's mother still sat on the dirty couch with her eyes glued to the TV. She didn't even bat an eyelid as Anderson walked through the room to the open door and the jungle of a side yard. When she reached the front sidewalk she had to pick leaves and small fragments of twigs from her pantsuit before getting into her car.

Year Unknown, Day 2

She awoke with her blood pounding in her ears and her veins throbbing throughout her body. It was dark, pitch black. She had been hoping it all had been a nightmare, but her mutilated fingers told her otherwise. The concrete floor pressed through the thin mattress into her spine and ribs. She felt stiff and tried to stretch her back, twisting this way and that. Eventually, her eyes adjusted to the dark and she could make out where the metal door and walls were. The room was now slightly lit up and she could see the scratch that she had worked so laboriously on the day before. She leaned over the edge of the bed and plucked the bobby pin up off the floor before she pushed up into a sitting position, her feet on the floor. The throbbing rushed to her head and turned into hammering. She quickly put her head between her knees and breathed deeply, sucking oxygen in and wishing it to her brain.

When she could lift her head, she maneuvered herself to the floor by her scratch mark, one of many scores to come. She brought the sharp end of the bobby pin to the floor next to the first one and went to work on a second scratch. The pin pushed into her swollen flesh and brought tears to her eyes. The small cutout on the bottom of the door scared her by suddenly opening. She jumped and blinked rapidly, trying to clear her eyesight. The sudden light had momentarily blinded her. Then with curiosity, she moved closer to the opening, craning her neck to see what was on the other side of the door. At first, all she could see was a pair of legs clothed with grey slacks outlined by light. As her eyes adjusted she was able to make out the room behind the legs. More cement walls and floors, but she could see cracks in the walls that had been poorly patched with caulking. The legs started to move and she scrambled backward.

A hand appeared and dropped an empty bucket on the floor inside the cell. It echoed slightly in the mostly empty room and her brain vibrated. She tried to keep her thoughts all straight as she watched the hand. It was gruff, calloused, and large. She looked at her own petite hands that were shaking in her lap. The hand then slid the bucket to the side before withdrawing from the room. Her curiosity quivered in her stomach and she tensed her muscles to force herself to stay put. The hand reappeared with a bright red plastic cafeteria platter with food on top. This too was set on the floor; promptly the small door slid shut again. The darkness was even harsher this time and she waited for her eyes to adjust. Her quivering made her fingers shake as she patted the cold cement, searching for the platter. She had been so terrified the last day that she had forgotten about hunger. Eventually, her fingertips brushed the rough plastic platter, and her stomach panged from the longing. Both hands began feeling and discovered an apple, a chunk of bread that was still spongy, and a bottle of water. She set to filling her stomach immediately and didn't stop until there was nothing left to chew and not a drop left in the bottle. With newfound energy she went back to work, scratching her score into the ground with the bobby pin pressing into her already cut up thumb. Her scabs cracked open and the metallic scent of fresh blood filled the air.

2017, Day 5

The sound of Anderson's cell phone vibrating on her wooden desk startled her out of a reverie. The pen she had been fiddling with launched from her fingers towards Luke's desk. He looked up from his computer screen with amusement in his eyes. The name "Tracy" flashed across her cell phone screen. That was the name of her father's new wife.

"Hello?"

"Emily, dear!" It sounded forced, it always did.

"What do you need?"

"Never waste a moment, do you? Your father would like to know if you're still coming to dinner this Wednesday?"

"That's the plan."

"Good. We made reservations at that Italian place downtown...Cafe Mare. Eight o'clock."

"Ok. Will Caleb be there?"

"Honey, you know we don't speak to him."

"One of these days he should join us."

"That reminds me, can we expect Charlie to be joining us?"

Anderson cringed. Tracy knew damn well that they had split up. "See you Wednesday," she said without answering the question.

Anderson hung up then, not bothering to hear her step mother's awkward, drawn-out goodbye. Her stepmother had a talent for taking a two-minute conversation and turning it into an hour-long phone call. It's not that she had anything of worth to say, she would just work her way through all the pleasantries that social norms dictated she should. Anderson could feel the bags under her eyes weighing her down. She needed more coffee.

"You look tired." Luke had come over to her desk and was already perched on the edge again, picking up and fiddling with one of her knick-knacks.

"I didn't sleep much last night."

"This case has really got you riled up. Is it because of your sister?"

She looked him in the eye, holding his gaze for a moment before going back to review the conversation.

"Ok, tell me, how did talking to Melissa go?"

"Well. She has the motive. She hated Kate Caldwell and was jealous of how similar they were and yet how horribly different their home lives were. She admitted to having an argument shortly before Kate disappeared. Even going to the party solely to piss her off. Since Kate disappeared, Melissa has moved up in the cheerleading squad and become part of the social group."

"Wow. Sounds like you need to update that timeline. You think she did it?" He put the paperweight down on her desk and shoved his hands in his pockets.

"I'm not so sure. As I mentioned, she has a motive, but I don't think she did it. She's a straight-A student and takes care of her younger brother, Danny, in her free time. That takes a lot of effort and time. Also, I think she would be a little less put together if she had anything to do with the disappearance. You should've seen her. Not a hair was out of place."

"Maybe that's how she deals with stress. Some people work that way. Especially if she's already a perfectionist."

"I'm just not sure. I want to explore a little more before following that lead. How's that hit and run looking?"

Luke's mouth was moving but Anderson wasn't hearing his words. She had tuned out and was nodding absentmindedly. His hands were waving about gesturing here and there to accent what he was saying, but she was in her own world, thinking about the party. And then she couldn't help herself. She interrupted Luke.

"High schoolers take a lot of photos at parties, right?"

He blinked for a moment. "I knew you weren't listening."

She held back a laugh and just looked at him, waiting.

"Yeah, sure they do." He crossed his arms in thought and waited for her to explain.

"So, there should be a photo somewhere of Kate or Melissa at that party that would either prove or disprove Melissa's story."

"Theoretically."

"Great. Thanks, Luke. I'm going to take a look at the list of kids that were at the party."

Luke's shadow remained on her desk for a moment as he hesitated before slumping back to his own desk. She had to blink her eyes at the page before she could actually make sense of the letters. Recognizing names from the cheerleading squad, she figured she should start there and highlighted the names. She picked up her office line and dialed the school's number.

"Hi. My name is Detective Emily Anderson. I'm looking into the disappearance of one of your students, Kate Caldwell. She was the captain of your cheerleading squad. I was wondering if I could stop by and ask the girls a few questions today during practice. It would only take a few minutes."

"Hold for just a moment while I confirm with the principal."

There was a small click and then some soft background music played. Anderson looked around the station as she waited. There were a few rookies starting today and they were pairing up and taking orders with their new partners. Detective Davis from Narcotics was by the front desk trying to flirt with Millie. Her sickly skin looked even more pallid with her bright red lipstick. It made Anderson wonder how anyone could find her attractive. Lieutenant Sanchez was in his office working on paperwork and looking aggravated, as usual. A rookie came in proudly marching a perp to booking. Everyone was busy and here she was sitting on hold. Luke was even hard at work running the plates for his case and tracking down the owner of the car.

There was a click and the music that was enabling her to space out was gone.

"Detective?"

"I'm here."

"Practice starts at three fifteen. Principal Murphy would like to meet with you at three and then I'll walk you to meet the coach and the girls."

"Thank you. I will see you at three."

Year Unknown, Day 5

The room was eerily quiet and she lay on the bed, ignoring the stains on the mattress. The first few days she had tried to avoid them but now she barely noticed. She rubbed her hands over her arms, feeling the grime that had built up. The stubble on her unshaven legs stood on end in the cold. Her pores felt clogged even though she had rubbed off the caked-on makeup long ago. Her hairspray had finally failed and ratted, stiff hair hung about her face. It still crinkled in her ears when she laid her head down.

Her fingers were still swollen from her bobby pin and throbbed every second she was awake.

Everything about the last few days had been unsettling. She had started tracking everything that happened. The man who had taken her was on a schedule. He fed her twice a day and her waste bucket was switched out daily for a fresh one, this was always done at what she thought was the morning. She had begun to wait as long as possible before using it because of the smell that would fill the concrete room. Sometimes all she could do was lay on the ground and tense all her muscles. There was nothing sharp or useful that came with her meals. Always finger food. Not just that, every meal was almost the same. Always a water bottle, a hunk of bread, and sometimes the apple was swapped for an orange. The bucket and food were served through the small cut-out panel by the hand, this way the actual door was never opened. Yesterday she had sat by it for only five minutes before it opened and in came her tray. She had snatched up the water bottle first. Her throat was still parched and raspy from her day of yelling to be released. It had done nothing. She was now certain no one could hear her, wherever she was.

She shuddered as she thought back to yesterday when He had actually entered the room for the first time. He looked to be in his late 40s but was still in shape. He was wearing blue jeans, tennis shoes, and a hoodie. His hair still had hints of brown in it but was grey for the most part. He had called her Alice, repeatedly. "Do you like it here, Alice?" He had said.

"My name's not Alice," she had tried to correct Him, but He acted as if she hadn't spoken a word. She became more persistent that she was the wrong girl. He slapped her in aggravation. Her face still burned from His calloused fingers. Instinctively, she touched a hand to her cheek and felt her swollen flesh. She could only imagine what it looked like.

As she huddled in the corner, He had continued to ask how John was doing and where he was. Who were John and Alice? It was a while before He would leave unsatisfied. She wondered when He would visit again and hoped it wouldn't be for a long time.

2017, Day 5

Anderson walked into the school's office at three o'clock sharp. The woman at the desk glanced up from her computer and stared at Anderson through big round glasses. The clacking from the keyboard never slowed down.

"Are you Detective Anderson?" the woman asked in a bored tone.

"Yes. I believe I spoke to you earlier on the phone." Anderson glanced at the name placard to double-check, "Ms. Thompson."

"Yes. Hold on just a moment while I finish this." The round eyes, amplified by the lenses of her glasses, shifted back to the computer.

Anderson leaned her arm on the counter trying to look casual. She wasn't really used to this. Normally all she had to do was mention that she was a detective and people just let her take command. She drummed her fingers on the counter and stared down at the receptionist for a moment before looking around. The room was small with a few chairs lining the opposite wall where two kids were sitting as far away from each other as possible. One was wearing dark colors and too much eyeliner. The other wore basic denim and a t-shirt with a cartoon of two squirrels sitting on a tree branch, one with an acorn and the other without, with big lettering underneath that said: "Don't Drop the Nutz" on the front. The one wearing a cartoon shirt had a book out and was reading. Anderson tried to read the spine, John Steinbeck possibly. A banner hung above the kid's head that said "GO SEAHAWKS" in sparkly blue block letters with a drawing of the mascot next to it. On the table in the middle of the room were a few magazines and a fake plant that had too much dust on it.

"You won't get much from them."

Anderson turned her gaze back to Ms. Thompson. "Oh?"

"They don't really appreciate talking to authority. And if they feel one of their own is responsible, they will do everything they can to protect them. That's how it was whenever Kate got into trouble." Her bright purple cardigan was off by a button and Anderson desperately wanted to lean over the desk and fix it.

"Thank you for the advice, but I have other reasons for wanting to speak to them."

Upon closer inspection of this woman's face, Anderson noticed big bags under her green eyes that were partially hidden under the weight of her glasses. Her round face was odd with her sharply angled nose and she wore earrings that stretched her lobes too much. They matched her oversized necklace, which was clearly compensating for her small chest. Again, Anderson's eye went to the buttons on the cardigan.

Finally, the receptionist pushed back from her desk, with her freshly manicured hands and led Anderson to an office next to her own desk. She opened the door after rapping the wood with her knuckles a few times.

"Principal Murphy, this is Detective Anderson." She quietly shut the door after leaving them alone in a small room. The wall directly to the right was covered in books that were supposed to look impressive, but Anderson could tell that they had never been opened and read. The wall on the left had pictures of previous principals and held framed certificates that showed his qualifications. The window directly across from the door that was behind his chair looked out onto the parking lot. They had tried to make the view prettier by planting a few bushes, but they hadn't grown enough yet.

"Please, have a seat," he gestured at the chair opposite the desk that was piled high with paperwork, "Thank you for meeting with me." His suit jacket was faded and clearly old. It hung off his body as if he had lost weight recently.

"I assume you have some restrictions you wish to discuss with me."

"Yes. Well, more importantly. How is the investigation proceeding?" He smoothed his hair back away from his face.

"There are a few new leads."

There was silence for a moment as the principal waited for her to expand on her statement. She met his gaze.

"I can't tell you any specifics of the case because it's still active."

"Yes. You are right. To the point then, shall we? I trust that your investigation won't disrupt any academic settings. If you need to talk to the entire student body I can arrange an assembly."

"I just need access to the girls Kate is friends with. Thank you for the offer though."

"Keep me apprised of the situation and let Ms. Thompson know if you need anything."

He stood and got the door for her. His suit pants were wrinkled as if he didn't own an iron. His belt held his pants up as they looked just as loose as the jacket. He gave her a firm handshake before letting the receptionist lead her through the hallways of the school to the football field. There wasn't a patch of green missing the entire length of the field. Flocks of blue and white were on opposing sides either giggling and stretching or throwing and catching the ball. The coach separated herself from the cheerleaders and met them midfield.

"Hello, Detective. I was told you would be here today." She stretched out a hand.

Anderson took it and shook. "Thank you, Coach. I appreciate your and the school's cooperation in this investigation."

"I have no guarantees that any of the girls will come forward with anything to say." Hard lines of worry covered her pretty middle-aged face.

"That's okay. I was just telling Ms. Thompson that isn't the only reason I'm here." Anderson turned to gesture to Ms. Thompson only to find that the receptionist had already started walking back across the field to the cluster of buildings. Her hips swung in her black slacks as she hustled away and the heels of her shoes stuck in the still damp dirt, slowing her progress.

The coach raised an eyebrow, intrigued. "Alright then. This way," she led the way over to the girls. They looked her up and down, hands on hips and weight on one leg with their hips jutting out, in the way only popular girls can. Their gaze was skeptical, challenging her authority. She recognized Mia and Melissa right away but didn't acknowledge them. They all wore matching gym shorts, white Keds, and fitted baseball shirts that showed a sliver of their stomachs.

"Ladies, this is Detective Anderson. She's here to ask you for a favor, so pay attention." Coach nodded at her and stepped back.

Anderson launched into the speech she had prepared about being safe, staying in groups, and being aware of your surroundings. Her eyes scanned the group as she spoke. Some of the girls weren't listening and some looked bored. Mia was trying to look unaffected but her eyes gave her away. Anderson's gaze strayed from the main group to the stragglers, those who were a part of the group but still stood back a little. The ones who weren't really a part of the main clique, those were the ones she was here for. One in particular stood a few feet away from Mia and kept shifting her weight. Anderson concluded by asking them to call her if any of them had any questions or information.

"I'll leave a few business cards with your coach so you can contact me if you feel the need."

"Okay ladies, stretch out! We will begin in a few minutes."

The girls separated into a few smaller circles and started talking. The coach walked Anderson out of earshot.

"Get what you needed?"

"I think so." Her eyes floated back to the girl by Mia and the coach followed her gaze.

"Tammi Calhoun. She wasn't close to Kate, but she was starting to get invited to the group hangouts."

"Would she have been at the party?"

"I don't know for sure, but probably. The whole squad was going."

"Here are some cards," Anderson pulled a stack from her jacket pocket. "Don't give her special attention or try to give her a card."

"You want her to come to you?"

"No, but I don't want to lose her trust by singling her out in front of everyone."

Coach nodded. "Good luck."

Anderson walked back through the halls, her footsteps echoing in the emptiness. She envisioned the ghosts of her own classmates lining the hallway and staring at her, their conversations paused mid-sentence. She had barely noticed at the time. She'd been too preoccupied blaming herself for Jamie's disappearance. She pushed the door open to the same scene of Ms. Thompson typing away furiously on the computer.

"I need Tammi Calhoun's contact information."

"Just a second," she said.

Both the kids were gone from the waiting room so Anderson claimed a seat in the middle and flipped through some of the parenting magazines. They were old issues, some of the ink had faded and was unreadable where fingers had previously held the pages.

"Alright, here's Miss Calhoun's information. You know where to find me if you need anything else." Ms. Thompson's eyes were back on the computer screen before Anderson had even crossed the room to take the post-it note.

Year Unknown, Day 32

The air was musty and stagnant. She could see the dust floating to the floor. Her eyes focused on individual particles and watched them fall past her, and the bed, to the ground. At this point, her feet had started leaving footprints in the dust. She had spent an entire day trying to figure out how to clean the floor, but there was nothing. No napkins with her meals, no sheets on the mattress, no cleaning supplies.

Slowly, with stiff joints, she sat up and swiveled her head, her eyes roaming the room, searching for nothing in particular. She stopped and stared at the bucket in the corner. It was placed specifically on top of the marks she had been making on the floor with her bobby pin. She wasn't sure if He would appreciate her keeping track of how long she had been down here, or if He would even notice. He was always so intent on her being Alice that He rarely paid attention to anything else. He hadn't even seen how swollen her hands were, although her body was getting used to the abuse from the bobby pin. Her white shirt was turning a rusted brown color from constantly drying all the blood off of the hairpin and her fingers.

The sound of the deadbolt turning echoed through the room. She slid backward on the mattress until her back hit the wall. The door creaked open slowly.

"Hello, Alice..." His voice sung the words slowly, filling the room with a hiss.

She hugged her knees to her chest and tried not to whimper.

He clucked his tongue at her. "It's polite to respond when spoken to. Say hello, Alice."

"H-hello."

"Wasn't that nice?"

She nodded in agreement as He approached the mattress.

"I'm sorry I've been gone for so long. I really did mean to visit you sooner. But Alice, you did too good of a job hiding John from me. I've been looking everywhere and I can't find him." He paused and tilted in His head to the side in a questioning way. "Where is he, Alice?"

She opened her mouth, but the words got caught in her throat and all that came out was a gurgling sound.

"Where is he?" His voice got louder.

"I don't know," she whispered.

The palm of His right hand dragged across the cold wall while He stared at her unfalteringly. She dug her fingernails deeper into the sides of the palms of her hands and struggled to maintain eye contact with Him. She refused to let it show that He terrified her.

"Oh, I think you know. You're just protecting him." The hand pulled away from the wall as He waited for a response. When she didn't say anything His hand flew through the air and she barely had time to blink before it connected with the side of her face. A shriek escaped her lips and both hands clutched her cheek, leaving her bleeding in crescent moons on her palms where her fingernails used to be.

"I think a day without food will help you remember."

He picked up her empty food tray and vacated the room. The door slammed shut behind Him but all she could think about was making sure she had the correct amount of lines etched into the floor. It was the only thing He couldn't take away from her.

She slowly let herself slide off the mattress and reached for the bobby pin underneath it. Her fingers curled around it and she clutched it to her chest as she made her way across the room, past the door, and to the waste bucket. Her face scrunched up at the smell. Once the bucket was moved she put the tip of the sharp pin to the floor and started working on adding two fresh marks to the thirty-one that were already there. One for today, and one for tomorrow.

2017, Day 5

Anderson's vision blurred and the scent of grease and coffee swirled around in her head. The conversation of other diners was a mumbled sound in the background, not even words in her mind. The booth's plastic-covered cushions squeaked as she slouched further into the seat. Her eyes closed and she started to sag to the side a little. Her head felt heavy and her mouth dry. The sound of a mug hitting the table in front of her snapped her out of her sleepy haze. Eyes flicked open, she sat back up and stretched.

"Maybe you should go home, hun," Bea drawled at her while shaking her head. "You look more tired than usual."

"Thanks for the coffee."

Anderson chose not to acknowledge Bea's comment on her appearance. She was well aware of how disheveled she looked. Bea shrugged and left Anderson to her work.

The pictures from the party that Tammi had taken were sprawled across the table. Her notes from the interview she had with her were somewhere underneath them. Red Solo cups were everywhere, in kids' hands, on the floor, on tables, and one boy was balancing a cup on his head while girls around him laughed. Her eyes scanned the photos, seeking out only two faces: Kate and Melissa. This was easy to do since Kate was in most of them, at least she thought it was Kate since there was always a large crowd encircling her. Anderson separated all the photos that didn't have either of the girls and put them back in the envelope. This left about half of the pictures still on the table. Next, she organized them according to time stamps. They didn't depict anything that she didn't know already. Arrival at nine and Melissa fifteen minutes later. At nine-thirty there's a picture of a few guys playing beer pong, but in the background, Melissa is facing Kate. Kate's face is contorted with rage and the girls around her look scared. Her face is flushed and her fists are clenched. Although

Melissa's back is to the camera, Anderson could tell from the body language that Melissa was trying, and failing, to have a power stance.

"Here are yur eggs, dearie. Oh! Where can I e'en put them?"

Anderson scanned the table before laughing. "I'm sorry, Bea!"

She gathered all the photos, making sure they were all in order, and put them in a pile next to the envelope. Bea put the plate next to the notepad with Anderson's scribbles from the interview with Tammi.

"Alright, hun, I want ya ta finish everythin' on that plate before you pull those pictures out again. Okay?"

Anderson pulled the notepad closer, picked up her fork, and shot Bea a cheeky grin.

"Ya damn workaholics," muttered Bea as she walked away.

She had barely taken a few bites and read half the page when someone slid into the seat across the table from her. She didn't bother to look up. Only one person knew she came here every night.

"Hey, what's up, Emz."

He reached over to her plate and stole a slice of bacon. He was happily munching on it when she looked up after finishing the sentence she had been reading. He smiled.

"I'm looking over some of my notes from my interview with Tammi Calhoun."

Luke's face remained blank.

"One of the cheerleaders from Kate's team." Anderson reminded Luke.

"That's right. How'd that go?"

"Tammi isn't one of the popular girls. She was trying to work her way into the group with Mia and Kate. Kate took advantage of this and made her do everything. From brushing her hair to doing her school work."

"Are these photos from the party?" He picked them up and started shuffling through them. "No wonder Tammi did as she was told. Kate is intimidating when she's angry."

"I haven't looked at all of them yet." She stabbed her fork into some fluffy egg and promptly put the bite in her mouth.

She slowly demolished her plate of breakfast foods while watching Luke start to flip through the rest, breezing past the photos where Mia pulls Kate into a different room and Melissa leaves. His hands froze.

"Whoa, whoa, whoa. Look at this."

He slapped a photo down on top of the notepad Anderson was trying to read from. It was Kate, Mia, and the three boys after they had left. They were illuminated by a lamppost above them. Kate was laughing with her head thrown back. The boy closest to her had his hand in the small of her back and a faint smile on his lips.

"Look at the background." Luke tapped a dark space in the background, behind Kate and the boy.

Anderson squinted and brought her face closer.

"Is that a shadow? Or a person?" asked Luke.

"I can't tell. But this could mean there was another person that night walking behind their group. Someone who saw what happened. Or..."

"Or that's the perp."

"Mia didn't mention being followed. They probably didn't know."

"Who took this picture? Tammi?"

"No. It was Tammi's camera, but she said..."

Anderson consulted her notes drawing out the last syllable,

"Nate took it home with him and gave it back to her on Monday at school."

"So… Nate took this photo. It's possible he saw who this person was. Add that to our list of things to do tomorrow." Luke reached across the table and stole another piece of bacon. "Speaking of future problems. Ready for dinner with your parents?"

Anderson released a big sigh, blowing air out through her mouth slowly.

"Not even a little bit."

"Come on. They can't be that bad."

"They aren't. It's just awkward. Some things happened— bad things. And they blame me for it. These dinners are more of a formality. It's to show that they're good parents and that they care. My stepmom cares a lot about appearances."

"So why isn't your brother included in these dinners?"

"My stepmother forced my dad to stop talking to him."

"If she cares so much about appearances, then why doesn't she care to have the whole family there?"

Anderson ducked her head thinking of how to describe her family. "Look, while I dealt with Jamie's disappearance by becoming a cop, my brother took a different route. My father became a lot stricter and needed to know where he was all the time. My brother lashed out calling him unfair. He got mixed up with some bad people and I wasn't there to pull him back. By the time my father tried to get me involved it was much too late. I tried talking to Caleb and he didn't react well to me trying to step in. After high school, he refused to go to college and my father kicked him out at my stepmother's insistence. Needless to say, they don't talk."

Luke was silent for a moment. "Since you clearly don't talk about family matters, what do you talk about then?"

"Well. There's some awkward silence followed by basic pleasantries and then there's some more awkward silence. But it's a big ordeal because my stepmom likes to get all dressed up and go someplace fancy."

"That doesn't sound like your style."

"No. I'd be happy if they took me to the pub down the block on Madison. I'm pretty sure my dad would be happy with that, too."

Luke laughed. "McCann's? My dad takes me there every week. We watch the games on Sunday with our jerseys."

"Whose do you wear?"

"Are you a sports fan?"

"No. I don't even know if the Chicago Cubs are football or basketball."

He laughed even harder drawing attention from other diners. "Neither. The Cubs is a baseball team."

Anderson sat back and stirred the last few bites of her eggs around with her fork. "I told you. So, that hit and run case. How's that going?"

"Oh. I ran the plates earlier like I said I was going to. Got a name. Derek Peterson. He's twenty-seven years old and has two DUI's this year alone. When I went to his address though, I found that he had been evicted four months ago. Probably couch surfing or sleeping in his car. Back to square one I guess."

"You haven't even touched your coffee, girl." Bea appeared at the edge of the table. "Oh. And you found a boy! Did you take my advice finally? He's cute, too."

"Bea, this is my partner Luke."

Bea drawled out, "Mmmmhmmm. I'm sure he is," then tossed her hair over her shoulder as she swaggered away.

Anderson stared at Luke in horror, "I'm so sorry."

"Is she always like that?"

"Sadly, yes. She is the small dose of attitude that makes me smile. Most days. That was just embarrassing though."

"So what advice did she give you?"

"Yesterday she told me to find a boyfriend."

"Well. I have heard I'm cute." He wiggled his eyebrows at her.

"At least Amy thinks so."

Luke smiled at the reference to his girlfriend.

"So," Anderson wanted to bring the conversation back to a work related topic, "Do you think we could scan this photo and zoom in on that dark spot? At least figure out if it's a shadow or a person there." She placed the photo on top of the stack and then back into the envelope.

"Probably. Again, tomorrow's problem."

She pulled a ten out of her wallet and placed it on the table before putting her coat on and gathering up her things. Luke followed her out of the diner and to her car.

"See you in the morning, Emz."

She cringed as she shut her door and started the engine. He knew she didn't like being called that nickname and she definitely shouldn't have told him about her nightly spot. Hopefully, this wouldn't be a regular thing. She glanced at her passenger seat where her sister's file hid underneath Kate's. Jaime would have to wait another night.

2017, Day 6

Anderson slammed the door of her car shut and walked towards the entrance of the police station. Detective Davis was a few paces behind her whistling a merry little tune she didn't recognize. She held the glass door open for him and paused at the sight of Millie. There was color in her cheeks for once and she had put more makeup on than just her lipstick. The mascara actually brought out the color of her eyes and made them pop. Her button-up shirt was low cut and the top button was left undone. Her black hair was swept up showing off her slender neck and her smile grew at the sight of Davis. His whistling stopped for a moment.

"Good morning, Millie."

Luke appeared at Anderson's side, chipper and energetic as ever. "We should get started by looking at the photo."

They scanned the photo into the computer and tried to zoom in to the shadow behind Kate. They tried brightening the colors, but nothing worked. The shadow remained just that, a shadow.

"There just isn't any data in this photo. I can't produce something from nothing and there's nothing there to enhance. It's just a shadow. But, I bet we can map how far away the perp was standing from the group based on the projection of his shadow." Luke suggested this after an hour of fiddling with the computer program. "I can check with Ramirez and see if he can take a look at it. This is a little bit out of my technologic know-how."

"I can talk to Mia and the boys again to see if they remember being followed." Anderson pushed her jacket sleeve up and checked her watch. "But they won't be done with school until after three so I have a few hours."

Just then Officer McDonald came hustling up to Luke's desk. "We have eyes on Derek Peterson."

"At his mother's?"

"No. At his girlfriend's house. Officer Williams is on-site right now. Saw Peterson through the window."

Luke grabbed his jacket and started for the parking lot alongside McDonald. Anderson followed at their heels.

"I thought we talked to Tricia yesterday and she said she hadn't seen him in a few days." Luke pushed open the station doors letting in the natural light.

"Clearly she lied," she interjected, the morning sun warmed her face as they jogged across the parking lot.

Luke stopped and looked back at her.

"I'm coming with you. Technically I'm on this case too."

He nodded. "I'm driving."

She hated when he drove because he was always so slow. She got in on the passenger side anyway. He was the lead, so she would follow his orders. They trailed behind McDonald the entire drive.

"The file for Peterson is on the back seat."

She reached behind her seat for it and started flipping through the pages, pausing over his photo.

"He's a greasy looking guy." His brown hair was slicked back out of his face. Tattoos stuck out from underneath his shirt and trailed up his neck. He was clean shaven and his brown eyes shone from under his thick eyebrows. The lines of his face were hard giving him a serious expression, his lips scrunched into a slim grimace.

When they finally pulled over, it was in the slums on the west side, just down the hill from the big houses that overlooked the cliff edges. The hillside kept the sounds of the waves crashing from piercing the quiet of this part of the neighborhood, but there was salt in the air that mixed with the sweet scent of weed that leaked out of most of the small and squished together homes on the block. Officer Williams met them at the edge of the property, where dead grass was the only thing separating them from the front door.

"He's been inside all morning. In the bedroom to the left. Idiot came right up to the open window to close the blinds."

"McDonald, Anderson. Go around back and make sure he doesn't try to sneak out. Williams, you're with me."

Luke headed up the front walk and banged on the door with a fist. Anderson led the way around the side of the house, ducking underneath windows and avoiding dead bushes that hugged the walls. McDonald was close behind, practically breathing down her neck. She froze at the corner, just before turning into what could only be considered as a backyard, even though it was just a patch of dirt with gopher holes creating small craters in the earth. She held a hand behind her signaling for him to stop too. She could still hear Luke's loud voice. He was probably projecting so that she could hear him.

"Good morning Miss Hearne... Yes, ma'am, we did talk yesterday. I wanted to check in just in case anything had changed..."

She heard a door close but couldn't tell if it was the front door shutting in Luke's face or if it was coming from somewhere inside the house.

"Is that pot? Do you have a medical license for that?"

She smirked and held back a laugh, of course he would use possession of drugs as an excuse to enter the premises. McDonald was getting restless behind her and was shifting his weight.

"Is there a reason why you won't invite me inside?"

Anderson heard the creak of a door slowly opening. She peeked around the corner of the building to see the iron screen door was open and there was a man's hand holding it open with his palm. She turned and silently lifted a finger to her lips at McDonald. He nodded and she looked again. The man had come outside and was walking towards their general location. There was stubble all across his jawline that wasn't there in the picture, but it was definitely Peterson. The tattoos on his neck and grimace on his face gave him away. Luke burst from the back doorway.

"Stop right there. You're under arrest."

Peterson took off running, right towards Anderson and McDonald. She stepped out from the side yard blocking his pathway, her hand rested on her holstered weapon and she had her jacket pulled away so he had a clear view of it.

"Put your hands in the air!" she yelled.

His hands shot up but his eyes darted around looking for another escape route. Luke walked up behind him, handcuffs at the ready.

Year Unknown, Day 56

The throbbing in her hand had stopped and her fingers were calloused. She no longer felt the pain as she etched line number fifty eight into the floor. She carefully placed an empty bucket over the top and then sat in the middle of the room. What would happen when she had so many marks that the bucket didn't cover them anymore? She could use the food tray. She would run out of space underneath that. Honestly she hadn't thought about the idea of running out of space until it had happened. Her eyes roamed the room again. She supposed she could use the mattress. Her shoulders slouched and she felt a tightness in her chest, what she could only label as all hope abandoning her. If she used the mattress to hide the marks of counting down the days, then she would be caving to the idea that this ordeal wouldn't be over anytime soon.

She pulled the sleeves of her shirt to cover most of her hands and wrapped her arms around her waist for warmth. It was cold, as it had been the entire time she'd been here. Her clothes had even started to feel damp and cling to her light skin. Her stomach growled, alerting her to the fact that she hadn't eaten in days. She looked down at her stomach, "Shhh. I know." Her lips felt raw from chewing on them to distract herself from the cold and hunger. The only good thing that came from His punishment was the knowledge that He hadn't broken her yet. She still knew who she was and had no idea who Alice or John was.

The panel on the door opened and a patch of light illuminated the floor and the empty food tray. His hand probed around the floor until He made contact with it. Seconds later a new tray was dropped in its place and the panel slid shut again. The darkness settled in her eyes for a few moments before she could see again. Today he had added a small dish of butter to dip her bread in for flavor. He did this on the days that she hadn't eaten for a day or two. It was like a small treat after being starved. She scrambled towards the tray and her fingers tore the bread into smaller chunks and she ravenously devoured it all. She drank half the water bottle even though she knew she should be saving it and making it last all day. Her mouth was just so dry that she couldn't stop herself.

When she had finished her meal she lay on the bed letting her stomach digest what felt like a feast. She stared at the ceiling, tracing all the cracks in the cement with her eyes. She wondered if it would crack enough to collapse and cave in. She knew she'd be crushed. Maybe that would be better than this. At least the inevitable would be over. The cracks left a spider web effect, crawling to the furthest corner from the door to the left, over the bed, and to the other wall. Her eyes drifted down the wall to the air vent. It was in the top corner and there was no way to reach it. Even when jumping, the tips of her fingers barely brushed the bottom of the metal frame. This only fed her agitation. She could smell the fresh air slowly oozing its way into the room, but she couldn't follow it to its source. She fidgeted with her shoelaces. Maybe if she moved the bucket underneath, but if He came in then her scratches would be in plain sight. She stared ruefully at the air vent while she debated the pros and cons of moving the bucket.

2017, Day 6

The interrogation room was small and musty. The air felt thick and oppressive on Anderson's skin. The table in front of her was small and cold, a contrast to the heat the air held. She wasn't sure if the A/C or her tiredness was making her eyes so dry. Peterson sat on the other side, seemingly at ease with the situation, leaning back and relaxed in his chair.

"You know this isn't my first time in one of these rooms, right? All this intimidation crap won't work." He didn't sound cocky, just bored.

She leaned back and tried to match his attitude, she slouched a little and crossed her arms. She kept her face neutral and blank. Luke paced behind her, raking his fingers through his hair.

"What I don't understand is how you could not even notice the other person involved in the accident was dead." Luke paused here and waited to see if Peterson had anything to say. "A little old lady on her way home from the grocery store."

Peterson's face didn't give anything away. No flinch, no guilt in his eyes, but his left thumb pressed into his right bicep a little harder.

Anderson pretended not to notice, "You know it would be easier if you just confessed."

He didn't say anything but he relaxed a little. Anderson glanced at Luke and waited for his move.

"Where were you two nights ago at ten pm?"

"Home. With my girlfriend."

"And if we haul her ass down here, she'll confirm that?"

"Yes." His thumb twitched.

Anderson uncrossed her legs. "Okay then. Hope you don't mind sitting here for a few more hours while I go do that."

He shrugged nonchalantly. Tricia would back him up no matter what. Anderson tried a different track instead.

"Not that it would matter. We have an eye witness who saw you coming home that evening."

His thumb gripped his arm. This was not how he expected this to go down. Surprise and worry fought for control over his face. He hadn't been expecting that.

"Which neighbor? Was it Mr. Donnelly? You can't trust anything he says. He has it out for me, you know."

"We can't tell you who our witness is, but it is solid. Either way, you're going away for this. It'll go easier if you just tell us what happened."

He remained silent, trying too hard to look passive. His thumb pressing into his arm gave away his stress.

"All right then. I'm going to chat with our witness." Anderson deliberately slid her chair back slowly and looked as if she was about to stand up, slowly closing the file on the table in front of her. His thumb was turning red.

She was out of her seat now and her hand on the doorknob before he said something.

"Okay. Fine. "

Once they were back at their desks and getting started on their reports Luke commented, "Well, that was easy."

She raised her eyebrows at Luke. "Shouldn't it be easy? All the facts were right there. It was just a matter of whether or not we could break him."

"Sanchez will be happy."

"Fuck Sanchez and stupid departmental goals. I get he wants to prove himself as Lieutenant, but he wants us to focus on a case about a little old lady who was probably gonna keel over soon anyway, when there's a teenage girl out there with the rest of her life before her, missing. It's not right." She rubbed her eyes. The dryness still bothered her.

"Emz...."

"Don't call me that."

"Ok. Stop. I get that you're mad about the Caldwell case, but I think you're taking this too personally. Maybe you need to take a step back."

"Take a step back from looking for a missing girl?" She couldn't believe what she was hearing.

"It's reminding you of your sister and you're getting emotionally involved. Don't forget that you're not the only one working this case. I let you take the lead on this, but that doesn't mean I'm not working it."

"Fine. I'll take the rest of the day off. Suit you ok?" She shoved back from her desk violently, sending knickknacks every which way.

"And don't just go to the diner. Actually, take the night off. Have a glass of wine, relax. Try to get some sleep. You don't exactly hide it well."

She shot him a glare before storming out of the station, wiping the smile off Millie's face as she passed the front desk.

2017, Day 6

The whispers had just begun to die down when that detective she had spoken to showed up at practice. After that, it was like starting all over again. Renewed whispers and stares. No one on the squad was talking to her, but that wasn't too unusual. Luckily, Melissa had managed to avoid all contact with Cameron at school this week. She had spotted him a few times in the hallways, but always slipped away before could he catch sight of her. She didn't even want to know what he thought of all this.

Today she was home with Danny. He had woken her this morning by jumping on top of her bed and jostling her excitedly. She tried to push her grogginess away for his sake and got up to make coffee. Ma was still asleep on the couch when she tiptoed out into the common area. She moved as silently as she could to get the coffee going and some scrambled eggs made. She added just a dash of cinnamon and sugar to Danny's toast and left an empty mug on the countertop for whenever Ma would awake.

He was still in her room when she returned, juggling two plates and her coffee. His sweet smile was enough of a reward for her. She quietly shut her bedroom door and leaned back into her armchair at her desk. He was happily curled up in her still-warm comforter.

"What are we doing today, Lissa?"

"How about the park?

He shook his head furiously.

"How about the comic book store?"

"Ya ya ya! And the candy store?"

Melissa smiled. "Sure. Why not. Go put your shoes on and we'll get going while it's still nice out. It's supposed to rain today."

The walk to the comic book store only took about twenty minutes. Danny was pulling on her hand the entire time with so much energy that she had to be careful not to trip on the uneven sidewalk. Sometimes she wondered where he got it all from. She reminded herself that he got more sleep than she did. The clouds hung oppressively in the sky, but they weren't quite ready to drop any water onto their heads. They walked past the field that led up to Miller's Forest. It was dark in the depths of the trees. She couldn't see any distinction between the trunks. She shivered and her feet automatically picked up the pace. The hairs on the back of her neck stood on end. Why did this feeling always follow her around?

"Come on Danny. Let's hurry before it starts raining. I don't want to get wet."

They raced the rest of the way to the shop, bursting through the glass door out of breath. Melissa took note of the surprised expressions on the two other customers near the door before steering her brother towards the back of the store. Danny quickly found his Spiderman comics and was digging through them, searching for the latest issue. Melissa wandered the aisles aimlessly, her eyes passing over the titles and just enjoying the overstimulation of bright colors emanating from the glossy covers. She liked the idea of losing herself in another world that was better than her own. There were just so many options it was hard to choose one. Instead, she let her mind wander and let the animated version of herself leap from one comic universe to another. She found herself in front of the posters in the back corner. She had always wanted to save up and get one for Danny's room. Now that her room was complete she wanted to help him get his room liveable as well.

"Hey."

Her head snapped around so she could peer at the acne covered teen. She recognized him from her homeroom. Timmy. Maybe. He worked here on the weekends. She had never come on a Saturday when he wasn't working. Usually, he just smiled from behind the counter and avoided all contact unless she was buying something.

"Um. Hey," she said uncertainly.

"You should go."

"Why's that?"

"Some of the other customers are a little uncomfortable having you here."

Melissa pointedly looked at the other two people, both of whom were watching the exchange with interest. "You've got to be kidding me. I come in here with my kid brother every Saturday."

He nervously glanced around the store, tugging at the hem of his Green Lantern shirt.

"Can you at least tell me why?" She didn't know why she was asking. She already knew the answer.

"Just with everything going on with Kate's disappearance, you know, some people are a little suspicious."

"Of me? Like I could've done something to her?" She rolled her eyes and hoped her loose sweater emphasised how small she was.

"I'm sorry." He looked at her apologetically even as he inched further away.

"Fine. Whatever. Sorry to inconvenience you." She turned away, but then looked back at him for a moment. "By the way. The Green Lantern is lame."

Melissa stalked over to the aisle where Danny was. What the hell was she supposed to say to him? Sorry kid, we got kicked out of the comic book store because the girl who went missing looks like me, and people think I did it. He was a perceptive little guy. She had barely even bent down to talk to him when he looked at her and asked, "We have to go, don't we?"

"I'm sorry."

He held out his hand and she gently gripped it as she led him out of the store. She glanced back and glared pointedly at Timmy. Maybe Timmy. Or maybe he was Joey? Who cares anymore.

"You still want to go to the candy store?"

Danny's blonde hair flopped up and down as he nodded his head without saying a word. They walked the two storefronts over in silence. She wasn't sure what to say so she just stood passively to the side while Danny stared into the glass cases of chocolates and gummies. She could tell that his own excitement had been squashed, but he wasn't letting it stop him from getting his snack.

Tammi's straight brunette hair popped into Melissa's vision. She had on a pale pink shirt with the name of the shop on it. She smiled awkwardly at Melissa, but didn't say anything rude. Melissa took it as a sign of kindness.

"Danny, you ready to order, buddy?"

"Yeah. I want the sharks!" Tammi chuckled a little at his enthusiasm.

"And can I get a regular nonfat mocha?"

After they had ordered and collected their goodies Melissa led the way home. "Hey buddy, I'm sorry about the comic book store." He didn't say anything, just squeezed her hand a little harder. She smiled. Seriously, this kid was so great. If this was as good as life would get, then she would be okay with that.

2017, Day 6

Anderson really did try to get her mind off the case. She went through her bookshelf, looking for something fun, and found *The Picture of Dorian Grey* to read. After thumbing her way through a few pages her mind wandered back to Kate. She forced herself off the cracked leather couch and grabbed a jacket from the hall closet before heading out the door. She pulled her denim jacket tight around herself as she walked down the dimly lit hallway to the elevator. It was quiet here; everyone was hiding in their homes and staying away from the storm outside. The lobby was void of life as well, and through the windows the downpour outside was visible. Even through the glass, the wind was howling loudly.

Anderson glanced down at her knee-high rain boots and the extra thick leggings, then shrugged her shoulders and pushed through the doors into the rain. The wind was so strong that it was pushing the raindrops in an obscure slant. She popped the collar up on her jacket to protect the lower part of her face and made slow progress to the end of the block where a small liquor store was still lit up. She had to push the door open against the strong wind and it slammed behind her, hitting the backs of her heels with force. The man at the counter barely glanced in her direction before going back to the book he was holding. He was leaning with both elbows on the counter and the book was open to the middle. His eyes drooped, clearly tired from a long day of standing still.

She made her way to the wine aisle, per Luke's request from earlier, and glanced through the reds. None of the names stood out to her and the selection was meager at best. She strayed to the whites, but these were all too sweet for her. Wine wasn't her drink of choice, she really only drank it when she was around her parents because that was their preferred drink. It was part of Tracy's perceived idea of the perfect family. Screw Tracy. Screw Luke. She ditched the idea of wine and took herself to the whiskey section, picking out a decent but not too expensive brand, and went back to the man reading his book. She placed the bottle on the counter and watched as he emphasized his exasperation at having to mark his spot and close his book to ring her up. She couldn't blame him too much. When you get to the good part of a book it was hard to put it down.

He mumbled some numbers at her and she pulled out a debit card from her jacket pocket. She took the paper bag he handed her and before she had even turned away from the counter, he had opened his book again and was oblivious to the real world. Back out into the storm she went, walking against the torrential downpour. The rain was angled so that it hit her in the face no matter how much her collar covered it. She was splashed a few times from cars driving by, quickly drenching her entire body. The lobby of her apartment building didn't seem to be much warmer than the outside. She shivered in her soaked-through clothes.

By the time she made it to her apartment, her teeth were chattering uncontrollably and she made a beeline for the space heater next to the couch. She stood there until her leggings had dried out and she was warm enough to take her jacket off. She still had goosebumps, but she wasn't shivering anymore. Out came the small glasses in the cupboard and the whiskey stones from the freezer. In moments she had herself perched at her desk with a chilled glass and both Kate and Jamie's case files side by side. Her phone buzzed next to her arm, sending up goosebumps that had just gone away.

> Luke: Hope you're not looking at the
> case files. I'm stopping by after work
> to check on you.

Anderson let out a deep sigh. Of course he's checking in. She decided to ignore it for the moment and instead reached for Kate's file. Jamie had waited for fifteen years, she could wait one more night since there was still a chance that Kate was out there right now waiting to be found. Again, she breezed through the timeline of the events leading up to the disappearance. Her fingers glided down the page underneath her own handwriting even though she didn't need to read it. At this point, she knew every detail by heart. She sat back in her little metal folding chair and listened to the rain impaling her windows as she stared at the photograph with the shadow in the background. How did no one notice the extra person tagging along? Whoever the perp was he must be experienced in following people. This couldn't have been his first time, otherwise, the snatch wouldn't have been so clean-

An abrupt knocking interrupted her train of thoughts. She quickly put away both files before answering the door. Luke was leaning next to the doorway looking completely at ease with himself, even though he was soaked from the storm. He raised an eyebrow at her casually. Even when he had dropped in at the diner she had been dressed for work. This was the first time he'd seen her in anything but a pantsuit. She pulled the door open wider and gestured for him to come inside. She felt a little self-conscious about her tight pants and her shabby apartment.

"The space heater next to the couch is on if you want to dry off a little," she offered.

He wandered around her small apartment and took everything in, ignoring the suggestion to sit. He inspected everything. The huge bookshelf that took up almost an entire wall in the living room. The tiny TV with a Roku plugged into it. The second-hand couch with the cracking leather and the matching armchair encircling the cedar chest she used as a coffee table. The few pictures that were framed and scattered around the room that had happy and beaming faces in them. He glanced at her desk in the corner with the folding chair tucked underneath. Her clunky, college-aged Lenovo laptop was shut and charging in the left corner, just opposite the case files that were all labeled and shut in the right corner. He wandered back to the door where her coat rack was and felt her damp denim jacket.

"Went out recently?"

"Yeah. I went to buy some wine and wound up coming home with whiskey. Do you want a glass?" She awkwardly stood next to the doorway to the kitchen, looking for something to do so they wouldn't be just standing there. So she wouldn't have to watch him judge her and her living space.

"Sure. Sounds good on a night like this. Warm up my insides in no time." He grinned at her and shoved his hands in his pants pockets.

She busied herself with getting another chilled glass ready, grateful for something to do. He laughed when he saw the whiskey stones.

"Of course."

"What?"

"Of course you have a small apartment with crappy furniture, but when it comes to alcohol, you do it right."

A smile played at the corners of her lips.

"No Charlie tonight? I would have thought he would be stoked you came home early."

Anderson took a sip of her whiskey, sliding it gently around her mouth before swallowing it. "We're not together anymore."

"I'm so sorry, Emz. You were so happy when he proposed."

She stared into her glass, not wanting to look at him. She didn't want to be talking about this, especially with her coworker. She liked to keep her private life out of the workplace.

"So, I'm assuming you've been looking at the file."
He said this with certainty.

"Hey, I tried to do something else, okay? I tried to
read a book as you suggested." She jumped at the change of
subject.

He glanced at the paperback on her coffee table,
The Picture of Dorian Grey.

"No wonder you couldn't get into it," he laughed.
"Why didn't you try some light reading?"

"You know I wanted to be an English major, right? I
was in AP English classes all throughout high school. I only
switched majors in college when Jamie disappeared."

"I actually didn't know that. By the way, I've been
meaning to ask," his eyes hovered down at her kitchen
linoleum floor, "if you want a second pair of eyes to look
over your sister's file."

Silently, Anderson wandered through the room,
passing by the space heater on her way to the desk. Luke
just watched from the kitchen doorway. She shifted through
the files until her fingers touched Jamie's. She smoothly
slid this one out from underneath Kate's and brought it to
Luke. "Don't worry, this is just a copy of the original and a
few of my own notes."

He sat forward in the armchair and spread out everything in the file on the coffee table, drying off the drops that had missed the glass and dribbled down the side with his sleeve first. A light ring was still visible in the wood before Jamie's picture covered it.

"She looked like you," he commented.

Past tense. It rang in her ears. "Have you eaten yet? I think I have a frozen pizza if you're hungry." She needed out of the room, something to busy herself while he looked through her personal notes and ideas.

He nodded without taking his eyes off the report from the responding officer. She immediately got up to preheat the oven and get the pizza onto a cookie sheet. She scrounged around for some paper plates and refilled her glass before putting the pizza in.

"I hope you don't mind the triple meats kind!" she called from the kitchen.

"Hey Emz, what is this?"

"I thought I told you not to call me that."

She turned away from the oven to find him in the doorway staring at the map that had all her pen markings and highlighting on it.

"Oh. Right. I was trying to figure out which route she was taking home so I could figure out where she was taken."

He glanced back at the map. "So there are two routes she could have taken."

"Right. But I can't figure out which one it is. There's the one route where it goes around the two blocks that scare her..."

Luke interrupted, "Why was she scared of these blocks?" He pointed to the middle of the blacked out streets which was also the most direct route to get home.

"Well, some of the houses were kind of run down and the trees were just huge and looming. She always said she got a creepy feeling walking down that street like she was being watched. When she started walking home from school in junior high she would take the extra fifteen minutes to go around those blocks. It used to drive my dad insane."

He nodded thoughtfully.

"Anyway, if she took that route, then that would put her close to the meadow right next to the forest. It would have been easy to grab her in the dark over there."

"Why's that?"

"Only the residential side of the street was lit up by lampposts. They only added in more lights when that area became a problem."

"That's Miller's Forest, isn't it?"

"Yeah, why?"

"She wasn't scared of that area? Most people avoid it, I thought."

Anderson shrugged her shoulders. "Jamie always thought Miller's Forest was beautiful because of how lonely it felt."

Luke made a judgemental sound but moved on from the thought. "And the other route?"

"As you can see, with this route, it would cut further into the neighborhood. If she took this route then whoever took her would have needed to have some knowledge of the area to get her to the forest. This small area is confusing to maneuver because the streets aren't in a grid, there are a few cul de sacs and dead ends."

"And what is this circle outline in orange?"

She glanced at the map and saw the orange pen marks that encircled her family home and a small part of both routes.

"Ah. Right..."

The timer of her oven cut her off as it beeped. "Hold that thought," she pulled the cookie sheet out, using an old oven mitt. The original color of the thinning fabric was faded and seared brown. She could still feel the heat from the pan on her hand. Luke watched as she clumsily dug through her silverware drawer trying to find her pizza cutter, the clanging of her utensils sounded extra loud in the awkward silence. She cut huge slices and pulled them apart to cool faster, her fingertips burning and turning pink from the hot, crisp crust. She handed Luke a plate and took his glass from him. Without asking, she refilled it and led the way back into the living room. They sat on the couch together, perched on the edge so they could peer at the map that Luke had spread on the table, with their pizza plates perched on their knees, the scent of it wafted up to their noses, intensifying the hunger that Anderson hadn't even noticed was there.

"So the orange?" he prompted her once they settled.

"That is the radius of the area in which she had to have been standing in which I could be able to hear her scream all the way from the house."

"Which means that she had to have been in either these two blocks here," he pointed to a corner between the woods and the house, "Or over here." Again, he pointed at a few blocks in a cul de sac a block from the house.

"One route means it could have been anyone. The other route means it had to have been someone in the neighborhood. Someone who knew the area. If I knew the route she took then I would know if..." She didn't finish the sentence. She wasn't sure what she was trying to say anyway.

Luke glanced at her. "I get it. It makes all the difference."

Year Unknown, Day 57

A day had passed and still, she laid on her bed and stared at the air vent by the ceiling. That's the thing about having an endless amount of time on your hands, there was never a rush to make a decision. She could sit there and contemplate that vent for a week if she wanted to. But she wouldn't do that. That would make her even more stir crazy and that was the other thing about time. If you thought about the same thing for even just a few hours at a time it would make you aware of how crazy you were becoming.

She broke up her thoughts about the vent by replaying memories of her family. Remembering the little yard she used to play in with her younger brother, pushing him on the swing and jumping in piles of leaves. Her eyes watered a little as she thought of how much she missed him. The best part of her day was always to come home and see how excited he was to see her and that he always had a story he wanted to share with her. His blue eyes would get huge and round as his voice got louder and he rushed through his words, the story would just pour out of him like he couldn't contain it; he just had to tell someone. It had always melted her heart that she was the one he wanted to tell.

Her gaze flicked back to the air vent. Moving the mattress underneath would do nothing; without a bed frame it would barely add any height and it sagged under her weight anyway. Her only option to reach it was the bucket. She dragged her fingertips on the floor all around her, sending shivers up her spine from the cold. Even if she could reach it, what would it really accomplish? She couldn't get the grate off, there was no way she could get the screws loosened with only her fingers. If somehow she did manage that, then what's the point of it? It's not like she could climb through it, the vent was too small. There was no way she would fit. So there really was no point to it besides it giving her something to think about and attempt.

She prodded to her left until her hand found the food tray on the floor beside her and she picked up the bread. Today she was being careful to make it last, little bites here and there. She had been hungry for so long now that she barely felt the pains in her stomach. It was always there, aching all the time, but they were so constant that it had just become a part of her day. She washed down the bread with a small sip of water, savoring the cool sensation trickling down the back of her throat, hydrating everything it touched. Yet when she swallowed, her mouth continued to feel dry and raspy. She assumed this was what they called cottonmouth. A few kids at school talked about it happening whenever they smoked but she had never experienced it. She licked her dried out and scabbed lips and held back a laugh. Her mother had always told her to refrain from licking her lips when they were dry since it only makes it worse. Lips actually need a thin coating of oil to moisturize and protect them and saliva doesn't contain that. She could feel her blood pumping through all the tiny crevices in her cracked lips. Instinctively, she licked them again.

She leaned back against the wall next to the door, wanting to feel the cold cement. Her fingers brushed over the series of scratch marks on the door frame. They weren't hers. This wasn't the first time she had felt them and they meant only one thing. She wasn't the first girl to be imprisoned here.

2017, Day 7

Anderson awoke to sun rays peeking between the blinds. Her eyes snapped open and she stared at the ceiling for a moment before tossing the sheets off and bounding out of bed. With a bounce in her step, she wandered to the kitchen to flip on the coffee pot. As she waited for the coffee to brew she decided to look over the Caldwell files. She had taken one step into the living room before noticing Luke passed out on the couch. She froze and glanced down at herself. Boxers, unshaved legs, ratty t-shirt, and clearly no bra holding anything in place. Her arms crossed her chest and she retreated to her bedroom. She dug through her dresser for sweats and a sweatshirt, by-passing the silky, short kimono hanging from a hook next to the bathroom. She made a mental note to get rid of it. There was no need to have any reminders of Charlie here. She slipped on her slippers that did barely anything for cushioning, but kept her toes warm and headed back to the living room. She cautiously bent over the couch and poked Luke on the shoulder. Nothing. She poked him a little harder. Still nothing. This time she gripped his shoulder and shook him. He shot upright, simultaneously ripping his shoulder from her hand. She drew back quickly and waited for him to remember where he was.

"Do you want some coffee? I already have a pot started."

"What time is it?" He ignored her questions and countered it with his own.

She glanced through the doorway to the kitchen and checked the clock on the microwave. "Eight A.M."

"Emz. It's a Saturday. Learn how to sleep in."

"I always get up this early on the weekend."

"Well, do you have tea?"

She laughed, "Luke, do you know me at all? No, I don't have tea."

She went into the kitchen and got out two mugs, both a little beat up and stained. There was little food in her fridge and cupboards so she settled for toast with raspberry jam.

"How do you take your coffee?" she yelled from the kitchen.

"I'm not drinking coffee!"

"All I have is toast. That okay?"

"Don't worry about it, I'll grab something on the way home."

The door to the fridge swung open at her touch and she stared at the emptiness for a moment. A block of old cheese, a few slices of sandwich meat, jam, half a gallon of nonfat milk, a carton of expired eggs, and a bag of baby carrots. "Hey, I hope you like your coffee black, because I don't have any cream."

There was a slight pause, "Yeah, that's fine."

She brought the toast and coffee with her into the living room and set it on the table in front of him. He already had Jamie's file out on the coffee table next to his phone.

"Is it still okay if I take your sister's file home with me and look it over?"

She nodded as she bit into her toast and the taste of raspberry filled her mouth. She sucked on the seeds in the jam before swallowing and letting the toast warm her belly. Luke sat back, completely relaxed on her couch. His eyes were closed as he sipped from the mug. She watched him as he tried to swallow the gulp without making a face and wondered when the last time was that he had coffee. "That whiskey last night was some good stuff."

She smirked as she flipped through the pages he had laid out.

"College taught me how to pick my alcohol."

"Well Emz, I'm gonna head home so I can shower and have breakfast. I don't want to intrude on your day off. Amy is expecting me to call her in the next hour anyway. Where do you want the mug?"

Right, Amy. Luke's girlfriend. She glanced up and saw that he had already drained his mug dry. "Just leave it there, I can take care of it later. How is Amy anyway? I haven't heard you mention her in awhile. I was beginning to think you guys had broken up."

"Nope, we're doing good actually. She's been busy with her own work and you know I work as much as I can." He shrugged as he collected his coat that he had thrown over the back of her folding chair and picked up his keys, wallet, and Jamie's file from the coffee table. With two fingers placed to his forehead casually, he nodded at her. "See you on Monday." He let himself out and Anderson finished her coffee before locking the door and heading to the bathroom for her own shower.

Hot water poured down her face from the showerhead and turned her skin red from the heat. She loved the heat, sometimes it was so hot it hurt. The room filled with steam so the air felt dense when she stepped out and grabbed a towel. Her towel was old and terse, refusing to be soft against her skin, instead, it rubbed and turned her even redder. She ran a comb through her tangled hair and then twirled it up and clipped it in place. She drew on thick lines of foundation underneath her eyes to cover the dark bags that were ever present. She rubbed it in with a finger and then flicked on some mascara. All this took only a few moments, it was such a routine that she didn't need to think about it.

The steam from the shower had found its way into the bedroom and covered the top half of the mirror on the sliding closet door. She pulled the door to the left and eyed her few pants suits. They were, for the most part, wrinkled, but in good condition. They were the one thing, besides her books, she owned that were good quality. When she had been promoted to detective her dad and his new wife had insisted on purchasing some nice suits for her. It was the only way they were able to congratulate her since they still didn't approve of the way her life was heading. It was hard work and it took a toll on her view of life and her happiness. She had become cynical and always saw the worst in people. Relationships didn't last long and sleep was just a concept. She knew they missed the old Emily. Her eyes wandered to the boxes shoved sloppily up against the back wall in the closet and quickly darted away. She really needed to go through those and get rid of them. For a moment she considered it and then immediately decided that today was not the day. There would be a day when it didn't hurt as much.

She pulled a black cable knit sweater out of the closet and threw back on her sweats. Glancing out the window she saw that the bright November sun was partially covered by a dark cloud and the trees' brown and orange leaves swayed heavily in the stormy breeze. Slippers were then slid back onto her feet. The mug stood empty on top of the dresser, so she went to the kitchen to fill it up again. The coffee had started to cool and was barely warm at this point. The microwave proved useful in this instance before she curled up on the couch and pulled a blanket all around herself. She perched the Caldwell case in her lap and slowly sifted through the pages. She pondered for a brief moment what Luke and Amy did on their days off. She always just continued to work on whatever case she was working on at the time.

Anderson's phone buzzed on the table beside her.

Sarah: Hey, how about a double date
tonight? There's a new guy at my
office that you would hit it off with. I'm
dying for you guys to meet.

She rolled her eyes and just sent a quick "I'm not ready yet." Every now and then she would go on a blind date that a friend would set up, but recently she had become tired of the dating rituals and preferred to stay home. After what happened with Charlie she just needed a break. A friend from college had set her up with him a year and a half ago. There had been an instant connection at dinner and from there it had developed into a serious relationship. There was a brief stint where he had moved in before he proposed. During the next few months, things became tense as she put in more hours on her cases and kept putting off setting a date. She would come home full of stress and lashed out at him without meaning to. He tried to be patient, but unless you actually worked the job there was no way to understand and be forgiving. They spent many nights barely speaking and picking fights over the most insignificant things. Eventually, he sat her down and told her he was moving out. He left the next day and she hadn't heard from him since. After two months of radio silence, it was almost like she could hear the static of how still her life was. She felt stalled, stuck, and she couldn't do anything to push forward. Her friends already wanted her to move on and start dating, but her parents still asked about Charlie. The one thing she missed was how he was able to keep the conversations with her parents going. The awkwardness that was always there with her parents disappeared when he was around. She could've sworn that they loved him more than her. He certainly fit their idea of the perfect family better. Weekly dinners with her parents weren't so bad with him there. She knew she was the toxic one, that she had driven him away, but she still missed him and wished he hadn't left.

She spent most of the day drinking coffee, re-reading portions of the file, and staring off into space, thinking.

Year Unknown, Day 65

He had visited her small living quarters twice this last week. He was also becoming more violent and it always came in spontaneous bursts. She had become more black and blue and swollen than she had been when she picked up lacrosse for a school year. There were only a few patches of smooth white skin. She truly appreciated the food and water on the days she received a tray. He had become inconsistent now and would feed her sporadically. She never knew when He would be coming anymore, nonetheless when He would come inside. Her sense of time had been completely thrown off. She didn't know how many days had passed and sometimes added a random amount of scratches to her day count. She was sure that she was behind in her count, if anything she might be ahead by a day or a few because of an overcompensation issue. At this point, she really had no idea.

Whenever He was in the room with her, she was covered in goosebumps. He didn't just scare her, He creeped her out. She wasn't motivated by the terror anymore. She was motivated by the hair on her arms standing at attention. The anticipation of waiting for Him to speak and break the first few moments of silence when He entered the room tore her apart inside. She was constantly catching herself, holding her breath, and biting her raw lower lip. He did it on purpose. She knew it. He would watch her silently for a few minutes before saying anything. He wanted to see her react; it was clear on His face that it amused Him. She was still trying to get her emotions under control. She didn't want to give Him anything to get off on. He enjoyed it too much and she squirmed with the knowledge. She also knew that she didn't want to bore Him too much. She wasn't the first girl to be held here, she knew this from her discovery of the scratches at the door. He must get bored at some point and whenever that happens then it would be time for a new girl to take her place. The next girl would find her scratches on the floor and the scratches at the door from the girl before her and know the same thing. She wasn't the first, nor would she be the last. She needed to hold His attention long enough to figure out how to get out of here, to escape.

She had exhausted the idea of the air vent and had tossed it from her mind. It no longer occupied any part of her thoughts. Now she was trying to figure out if there was anything in the room she could use as a weapon. There was no bed frame, so breaking off legs wasn't an option. There were no bedsheets, so tangling him in sheets wouldn't work. There weren't even plastic utensils with her food. All she had was her sharpened bobby pin. Was she really willing to use it against him? If her attack didn't work then he would take it with him and she would lose the bobby pin. She wasn't ready for that yet. Even if she was off count, it was still her little crutch that brought her comfort. It would be her last defense, her last resort.

She rested her head on her knees which were pulled up to her chest and let her eyes fall to the floor. She stared at her shoes, the black high top chucks that had writing on the white rubber parts from close friends. They were beginning to wear through and her pinky toe of her right foot was starting to fall out through a small hole. She wriggled her toes and watched her pinky wave up and down at her. What about shoelaces? How long would they be if she tied them together? Slowly she reached around her knees and started pulling the shoelaces out of her shoes. When she finished pulling them out she laid them on the floor side by side. She didn't know how she was going to use them yet, but it was something. It was something that she didn't have just moments ago. Did she need to tie them together? Maybe she could use them separately. This would give her two attempts.

If she was going to plan an attack then she would need to regain her strength. Sitting and sleeping for sixty-five (give or take a few) days had definitely weakened her. She thought about her old soccer warm-ups. The calisthenics and stretches. Both would help her regain her strength and limberness. She decided it would become a part of her morning routine. Wake up, scratch a line into the floor, have some of her bread and water, do some stretches, and then some calisthenics. It would be slow going, but eventually, she would feel ready.

2017, Day 6

Anderson couldn't stay at home all day and do nothing when there was a terrified teenage girl being held somewhere against her will. After a quick lunch and ignoring more of her friends' pestering texts, she went into the station. Luke was already there and working on paperwork. She took a seat and immediately pulled the Caldwell file out of the bottom right drawer. She glanced up, Luke made eye contact.

"What are you doing here? It's your day off."

"It's your day off, too. I could ask you the same thing. Anyway, I thought you had plans with Amy," she replied.

"She canceled."

"Right…"

"Is Millie wearing more makeup than usual?"

She couldn't stop the smile that spread across her face. "You've noticed it, too?"

"And Detective Davis is standing a little taller."

"It's not going to last."

"No, but they needed the confidence boosts."

Luke took a swig of his tea and went back to his computer. Anderson sat at her desk staring at the open file that was staring right back at her, mocking her. Her foot tapped the floor in irritation and her coffee sat untouched next to the file. Luke sat at his desk across from hers and quietly watched, taking in how much this case was actually bothering her. It was evident to everyone walking by. It took her much too long to become aware of his gaze, but eventually, she looked up and saw him. Her foot froze and she reached a hand out to drink her coffee. She sputtered a little as the cold sludge slid down her throat. She struggled to swallow it. Luke smirked and looked down at his own desk for a moment. She knew how he felt that morning trying to drink the coffee she had made for him.

"So… You sent me home before we wrapped everything up. You know and put a bow on top." For once, Anderson wanted the distraction of another case.

"Yeah. You were there for all the excitement. Really just missed out on paperwork. Honestly, there wasn't a lot for him to argue with. There's a credible witness that saw the whole thing, placing his car at the scene. There is a scuff mark on his car where he hit the vic. Even his girlfriend, Tricia, wound up turning on him and admitted that he had taken the car out for the day and had returned only a little later after the incident. She even told us what bar he had been at. I tracked down the bartender who worked that night and he told me the guy had left shortly before the accident. Felt bad he hadn't called the guy a taxi because of how much he had to drink."

"Wow. You really nailed the guy."

"Yeah. Wrapped up all nice with a bow and everything." He grinned at her.

"So, what now?"

"Well, how's it looking for Kate Caldwell?"

"The pictures with the shadow of someone following her and the guy's home proved useless. I think we need to interview the kids again and see if any of them remember being followed."

"I don't know. They were all pretty drunk."

She stared at him for a moment.

"This is our job," she reminded him, "we need to look into it. We need to exhaust all of the possibilities before we can give up. If we have a lead then we have to follow up."

He shifted under her stare. "I know, I just don't want you to get your hopes up that something will turn up when most likely, nothing will."

"Luke, there's only room for one pessimist in this partnership, and that's me." She choked down another gulp of coffee sludge.

He laughed. "Alright. Let's have them down here this afternoon?"

Anderson made the necessary phone calls, continued to stare at photos and notes, and made a small list of things to ask the kids. It's not like she really needed to, it was just something to do while she waited. Luke worked on finishing up paperwork from the hit and run. They only stopped for coffee refills and lunch at the little Mexican Taqueria at the end of the block where the waiter knew their orders by heart. On the walk back to the station Anderson's phone rang. She answered without checking the caller ID.

"Hello, this is Detective Anderson."

"Oh good Emily, you answered. Your father and I were wondering if we could move dinner to a different restaurant. Cafe Mare closed apparently."

She shut her eyes and took a deep breath. She covered the speaker on her phone for a minute and looked at Luke, "I'll meet you in there." He nodded and wandered ahead of her into the station, greeting Nate and his parents who were just approaching from the parking lot. He gestured with one hand and held the door open for them.

"Emily, dear?"

"Yes, I'm here. I was just thinking about where we should eat."

"Yes well, we were thinking of that place on fifth?"

"That's specific, there are at least ten places on fifth that you could be talking about."

"Emily." The stern tone to her stepmother's voice wasn't hard to miss but she had learned a long time ago to ignore it. She wasn't a child so why should she let it bother her when she was treated this way? The woman didn't raise her and only came into her life when she was already full grown and in college. She had zero authority.

"How about I pick the place for once?"

"Well, I suppose that would be alright."

"Great, I'll see you at McCann's at eight on Wednesday."

"Isn't McCann's-"

She hung up before her stepmother could argue with her. Luke was waiting for her at her desk. "What was that?"

"Nothing."

He waited a little more, but when it became evident that she wasn't going to expand her statement he continued on. "Nate and his parents are here."

Her hands were in her pockets now. "Lead the way."

Luke picked up the file from her desk with the pictures in it and led the way to a cozy room down the hall. There was a couch on which Nate and his mother were uncomfortably seated. He wore tan shorts, Nikes, and a Seahawks sweatshirt, while she wore low heels and a sweater dress that hugged in all the right places. His father stood by the window and was staring outside at the view of the parking lot, the light illuminating his broad shoulders. Anderson and Luke pulled up two folding chairs to the coffee table in front of the couch. The lamp on the side table set a yellow glow on Nate's face.

"We're sorry to ask you to come down here again, but we appreciate your cooperation. We just have a few more questions to ask," Luke started. He still held the file, carefully making sure nothing fell out. He waited for the mother's approving nod before carrying on. "The night Kate disappeared when you were walking home from the party, do you remember anything odd?"

"Like what exactly?" The father finally turned from the window to face the detectives. His arms were folded in front of him and he frowned in displeasure.

"For instance, the feeling of being followed. Or like there was someone else there."

Nate looked at his parents with his hazel eyes and both nodded at him encouraging him to be honest.

"I don't remember anything exactly. I mean, we had been drinking quite a bit."

The corners of his mother's painted lips edged downward and she glanced at him. Disappointment was clear on her face but she remained silent, merely pursing her lips in response.

"We were all just having a good time. Laughing and goofing off while we walked. Although, I do remember Josh kept looking over his shoulder every now and then."

"So it is possible that someone else in the group thought you were being followed?"

"I guess." He shrugged his shoulders.

Luke placed the file on the table and opened it to reveal the photo of the group walking.

"Do you remember who was taking the photo?"

Nate was staring at it, the sweatshirt tie that he had been chewing on dropped from his slack mouth. His attention had been captured. "Is that shadow a person?" he asked while pointing at the dark splotch.

"It's possible that it is. We tried to lighten the photo but there was no way to make it any clearer. However, whoever took this picture could have seen this person."

Nate continued to stare at it.

"I really didn't notice anyone following us."

"Hey, Nate," Anderson called his attention away from the photo, "it's not your fault. This person who took Kate was very stealthy. He knew what he was doing. There isn't anything that you could've done to stop it. But you can help us now. Do you remember who took the photo?"

"I think it was Mia."

Luke and Anderson glanced at each other. Why did it always lead back to the girls?

"Thank you for coming in. If you remember anything else that you want to tell us then just give us a call." Anderson gave Nate's mother her card. They walked Nate and his parents out and in the process greeted Josh and his parents, leading them back into the same room. Josh's mother wanted water so Anderson fetched all three of them water cups. They started off the same, casually asking if he remembered anything being off during the walk. He was less than forthcoming, claiming that nothing had been amiss. He sat stiffly in his jeans and his t-shirt and kept his tired eyes staring at the floor.

"Josh, can you explain to me then why Nate says that you were looking over your shoulder frequently?"

"You don't think I did something, do you?" He raised his gaze so that he could meet Luke's eyes.

"No. But I think you knew something was wrong. Even if you don't know what it was, that's fine, we just need to know."

"Well. I didn't see anything. I just felt like we were being watched. I kept looking around to see if I could spot anything, but there was nothing there. The whole point of walking the girls home was to keep them safe. I thought I kept hearing an extra set of footsteps, but then you know, I wasn't exactly sober either. I thought maybe I was hallucinating."

"I don't think you were." Luke placed the file on the table, same as he had before. "Do you see this shadow?" he pointed at the splotchy spot, "We think this may be the shadow of whoever took Kate. This means that you were right. You were being followed."

Jost stared at the photo for a minute. "So I did hear footsteps?"

"Yes. You probably were hearing footsteps."

Josh expelled a huge breath he had been holding and sat back on the couch, running a hand through his thick black hair... His eyes moved from the photo to both detectives for a moment, shock and guilt shining through.

"Do you think if I had said something, then, you know...she wouldn't be missing?"

"No. I don't think there is anything you could've done. This guy, he was able to lure Kate away from you guys even when you were moving as a group. He would've been able to do the same if you guys had been standing and calling for a ride."

"So it's not my fault?"

Anderson answered before Luke could. It was her turn to jump in. "No. I don't think it is. But I think it's natural for you to feel this way. Do you remember anything else that could help us?"

"Mia took the photo, so if anyone saw anything, it would be her."

"Okay. Thank you for coming in. If you remember anything else, please don't hesitate to call." She handed her card to the parents and again, walked them out of the station.

"Poor kids," Luke commented, "I would be feeling pretty guilty too if I was one of them."

Anderson shuffled her feet without responding.

"Sorry, I didn't mean anything by that."

"Don't worry about it." Mia and her parents walked into the room. "Hello, please have a seat."

They all squeezed onto the couch together. Again, Anderson fetched some fresh water glasses. When she came back it was to utter silence as the parents took in the surroundings of the room, the watercolor paintings on the walls, the blinds open on the window letting sunlight in. Mia sat between them on the couch. She was slouched and leaning back with a somewhat pouty expression on her face. The parents were sitting primly in their pressed and proper clothes. Mia had on a pair of jeans that looked so tight they couldn't have been comfortable.

"So, what are we doing here again?" asked Mia's mother.

"We have some new leads that popped up and we just wanted to ask a few more questions. Is that alright?"

She nodded without trying to hide her irritation.

"Great." Anderson glanced at Luke, signaling that he could start things off.

"Do you remember anything weird about the walk before you and the guys noticed that she was gone?"

"Not really. Everyone was in a good mood. Josh was like a scaredy cat, looking around everywhere every five seconds." She rolled her eyes for emphasis.

"Do you remember taking any photos?"

"Yeah. I had Tammi's camera and we were taking a lot of pictures."

"Do you remember taking this one?" Luke placed the open folder on the table in front of her.

"Yes. Kate was begging me to take a group shot of her with all the guys so I started taking a million candid pictures of them all together. They came out so bad." She let out a little laugh.

"Do you see this dark spot?"

She squinted where he was pointing.

"Yeah. What about it?"

"We believe it to be the shadow of the person who took Kate."

She looked them both in the eye.

"So, what are you saying? That I saw this guy and didn't say anything? Do you know how bright flash is at night? I was blinded. Everyone was blinded." She attempted to remain calm but couldn't hide the franticness that seeped into her voice.

Luke glanced at Anderson for help. "We're just saying that you could have seen someone. It's a possibility. If you didn't, that's okay, too. We're just asking if you did."

"Well I didn't," she insisted. She looked at her parents and then at the detectives again. "I didn't see anything. Can we go now?"

"Yes. You can go."

Mia and her parents left. Her mother led the way with her head held high, not even checking to see if her family was following. Mia trailed behind, attempting to imitate her mother's self assured movements. The father brought up the rear, with none of the attitude that both of the women possessed. This left Luke and Anderson watching from the doorway until the procession was gone before heading to their desks.

"So, Mia seemed a little too insistent that she didn't see anything. She reacted to it all differently than the boys," commented Luke.

"Yeah. I think she's lying. The guys felt guilty that they didn't notice something was wrong, whereas Mia seemed frantic like she was hiding something."

"Do you think she saw something and just didn't say anything?"

"But then why wouldn't she just say so when we asked?"

"I don't know. Make a note of that. I know you have a list of things to look into."

She smirked at Luke. Partners, people who know too much about each other without actually being in a relationship. "Also, she was the only one to mention that the flash was blinding. I don't doubt how bright it was, but she made a big deal about it and neither of the guys even mentioned it. If the flash was going to blind anyone it would've been the boys."

"That is a little odd," agreed Luke.

Anderson propped her elbows on the desk and leaned forward. "This is just aggravating. Everything just leads to more questions."

Luke glanced at his watch. "It's just about time to call it quits for the day."

"Hey, are you, by chance, done with my sister's file?"

"Nope. Not done yet. Sorry. You want to go to your diner, don't you?"

"Yeah, I was hoping to." She fiddled with a pen in her hands, not sure what to do with herself.

"Your evening at home seemed to do you some good. Why don't you just go home and I'll see you on Monday?"

She would rather do anything than going home and stare at the mostly bare walls that she used to share with someone else. She didn't move, instead, she sat frozen at her desk, staring at the notepad in front of her. Mia was hiding something about that night, Anderson was sure of it. She didn't think Mia was personally responsible for Kate's disappearance though. So what was she hiding? She had inherited head cheerleader and head of the popular clique. Her gut twisted a little. Mia was clearly a petty person and cared what people thought of her. Was it possible that she felt guilty for enjoying her new life? Definitely a possibility. Anderson added this train of thought to her notes from the interview.

"Still stalling going home?" asked Luke from his desk.

"Yeah. Well, I'm trying to pinpoint why she felt so off. I'm thinking that she might like her new life without Kate."

"And she's feeling guilty about that."

"Well yes. If Kate was here, nothing would have ever changed."

"I'm really surprised Mia didn't see anything. From what the boys were saying, and with the flash on and illuminating everything behind them, she should have seen something. The flash should have blinded the boys."

"Do you think she's lying about it?"

Anderson sat back in her chair, elbows propped on the armrests and fingers laced in front of her face.

"If she did, then she'd be an accessory to kidnapping since she's not saying anything. At this point, possibly a murder," mused Luke.

Anderson flicked her eyes at him, acknowledging his comment even though it left a bad taste in her mouth, accusing a kid of something so horrible.

Year Unknown, Day 66

She wasn't sure how long the shoelaces were, but they were definitely long enough for her purposes. She would use one and hide the other. For now, both were tucked underneath the mattress and she wandered around in shoe-laceless shoes. They flopped around on her feet and every time she took a step she thought one of the shoes would come flying off. Without the shoelaces holding the canvas close to her skin, her ankles were exposed to the cold. This took a while to get used to. With nothing else going on, it was all her mind could focus on.

Her new morning routine consisted of drinking half of the bottle of water, to hydrate her system beforehand, and eating only half of the piece of bread. Then she proceeded to work out. She didn't know how long most of her workouts were, but for the first day, it did not last long. Hopefully after a week of consistent daily workouts that

would change. She started with basic cardio exercises;
jumping jacks and jogging around the room, it was so small
she couldn't really do sprints. Once her heart rate was up
she started her calisthenics. When she felt her heart rate
dropping she would throw in another jog. She tried to do
push-ups, but sadly found that her arm muscles had
weakened over the last two months. She did crunches,
squats, and mountain climbers. After the actual workout
was over she would then stretch out her hamstrings, back,
quads and shoulders. Once all of this had been completed
she then finished her water, bread, and whatever fruit He
had brought her for the day. Today, for instance, she had an
apple. When dinner was delivered she then repeated all this
again. Her legs and abs were a little more sore than she was
expecting and she was disappointed in her own abilities.

In her free time between workouts and mealtime,
she would sit and think about how she would attack.
Mostly it was just daydreaming about how it would go well
and that she would be able to find a way out.

2017, Day 7

After practice Melissa headed to the locker room for a quick shower and change. Ma had complained about her being too sweaty when she got home this week so instead of walking straight home, she figured she should clean up first. She also needed to run to Danny's school a few blocks away to pick him up. Practice had gone well; as they had been since Kate had gone missing. She opened her locker, next to Lauren's, and dug through her gym bag for her shower gel and shampoo.

"Hey, we're studying for Mr. Roger's exam tonight at my place. Want to come?"

Just another event she wasn't invited to. She knew she'd be up late tonight studying for the same exam anyway. It would just be nice to be invited. To not be an outcast. She sighed and didn't even glance in their direction, no point in letting them know that all this bothered her.

"Hello?"

Her fingers found the evasive shampoo bottle, she pulled it out and shut the locker in one fell swoop as she turned towards the showers. She stopped short when she realized that Lauren was staring at her, arms crossed over her chest.

"What?" asked Melissa.

Lauren let out a big sigh. "Do you want to come study at my place tonight?"

"You were talking to me?"

"Duh. Do you see anyone else around?"

Melissa looked around the room. There were plenty of girls standing around and chatting at their own lockers. She could've been talking to anyone. Wait, Lauren was talking to her with witnesses. This was huge, she probably shouldn't be ignoring Lauren right now. "What time?"

"Seven. My mom is making a casserole so come hungry."

That wouldn't be a problem. "I don't have your address."

"Give me your phone." Lauren was giving off airs of being impatient, but Melissa could tell she was enjoying this.

"Now you have my number and address. Call if you get lost." She handed the phone back, shot a shiny, glossed smile at Melissa, and then pranced away. Melissa couldn't hide her smile all through her shower. Was it possible that she now had a friend? Who would have thought that one bad thing could bring so many good things? She could see a new version of herself forming and she was loving it. Life was going to be good from here on out. She rushed through getting dressed and hurried to pick up Danny.

He stood by the gate, waiting for her. She called hello to his teacher who was talking to the parents of another student. The teacher smiled and waved back.

"Ready to go, kiddo?"

"Yeah!" He readily grabbed at her extended hand and trotted by her side all through the neighborhood.

It only took them ten minutes to get home from his school, but for once she stopped at the sidewalk and stared up at the house. He peered up at her face expectantly. She squatted down so she could look him in the eyes. "OK kiddo. I'm going to a friend's house tonight to study for school. Will you be okay for a few hours on your own?"

"What about dinner?"

"I think I have that covered. My friend's mom is making a casserole. I can try to bring some home for you. But if you want food before I go, then I could make you mac and cheese."

"What's a casserole?" He grinned up at her.

She ruffled his hair with one hand. "You're too good to me. You know that?"

His smile spread across his small face and dimples appeared on both cheeks. She loved that smile. Danny was just the cutest kid, not that she was biased in any way. She took his hand again and led him into the house. She nudged him towards the hallway and waited for him to be out of the room before she addressed their mother.

"Hey, Ma?"

"Yeah." She didn't even look up from the telly.

"I'm going to a friend's house tonight to study for an exam tomorrow."

Ma stared at her blankly. "You have friends? Since when?"

"Since now." She tried not to be offended.

"Just come home at some point. And make sure they feed ya. I don't got food here."

"Her Ma made a casserole for all the girls who will be there."

Ma went silent. The conversation was over and daughterly duty was completed. It saddened Melissa that her mother hadn't even asked about making dinner for Danny. She quickly used maps on her phone to navigate her way to Lauren's house. She grabbed a light blue hoodie from her color-coded closet and packed a small bag of the books she would need and then she was out the door.

Lauren's was only a twenty-minute walk away. Leaving at six-thirty, she should be there ten minutes early. Every few blocks she found herself looking over her shoulder. This was a habit she picked up a few months ago. She had felt as if someone was following her, a shadow of some sort. But this last week it was gone and now she just had a weird habit. Maybe it had been Kate's presence in her mind, always there, always angry. Whatever it was, she was glad it was gone.

Lauren's house was nice, as were all the houses on this street. It reminded her of Kate's house; big, two stories, bright green lawn with a white picket fence. There was even a jacaranda tree in full bloom by the steps up to the veranda. She tried not to smoosh the lavender blossoms into the wood steps.

She rang the doorbell and it was opened almost immediately. A middle-aged woman with an apron thrown on haphazardly over her jeans and button-up plaid shirt shot her a beaming, white-toothed smile.

"Hiya Hun! I'm Lauren's mom, Diane. You must be Melissa."

"Uhh, yes, I am."

The woman peered out into the street and looked around, "Where's your mom?"

"Oh. I, uh, walked here."

She frowned for a moment. "Well, don't worry. I can give you a ride home later. Next time just call if you need a ride." Her smile came back.

Melissa's stomach twisted with butterflies, *Next time!*

"Are you hungry, dear?"

Lauren's mom led her into the house. Melissa took note of the shoe rack and quickly removed hers before being led down a hallway and into the kitchen where Lauren and two other girls were already seated and starting on dinner.

"Hey! Grab a plate," Lauren called from across the room.

Melissa cautiously picked up a plate from the stack that was on the countertop next to the glass dish of what looked like ground beef and cheese layers. She served herself a small, but polite portion. When she looked back up, Diane had already left the room, but the three girls were all watching her.

"Is that all you want? You can have as much as you want…" Lauren almost sounded offended that she hadn't taken a larger portion.

She looked at her plate and thought about her empty stomach and the empty pantry at home. Without thinking, her hand reached out and she served herself a much more, filling her plate.

"Cups are on your left. Help yourself to anything in the fridge."

It was an out of body experience to be this friendly with Lauren's house, but Melissa's hand reached out and pulled open the fridge door anyway. She had never seen such an awfully stocked fridge before. Each shelf was bursting with food, leftover containers, and jugs of different liquids. She stood motionless while her brain processed the view in front of her.

Lauren appeared at her side. "Can't find what you want? We have another fridge in the garage."

"No. I just…I've never seen a kitchen this well stocked. I don't even know what I want. There are so many options."

Lauren let out a small laugh. "Really?"

"Oh yes. On a good day, we don't have expired milk for my cereal." Was she really sharing her home issues with these girls?

"No way!" Camille wasn't on the cheerleading squad but was in Mr. Rogers' class with them. "That's insane. My mom is so terrified of expired milk that she dumps it out two days before the expiration date."

"I can't imagine that it's such a waste."

"Soooo…do you want milk?" asked Lauren.

"Sure."

"We have nonfat, 1% and 2%. Which do you prefer?"

"Uhhhh."

"No way! You don't even know which one you like?" Camille butted in again.

"Well. Ma always gets 2%. But I've never tried the other two. Why do you have all of them?" Having all three just seemed excessive. Who needs this much milk?

Lauren rolled her eyes. "My dad only drinks 2%. My mom only drinks nonfat. Brandon and I go for 1%."

"Brandon?"

"You've met Brandon. He's on the football team."

"He's your brother?"

"Duh."

It was Melissa's turn to say no way. "I didn't know you guys were related. I've had a crush on him since junior high." Did that seriously just pop out of her mouth? Blood rushed to her cheeks and she could feel herself turning pink. Cassie, who was still sitting at the table, giggled with a hand over her mouth.

"It's okay. A lot of my friends growing up had crushes on him. I'm used to it. Here, I got you 1% so you can try something new. Kinda." Lauren handed Melissa a tall glass and they all sat down at the table with Cassie.

"I have a brother, too. But he's younger than me, still in elementary school. You guys probably don't know him."

"Aww, do you have a picture?" asked Lauren.

Melissa pulled her phone out and flicked through her photos. She found some good ones from the time a few weeks ago when she took Danny to the park nearby. The other girls oohed and ahhed over him for a few minutes.

"He's adorable," commented Cass, "How old is he?"

"Nine."

"So cute!"

She tucked her phone away again and took a bite of the casserole. It was like heaven in her mouth. She hadn't tasted anything besides her own basic cooking and cafeteria food in a long time.

"Oh my god, Lauren. This is amazing. Remind me to thank your mother before I leave."

"You want to take some home?"

"Really? Can I?"

Lauren nodded.

"Thank you so much. Danny will love this."

She went back to the counter and started cutting a slice for him.

"Get enough for dinner tomorrow too. If you want."

Lauren knew what Melissa's home life was like. She remembered from when they were kids, and this was her way of helping out without bringing attention to it in front of the other girls.

"I know this is mean but, who here doesn't miss Kate?" asked Camille.

"Oh my god. I never liked her. I mean, I feel bad for her parents now that she's gone, but she was a bitch."

Cassie shut her mouth and glanced at Lauren. "Sorry. I know you guys were close growing up."

"Yeah, growing up. Not anymore. She just got really mean, and unnecessarily so. I always felt bad for you though," Lauren nodded in Melissa's direction.

"Why?"

"She took out so much anger on you. And she never let us talk to you. When she went missing, I told myself to be nicer to people, starting with being friends with you. Maybe it's just karma. Maybe she's gone because she was so horrible all the time."

"Maybe…" Cassie's face was clouded with thought.

"Hey guys!"

All four heads looked up and all four sets of eyes were surprised by the silent approach of Mia. She stood in the doorway, backpack slung casually over one shoulder. She wore light blue jeans that hugged a little too tightly on her hips, a white cap-sleeved shirt, and black flats with bows on the top. Her hair hung loose barely touching her shoulders, brown curls covering half her face.

"Hey, girl. Grab a plate."

"Thanks. I'm freaking starved. I had to go to the police station yesterday. Again." She rolled her eyes as if this was the most inconvenient thing ever. She was already shoveling food into her mouth as if she hadn't eaten in days. Melissa didn't like it, there was never a reason to be this rude when it came to food and being in someone else's house.

"What did they want now? More questions?" This time it was Lauren trying to force information out of Mia. The power struggle between the two was evident. Clearly one of them would replace Kate, but the question was which one? Although Mia had become the new cheer captain, Lauren was better with people and everyone liked her better.

"Yeah. Just a few more questions about that night and the few minutes leading up to us noticing that she wasn't there anymore."

"You must feel just terrible about that," stated Camille.

No one else noticed, but because Melissa was staring Mia down she saw the slight shift in her weight and the brief flash of fear in her eyes. She was scared of something being discovered. Mia recovered so quickly from the fumble that the others didn't notice. She dropped her backpack on the floor, drawing attention away from her face. The other three looked down but Melissa made eye contact with Mia, just a small warning that she knew something was up. Mia cocked her head slightly. A challenge.

"Yeah, I just feel… so guilty that I didn't see anyone." The other three looked back at Mia's face.

"I can imagine," commented Lauren, "but you know it's just survivor's guilt."

"I guess so," Melissa thought Mia was over-acting the thoughtful bit, but the others were buying it completely.

"Should we get to studying now that we're all here?" asked Camille.

"Oh, by the way, when we need to take a study break later. My mom made us a cherry pie for dessert." Lauren gestured across the room where a cooling rack was set away from the rest of the dinner that was laid out for the girls. Melissa thought she would die of happiness when she noticed the perfectly latticed pie crust covering the top. She didn't necessarily condone the 50's housewife persona that exuded from Lauren's mother, but it was nice that some effort had been made to make her daughter and her daughter's friends enjoy coming over.

Cassie turned to Melissa, "Lauren's mom makes the best pies on earth. I'm not kidding."

2017, Day 7

Anderson was curled into a small ball on her couch. Between her chest and her knees was perched a book that she had desperately tried to read. At Luke's suggestion, she had tried to read something a little less challenging. There was a glass of whiskey on the table beside her with drips of condensation leaving a watery ring on the table. She didn't notice it, nor did she care. She clutched her phone tightly in her left hand. It was a day where she had hoped it would light up with his name on the screen and the picture of him she had taken in a microbrewery they had liked to frequent. Earlier her phone had lit up with a message from a friend reminding her that if she was still free that there was a perfectly eligible man who would love to take her out for the evening. She didn't understand why her friends kept doing this to her. They just kept pestering and nudging. And she kept saying she wasn't ready to move on yet. It would be a long while before she would want to date. They just kept poking at her open wounds.

Without her sister's file, she had nothing to do. Nothing to distract herself with. Bea was probably wondering where she was. She really had tried to read. But her attempts to do anything but sit and pine for Charlie had failed. Within two pages her eyes had watered so much that she couldn't see the words in front of her.

Eventually, she gave in to the sobs. They were more violent than she remembered them being. Her entire body shook and she couldn't breathe. They came out as short, rattled, muffled screams. At least that's what they sounded like to her. It had been a long time since she had allowed herself the luxury to cry like this. Her world had shattered when he walked out that door. She had lived with puffy, red eyes for weeks. She knew everyone at work had noticed but had kept to themselves. A few of the girls, like Millie, had tried to reach out, but she had told them to back off and leave her alone. Even now, it took everything she had in her to get herself out of bed and to put on the little amount of makeup that she wore in the mornings.

He was the first person she had really let into her life on that intimate of a level after Jamie had disappeared.

He was the only one she talked to about that night. Sure, her friends knew about it, but she didn't talk to them about it or how it had altered her and how that had changed the trajectory of her life. But he knew. He was the only one she felt safe enough with to talk about such private things. Charlie was also the only person she talked to about Caleb. In fact, none of her college friends even knew she had a brother. When she lost Charlie, she lost her emotional outlet as well as her partner. As a result, everything was continuing to build up. She felt full and frustrated and didn't know how much longer she could handle the pressure on her own. People always said it'll get easier with time. They were all wrong. It was getting harder instead and she felt like she was losing herself in the process. She had thrown herself with renewed vigor at Jamie's case. She had no reason to go home and no one to check in with and that's how the diner evenings began. Now she had to check in with Bea every night. Maybe she should go even though she didn't have the files. She could still take a notepad and work from memory. She didn't really need the files anyway. She had frequented them so much that they were etched into the depths of her mind.

Her body acted before she had made an actual decision. Her keys were already dangling from her fingertips and her denim jacket was now slung over her shoulders and pulled tightly around her torso. The hallway outside was a drabby gray. It looked dirty as if it hadn't been cleaned since the seventies. Honestly, it probably hadn't been. There was still a slightly green shade to it, making it a puke color when it probably used to be closer to lime. It was worn down now with a clearly trodden path in the middle where it was dirtier and the carpet was thinning from years of use. One foot in front of the other, it was muscle memory that propelled her forward towards the elevator and the staircase on the left. She never took the elevator. She always felt claustrophobic and she enjoyed the exercise the stairs provided. Not quite a workout, but at least she wasn't being lazy. Her stomach panged with hunger. Good thing she was already on her way to the diner. She had nothing in her kitchen. Only her dwindling supply of whiskey and crackers. She stepped outside into the crisp night air. Traveling by bus was a little sketchy, but she had been drinking and taxis never just happened by in this neighborhood. The ride seemed to drag on, but maybe that was the liquor in her system. The streetlights blurred through the dark sky as the blocks dropped away. She got off at the Ocean Street stop and walked the one block to the diner.

It was the only building on the block with its lights still on, like a beacon seeking all the lonely night owls. It wasn't raining as it had been the other evening but there was a light mist that brought a chill to the air. The hairs on the back of her neck stood at attention so she shook out her ponytail and shivered. The door clanged a bell over her head as she entered.

"Darlin'! You were beginnin' ta worry me. Where've ya been the last few days?"

"I took some advice from a coworker and took some time for myself. Even went home early on Friday." Not quite the truth, but close enough. Bea didn't need to know the details. She didn't want to seem like she was completely losing it.

"You look different."

Anderson surveyed herself for a moment. "Besides the sweats?" Or maybe it was her tear stained face. She hadn't even washed her face before coming.

Bea shrugged, looking exasperated. "Your booth is open, hun."

Anderson made her way to the back of the dining area and made a hard right into her little nook. It was dimly lit, which she preferred because most people walking by didn't notice her lonely presence. Her fingers fiddled with the bent menu edges, but she didn't look at it this time. When Bea rounded the corner she already had the steaming cup of coffee in her hands. "No file tonight, sweetie?"

Anderson shook her head, her brown hair bouncing around her shoulders. She was still trying to grow out the pixie cut that Charlie thought was so adorable on her. She never liked it. He had always liked things about her that she hadn't. He had seen the silver linings while all she could see were dark clouds. But that was also why they worked so well together. They had challenged each other.

"I'm not even askin' what ya want to eat. I'm just goin' ta put yur order in."

Bea retreated, leaving Anderson alone. She wasn't really alone though. Faces from the posters stared down at her. Letters of initials carved into the wooden walls told of many love stories that had at some point been inside this private cubby hole. She was surrounded by people and her loneliness eased. Home had too many ghosts. She pulled her small notebook and pen out of her pocket and took a sip of her coffee. She nestled herself into the corner, feet on the booth next to her, and set to work hashing out all the details from memory.

Year Unknown, Day 63

She sat motionlessly. The stillness of the room was unsettling, but she had become accustomed to it. The air in the room seemed thick. She had her back against the wall and faced the door from across the room. He had just been here. He was beginning to be more aggressive and He could tell she was up to something. She was acting differently even though she tried not to. It was difficult to be ignorant of how her muscles were starting to take shape. She was becoming leaner and more toned, at least comparatively to a week ago. The problem with her workouts though, was that they made her even more aware of her hunger. It was getting impossible to ignore.

The lower right side of her lips was already starting to swell and her mouth was filled with the metallic taste of blood from where her skin had split. Her pulse pounded in her ears and it throbbed through her lips. She took deep breaths, trying to calm herself after the adrenaline rush. Her heart was racing, faster than she ever remembered it beating. She forced her mind to think about other things, pleasant things that would distract her. She thought of her brother, Jimmy. Of pushing him on the swing set in their backyard under the oak tree. His squeals of laughter and pleasure. He was her only link to innocence. Without him, life would have been dark and fucked up. Not worth waking up for every day. But he brought light into her life and made her smile when no else could.

She thought of the nights that she would cry herself to sleep and he would crawl in bed with her and she would wrap her arms around his small frame. He would let her tousle his brown hair. He would always go back to his own bed, across the room from her, before the sun came up. But he knew that on the bad nights she appreciated the comfort that he brought her just by simply being there. It was all she needed. And it was what she needed now. She needed to feel that second heartbeat and second breath in the room. It was too silent with only her own filling the space. It didn't really fill it. The room was hollow and she was insignificant in it.

She was conscious of the fact that she was spiraling into a depression. She couldn't do anything about it besides what she was already doing. Work out and plan and wait. Other than that all she had to do was sit. And do nothing. And feel her ass go numb and cold from sitting on the floor. Her fingers played with the loose flaps of her chucks and ran her fingertips over the empty shoelace holes. She just couldn't sit still anymore.

2017, Day 7

It was almost midnight and she had fallen asleep on the table in front of her. Bea had woken her with a shake of her shoulders. Anderson blinked at her.

"Darlin, it's time for ya ta go home."

Anderson didn't argue and collected her things. The streets were quiet, no one was out this late on a Sunday. Without cloud coverage, the air was freezing so she rushed from the bus to her apartment building. Even as sleepy as she was, she forced herself to take the stairs. She pushed open the door to her hallway and saw a small figure huddled on the floor by her door. She couldn't tell who it was so she approached cautiously. He had brown hair and wore dirty jeans. His tennis shoes were old which was clear from the excessive lines and creases that were created from so much use.

"Emz…"

She rushed forward when she recognized the voice.

"Caleb, are you okay?" She helped him to stand and looked into his red-ringed eyes. He did not look good. Last time he had stopped by he had been in the middle of a detox. It hadn't lasted long.

She unlocked her door and ushered him inside. He looked around briefly.

"Where's Charlie?"

"We broke up a couple of months ago."

"Why didn't you tell me?"

"Caleb, you're never around anymore. You don't keep in touch. I never know when I'm going to see you again. Especially when you just take off without telling me like you did last time."

He didn't even look sorry. He just sat down on her couch and emptied his pockets onto the coffee table, wallet and phone, his only two possessions. "You have anything to eat here?"

She sighed and shut the front door. "Wait here," she instructed.

She went into the kitchen alone. She needed to hide the whiskey bottle before he found it. She knew it would be gone before morning if he did. After that was effectively hidden in the broiler underneath the oven, she rummaged around the fridge and wished she hadn't made the frozen pizza for Luke a few nights ago. All she could manage was making a small sandwich. When she returned to the living room he was standing in front of the wall with all the photos. He was staring at one of him, Jamie, and herself from when they were all fairly young.

"This picture is a lie. We were never this happy."

"Caleb. Don't. I don't have the energy to do this right now."

"It's true though." He turned away from it and looked at her offering the sandwich to him. "You're as bad off as I am, aren't you?"

"What makes you say that?"

"You don't have any food in the house. I know that because you're trying to give me this. Charlie always used to have all kinds of foods prepared for you when you got home from work."

"Can we not talk about Charlie, please?"

"Why not, Emz."

"It's still painful that he's not here. I don't want to think about it right now."

He took the sandwich from her finally and silently devoured it. She just stood and watched her little brother. It was probably the first thing he had eaten in a while. He was pale and gaunt. Worse than last time he had been here. When he was licking his fingers she spoke again.

"What do you want, Caleb?"

"What do you mean?"

"You never just stop by here without a reason. Just like how I don't call our stepmother just to chat."

"That woman is not part of our family."

"We're on the same side here."

He didn't look like he believed her and looked everywhere else in the room besides her face. She glanced at her watch, one-thirty. She needed to go to bed.

"I have work in the morning. You're welcome to stay the night. I'll leave some money for you on the table for breakfast. I don't have very much food here."

He still wouldn't look at her.

"Night Caleb." She started toward her bedroom. It was very quiet, she almost didn't hear it, but she thought she heard him say "thank you." Although she knew he was being nasty because he was coming down, it still hurt. Caleb had a knack for poking at all her scars. How had the same tragedy affected them both so differently? She was doing much better than he was, but she wasn't really handling it well. At this point in life, she had hoped to be more financially secure. That was definite. Charlie had never liked how much she helped out Caleb. It was just another wedge that drove them apart.

2017, Day 8

Anderson's alarm pierced the silence, but she was already awake and staring at the ceiling. She glanced at the clock. Six-thirty. She had barely slept at all. The covers fell from her shoulders as she sat up and the hairs on her arms rose from the morning air. Mondays were always the hardest. After a weekend alone with her thoughts, she was sluggish and dragged her feet. It was a struggle to get her mind in order and ready to focus. Thoughts of Charlie swam in her head as she showered and dressed. She wandered into the kitchen knowing she had no food to cook with. She tried to be quiet so that she wouldn't wake up her guest. The coffee pot was clean and ready, she put a filter in the top compartment and opened the jar to the right. Empty. No coffee grounds left. No coffee. This was not a good way to start the day.

"Mondays…" she grumbled to herself.

She would have to settle for the sludge at the station. She snuck into the living room and pulled out a ten from her wallet. That should get him something from Starbucks. She let herself out trying to be as silent as she could. Caleb didn't even budge an inch. He was draped on the couch awkwardly, his long, muscle-less limbs poking out at random angles. His snoring was loud and even, uninterrupted by the door clicking open. His face showed an amount of peace that he never had during his waking hours.

It wasn't raining, but there were storm clouds blocking the sun. The little light that shone through made a blinding glare on the front windshield of her car. It had been far too long since she had taken her car in to get washed. She didn't really care, it was old and falling apart.

It would surprise her if the car lasted the rest of the year. The grey dented Corolla was her stepmother's old car that was given to her when her previous car had died on her. She had been away at college and needed a car to get home for the holidays. She was only gifted the car because her stepmother wanted to buy a new one for herself. Generous people her parents. She should really cut her dad some slack. Losing a child isn't easy, she knew that from losing Jamie. However, her dad had married an uptight shrew who always treated her like she was an inconvenience. Instead of being supportive of her life choices, her stepmother wanted to be able to choose for her how her life would play out. She hadn't had any of her own children. This was probably for the better. The woman settled for forcing civilized dinners once or twice a month in restaurants of her approval. By never once stepping foot in Emily's apartment, her stepmother could imagine that she didn't live in a small, rundown hole. She didn't want to see the truth, but merely projected what she wanted to see. Without seeing the real place, her stepmother could imagine a spacious open floor plan in a nice part of town with a fresh paint job. Something that every parent would want for their child.

The station lot was still fairly empty, but Luke's car was already there. Emily's car shuttered when she slammed the door behind her. One day it was going to fall apart. She passed by Millie on the way to her desk and then froze. She backtracked and looked at Millie.

"Good morning, Anderson." She sure was chipper for a Monday.

"Are you wearing a pushup bra?"

Millie's face flushed and she shifted in her seat uncomfortably. "Is it that noticeable?"

"Just do the top button on your shirt and you'll be okay. There's no need to be showing that kind of cleavage around here."

"He hasn't talked to me all weekend and…"

"Stop." Anderson cut her off. "You know I don't do guy talk with the rest of you girls. I don't want to know."

Millie's face drooped and a glimmer of disappointment and confusion could be found in her eyes. This didn't concern Anderson, just like her break up with Charlie didn't concern the rest of the station either. 'Leave your personal life at home' was her philosophy.

She noted that Luke wasn't at his desk as she seated herself in front of her computer. She pulled up the photos from the party and started to scroll through them again. Perhaps she had missed something the first few times she had gone through them. She paused and studied each one of them.

Mia had tactfully stayed behind the camera lens and wasn't in very many pictures. They mostly consisted of Kate and the boys laughing while they walked. In the house there were pictures of Kate running into Melissa and then Mia dragging Kate out of the room. Then there were just pictures of drinking games. Kate was always the center of attention, whether it be the people in the photo gathered around her or just posing for the photo, stealing the attention from anyone else around her. The social world seemed to revolve around her. Anderson was about to keep scrolling past a photo that was taken in the living room but something made her stop and examine it a little more carefully. There was a group sitting on the couch, Kate was amongst them. Plastic cups littered the table in front of them and one of the girls looked as if she was in the middle of telling a story to her friends. Behind the couch was Mia walking past, her head turned back to look at the group. The look on her face was unpleasant, to say the least. Distaste oozed from her. She looked as if she had bitten into something sour. Did Kate and Mia have a disagreement shortly before Kate went missing? This was certainly news. There was no way that Mia was responsible for it, but it supported Anderson's theory that Mia saw something and didn't say anything.

She jumped when a coffee mug smacked into place next to her arm on her desk. She looked up from the computer screen. Luke was standing there, holding his own steaming cup.

"I just made a fresh batch, figured you'd want a cup."

"Thanks," and then a half a beat later, "are you switching to coffee?"

"I thought I'd give it a shot. I was up a little late last night. How was the rest of your weekend?"

"The usual. Stayed at home, read a little."

She tried not to notice that he was getting the topic of discussion off of himself. He shook his head. He was clearly disappointed but didn't verbalize it, he didn't need to. He gestured at the computer, "What've you got there?"

"This photo proves that Mia wasn't happy with her friendship with Kate."

"You're beating a dead horse, she didn't do it."

"I know she didn't. It's just another layer pulled away. You know? One less thing to wonder about. We could sit here all day and theorize about it and the relationships all these people had to Kate, but now we have tangible proof that she wasn't even liked by her own best friend. Being a cruel leader does not make lasting friendships."

He nodded in agreement. "So what now?"

"I have no idea." Anderson propped her elbows up on the desk and tiredly leaned her chin into her hands. Her shoulders sagged and she let her eyes close. "Maybe Lieutenant Sanchez was right and this case is at an impasse."

Luke remained silent and let her battle the war going on in her mind. She didn't need him to weigh in and he was aware of that. Her mind would provide both sides of the argument and they both knew what she would decide.

"Everyone deserves a chance to come home. At the very least, her parents deserve closure." She tilted her head to look at Luke. He wore an expression of approval.

2017, Day 9

Lauren was waiting for her right outside the classroom door after second period Calculus. She was leaning with her back up against the wall, backpack at her feet and cellphone out, texting of course. Her long, straight blonde hair hid her face from view, which is why Melissa almost walked right past her without noticing. Lauren reached a hand out and caught the inside of Melissa's elbow with her fingertips.

"Hey there! Wait up."

Melissa felt like a fish that had just been caught on a line and was pulled back by Lauren. She blinked for a moment, not really sure what she was supposed to say or do. "Umm. Hi. What's up?" That felt awkward and she winced inwardly.

Lauren smiled at it though. "Some of us are going off campus for lunch. Want to come?"

"We have a closed campus though."

"Yeah, well, it's just something we do every now and then." Lauren had fallen into step beside Melissa as they walked to third period World History together.

"I guess so. That sounds fun. Yeah."

"Cool! You feel ready for the exam? I'm so glad we had that study sesh the other night."

"Well, um. Yeah. The flashcards we made really helped so I feel pretty prepared."

Lauren crinkled her nose in distaste. "You and those silly flash cards. Seriously. Those never help me."

"Well, it's not the actual quizzing each other that helps, it's the action of sitting down and writing the flashcards out that commits the information to memory. For me at least." Melissa shrugged trying to play it casual.

Lauren had stopped walking and Melissa looked back at her. Her mouth hung slack a little and confusion hung in her eyes. She attempted at a grin, "You're a bit of a bookworm, aren't you?"

"Just when it comes to school."

They started walking again, down the hall to the classroom on the left at the end. They went to their assigned seats, which weren't too far from each other, but far enough to end their conversation. Melissa was glad for the reprieve though, she needed a break from being social. She hadn't realized that having friends took this much energy and thought. She carefully placed a notebook and pencil side by side, perfectly parallel to each other on the desk. Lauren was only two desks away, but Melissa could hear her chatting excitedly with Camille, who was in the seat in front of her. Camille glanced over and then waved and grinned at Melissa. So this is what it feels like to not be invisible. It was exhausting. A smile crept over her face as she sat back in her chair to enjoy the feeling. The feeling of no longer being completely alone. This feeling would take a while to get used to.

Mr. Rogers walked in and took a look around at his classroom and all the small conversations taking place. "Looks like everyone had a good weekend. I'm going to give you all five more minutes to review your notes before handing out the exam. At that point, all extra books, papers, and cell phones need to be stowed away. The only thing on your desk should be the exam, one pencil, and your perspiration from last minute cramming." He paused to chuckle, but then collected himself when he realized no one else had found it funny. The class stared back at him blankly. He glanced at the clock on the wall, "I suggest you get started, the five minutes started when I started talking, you now have four minutes left."

The students erupted into a flurry of activity and the room was filled with the sound of papers being flipped and quiet murmurs of kids reading to themselves. Melissa calmly opened her forgotten notebook. She wasn't worried. She had been studying all week, when she met with the girls to study, that was her cram session. She was ready.

Exam completed, and she was waiting outside for the rest of the girls to finish. She figured since Lauren had waited for her earlier, it was only polite for her to do the same. Mia was the first to join her in the hallway. Melissa still didn't like her, couldn't place why, just had a feeling that they would never quite get along.

"Oh hey."

Mia nodded back in response but didn't say anything. She placed her backpack at her feet and leaned back against the lockers, cell phone out. Exactly how Lauren had been standing earlier. Weird. Were they trained by Kate to be clones of each other? She wouldn't be surprised. That was Kate's style.

"What are you looking at." Mia had caught Melissa staring.

"Nothing."

"No really. What?"

"Well, uh, I just thought it was weird. That you're standing exactly how Lauren was earlier."

Mia raised an eyebrow. "What? Training to be a cop?" She spat the words out as if they were poisoned.

"No…"

"Then keep your eyes to yourself."

Melissa looked down at the floor. Her attitude had gotten worse since Kate had gone missing. Curious, since everyone else's attitude had improved.

A few more kids left the classroom, giving the two silent girls awkward glances as they walked by. Maybe she should just go… Maybe they would find it weird she had waited…

"Oh hey! You waited!" Lauren.

"Yeah, of course."

"Coolio, they're going to meet us for lunch, so we can take off if you guys are ready?"

"Um…yeah, sure."

Mia rolled her eyes at Melissa's hesitation.

"It's really not that hard to sneak out of here. We usually just walk out the door." Lauren laughed and ran her fingers through her silky, light hair.

"Lead the way," Melissa faked being calm and collected. Don't show any cracks in the facade. They might leave you behind.

With Lauren only slightly in the lead, the three girls started walking down the empty halls towards the main entrance. Before reaching the main entry area, Lauren and Mia veered to the right, the door to the football field. Lauren laughed at Melissa's expression of surprise.

"I said we usually walk out the doors. I didn't say which door."

Melissa let out a nervous laugh but followed the other two girls. They hugged the wall of the building and ducked under the window sills. Wind whistled past their ears and their footsteps in the wet grass made swishing sounds. Opening the gate of the chain-link fence without making a noise was impossible. The top hinge always squeaked. They opened the gate just wide enough to squeeze through to keep the noise level to a minimum. After that, it was home free. They simply walked through the parking lot and off campus. Just a few blocks and then they turned up the walkway to Jon's, a local burger shack. Anyone who was anyone of importance ate here. She was officially a somebody.

Melissa excused herself to use the restroom. She stood in front of the sink and stared at herself in the mirror. Stick straight blonde hair that refused to do anything and pale blue eyes blinked back. She wore basic concealer and little amounts of mascara that did nothing but clump. She brushed her fingertips along her chapped lips that were still berry red from the cold and matched her cheeks. She didn't belong here in this group, but who was she to question it. She quickly splashed her face with cold water and patted it dry with a paper towel. She pushed open the door and back out into the little shack. The other two had already grabbed a table in the corner, with a window on either side. Lauren was watching traffic stop at the four way stop sign while Mia talked.

"…Kate is gone, all goes to hell. Now we're letting losers into the group? Come on, Lauren."

Lauren pulled her eyes away from the traffic to look at the girl across from her. "She's not a loser. Just ignored. It's a social injustice. I always liked her, even in grade school."

"What for? She's awkward and a nerd."

Melissa didn't need to hear anymore. Her own doubts were being echoed right back to her. She got out of there as fast as she could. She didn't slow down until she was close to campus again. Anxiety clutched at her and she looked back over her shoulder. She hated that prickly feeling of being followed, it went everywhere with her. It was less often now, but it still lingered.

"Hey, where are the others?"

Melissa swore she jumped six or seven feet in the air. Camille and Cass burst into hysterical laughter.

"Whoa, girl. It's just us. Why are you so jumpy anyway?" Camille continued to laugh.

"Sorry. I didn't hear you walk up."

"Clearly."

"They're still at Jon's."

"So why aren't you there?" asked Cass.

Melissa didn't know how to answer that. She opened and shut her mouth. How was she supposed to gracefully respond to that? Thankfully she didn't have to, Camille answered the question for her.

"It was Mia, wasn't it? She doesn't know when to shut up. That was the one thing about Kate, she knew how to tell Mia to shut it."

Cass nodded emphatically in agreement. Camille linked arms with Melissa and turned her back around. The three started walking back the way she had just come from.

"She'll get nicer once she gets to know you. She's just protective of our little group," Cass interjected from behind her.

"Can I ask something without you guys judging me?"

"Of course!" said Camille, squeezing her arm closer for a second, in an attempt to display comfort between friends.

"Why are you guys being so nice to me?"

Cass threw her arms around Melissa's waist in an awkward hug from behind and laughed. "Because we like you, always have. Kate just never let us talk to you."

Melissa glanced sideways at Camille for confirmation, which she got when Camille nodded. "Totally true. Lauren and the two of us agreed that you needed to be a part of our little group."

They turned up the walkway to Jon's Burgers again and this time she went to the counter with the two. Lauren came dashing up, "Oh my god! You scared me. Where the hell were you? I checked the bathroom and you weren't there."

"Sorry, I just…" She didn't know what to say to defend her behavior.

"She overheard Mia being a bitch and thought that she wasn't welcome here. We ran into her and talked some sense into her. Right?" Camille came to her defense again.

"Yeah. Not the words I would have used… but yeah."

Sympathy immediately oozed from Lauren. She hugged Melissa.

"I'm so sorry. If you had stuck around any longer you would've known that I put her in her place. She was being unreasonably mean." Lauren held Melissa at arm's length and looked so sincere.

"Yeah okay. Well, I'm back. And I'm hungry."

"Perfect. I'm buying."

"No, you don't have to do that!" Melissa was dismayed. She was not a charity case.

"No. Mia was a bitch, I got this."

Lauren marched up to the counter and ordered for her. Melissa glanced at the corner table where Mia sat by herself, glaring at Melissa. What was that girl's deal anyway?

"You're gonna love this. Best french fries in town."

"You said that about Cass's mom's pie."

"And was I wrong about that?"

"No, you weren't." Melissa smiled. "Thanks."

Lauren led her back to the table while the other two girls ordered their own meals. "Here, try one of mine. Dip it in the shake. I hope you like shakes, I got one for you." She grinned at Melissa as Melissa cautiously took a french frie, dipped it in the chocolate shake, and took a bite. Lauren wiggled her eyebrows at her. "So?"

"Yeah, best french fries in town," Melissa laughed.

Lauren looked pleased with herself as she leaned back in the booth. Camille and Cass took their seats on either side of Melissa. This still felt weird to be surrounded by people who called themselves friends. People who were standing up for her. Laughing with her and waiting for her after class. It was the best feeling. It was starting to be less out of body, but still not natural.

"So, is sneaking back onto campus as easy as sneaking off?"

The girls exchanged looks, "Yeah…sure. Totally as easy."

Melissa didn't believe them for a second. She knew there was a P.E. class at that time and as long as it wasn't raining, they would be outside on the football field. They were only a block away.

"Seriously guys. What's the plan?"

"Just follow me," Lauren seemed to be the new leader.

She led the way around back to the chain-link fence. She peeked around the corner and then checked her phone for the time.

"Okay, we have five minutes to get inside before the P.E. class should be starting. So we gotta be quick."

She held the gate open a couple of inches and winced at its squeaking. One by one they slid through, crouched down under windows, and tried to move as fast they could. Instead of turning in at the door they had come out of, they continued past it to the locker room door. They filed in and blended in with the girls that were already in there until they made it to the hallway door. Just as they were leaving they ran into Coach.

"What are you girls doing? I know I don't have you in my next class."

"Um, I left something in my locker…" Camille tried to cover.

"And that required all five of you?"

"You know how we travel in packs."

"Mmhhmm. Alright. See you at practice."

They filed past her and waited until the door swung shut before bursting into laughter.

"Coach totally knows."

"Why doesn't she bust us?"

"I have no idea. It's not like we're hurting anyone though."

Melissa started to break off from the rest of the group, "See you guys, I need to get to AP English." She waved and took off down the hall to her locker. She needed to switch out books before heading to class. She got to her locker, pulled it open, and started rifling through her backpack for her British History textbook. Her blonde hair fell from her shoulders, blocking her view of the hallway. Her fingers finally found the book and pulled it out. She placed it in her locker and started looking for her English books. Her hair fell from her face and she glanced down the hall. Cameron was at the end standing next to his own locker, talking to some of his buddies. One of the guys caught her looking and nudged Cameron. She immediately averted her gaze back to the books in her locker. She couldn't find her book. Screw it. She slammed shut her locker and rushed down the hall, passing the boys at the end. She couldn't stop herself, her eyes looked up from the floor and found that Cameron was watching her. Their eyes connected for a second and then she was back to staring at the floor. She was gone before he had the chance to say anything.

2017, Day 10

Luke had picked up another case from Millie in the morning. Anderson was glad for the distraction since she was stuck on the Caldwell case. They spent all day working on the new case, but she couldn't seem to stay focused. Her car shuttered to a stop in her parking spot in the underground garage. She sat for a moment and thought about it. Today they had been called to the scene of a convenience store robbery. It was a seedy neighborhood corner store. It hadn't been too hard. The store clerk recognized the guy's voice as a local who frequented the place. Emily smiled to herself as she walked up the last flight of stairs to her floor. Who would be stupid enough to rob a place they go to all time? That would be the equivalent of her trying to rob Bea at the diner. After they had arrested the guy, she let Luke take charge and lead the interview. She turned the key in the lock to her apartment door, number 469. There was silence in her apartment which was weird. Caleb had been there for two days. He was always there when she left for work and when she got home. She had consistently made him dinner and left him money for breakfast. Today there was no sign of him when she entered her living room. She walked through the entire apartment. No sign of him. She started to get an icky feeling. She looked through the kitchen. She wasn't sure what she was looking for until she found it. The empty whiskey bottle in her recycling bin. She dashed into her bedroom and slid open her closet door. She dropped to her hands and knees and pawed through her shoes and shoe boxes looking for the right one. She found it exactly where she had left it. She pulled it out in a frenzy and threw the lid off. The cards and little notes were still there.

Everything that Charlie had written to her was in this small Nike box. She dumped the box out on the floor and sorted through them. Eventually, she had to admit defeat. She had never thought that Caleb would stoop this low. Sure, he had stolen cash from her wallet before. But this was a whole new level. The small black velvet box was empty. She could still vividly see Charlie down on one knee, holding out the open box, the ring sparkling at her. They were at the botanical gardens in the middle of Spring, the roses in full bloom all around them. She sat on the floor in her closet and stared at the empty box in her hands. Her heart felt like it had dropped out of her chest.

Year Unknown, Day 89

"Alice…"

It sounded far away as if she wasn't quite in the same room. The voice was distant and pulled at a memory that she had tucked away in a far corner of her mind so she could sleep.

"Alice…"

Her hair tickled her face and her nose twitched involuntarily pulling her further from her dreams. Maybe it wasn't a memory. Whoever that was needed to keep the noise down. She felt around for a blanket to pull over her head. When she couldn't find one she settled for covering her face with an arm and hoped that whoever it was would leave her alone. She clearly wasn't ready to get up yet. Whoever Alice was, she really needed to answer whoever was calling to her.

"Alice!"

That was directly in her ear. The grogginess was gone in an instant and she flung her arm from face, opening her eyes wide. He was in the room with her. Nonetheless, His filled out face and silver-rimmed glasses were inches from her cheek. She held back the whimper that wanted to rip from her throat. He had never been this close to her and she didn't like it. She had always tried to avoid eye contact at all costs, but this forced her to look at Him. His eyes were a muddy brown, and all the glow of life had been sucked out of them. This rivaled the fear that she had of the fact He had broken several unspoken rules. He had entered the room while she was sleeping, which He had never done before, at least to her knowledge, and now he was inches from her. He didn't draw away, He remained close. She, in turn, remained on the bed, motionless, waiting to see what other boundaries he'd be willing to cross.

Irritation crossed his face. "I'm tired of playing games, Alice." He paused and waited for a moment. When she said nothing He continued, "I need to know where John is."

"I don't know who John is," she whispered, exhaustion seeping into her voice. She was tired of these questions. He never stopped with them. When would He get it? She wasn't freaking Alice. He kidnapped her, shouldn't He know who she was?

He slammed a fist into the wall by her head. She couldn't help it, she flinched away from Him and the wall. She needed more distance. He honestly couldn't feel the pain in His hand, or if He just had the mental capacity to ignore it. She didn't know which one was more terrifying.

"Yes, you do, Alice. Just tell me where you hid him and all this will be over."

She shook her head, refusing to say more. Even if she did know who or where John was, this wouldn't be over. He slammed His palm on the wall again. She tried to hold her ground but her gut was churning. He reached out, grabbed her by the forearm, and pulled her up to standing. His fingers were rough on her skin, but the warmth of his touch sent a chill rippling through her. She thought of her brother, and of pulling close to her as he fell asleep. She quickly shook the thought from her mind. His grip was turning her arm red, but she didn't want to anger Him further by trying to pull her arm away. He smelled like the outdoors, it filled the air around her and she tried to enjoy this small thing, a gift He had unknowingly brought to her.

"Where is he?"

"I don't know."

He shook her.

"I don't know!" She shrieked.

He pushed her against the wall, smacking the back of her head against the cement. She closed her eyes tight from the pain that coursed through her skull. The blood was pounding in her ears again. He placed a hand on either side of her head on the wall and brought His mouth close to her right ear. Distance was seemingly gone.

"One more time. Where is he, Alice?"

She shivered from the vibration of His voice. Goosebumps covered her bare arms and shoulders. She could feel His body heat radiating off Him. This sent more chills down her spine. She didn't want to feel His body heat. She wanted Him to back away. She wanted the shoelaces that were tucked in her bra right now. She wanted to be just a bit stronger so she could overpower Him and run out that slightly ajar door. Instead, she remained where she was, back against the wall like a cornered animal. She tried to control her breathing, to keep it level, to keep the panic out. Anything to hide her true feelings from Him. He grabbed her face with a hand and jerked it up so that she was forced to look Him in the face. She didn't want Him touching her like this. What if she head-butted Him? How much does that really hurt?

"Alice. I need to know where he is. I need to know he's safe."

"I don't know who John is, but I do know he wouldn't be safe with you." She surprised herself with her own aggression.

He didn't take kindly to this, she didn't expect Him too. He grabbed her shoulders and shook her hard enough that her head cracked into the cement again. Black spots passed over her vision and she struggled to stay upright. Something wet was dribbling down the back of her neck.

He had a disgusted look on His face, but He dropped His hands from her and stood back.

"I'll be back tomorrow, I hope you'll have a different answer."

He turned His back to her and headed for the door. She waited a moment before dashing after Him, reaching for the door with one hand outstretched in front of her. She was too late and it slammed shut behind Him. It was too quick and she couldn't stop her body from catapulting into the shut door. She crumpled to the floor in front of it. She wasn't able to keep herself standing anymore. She reached a hand to the back of her head and felt for it. It wasn't hard to find. Blood covered her hair and briefly, she wished for a hair tie. The black spots were back and swimming in front of her. She crawled to her food tray and felt for the water bottle. She pulled her shirt off and got a piece of the fabric wet and tried to haphazardly clean the back of her head and her hair. She couldn't see what she was doing and she had no idea if it was even helping but she didn't stop. It was soothing to feel as if she was doing something useful for once.

2017, Day 11

Anderson stood in front of her mirror. For once they weren't going to a fancy restaurant and she didn't need to dress up too much for dinner. Her stepmother would still expect her to look decent, as opposed to her normal haphazardly thrown on outfits. She paired dark skinny jeans with a loose deep purple sweater and brown knee-high boots. By pulling back her hair from her face with a simple clip, she hoped she could smooth out the tired wrinkles on her face. Attempting basic eye makeup took longer than she had thought, and she always felt like she had raccoon eyes once eyeliner had been applied. It brought out the redness in her eyes that she shared with Caleb- his from the heroin, hers from the lack of sleep. It would have to do since it was all she really knew how to do. She turned her face this way and that, picking out all the flaws that she knew her stepmother would point out. She picked a simple brown purse that matched her boots and threw in her wallet. Her denim jacket was still on the coat rack right where she had left it. Her car keys jingled as the vehicle sputtered to life and the windshield wipers smeared water across the window, making it even harder to see. She made a mental note that she needed new wiper blades.

It was a short drive to downtown where she pulled into the only free parking structure. She never found a spot in it, but she always attempted it anyway. One day she'd get a spot. Today was not that day though. She circled a few times before she gave up and went to one of the many paid structures. She took the wax-like ticket from the machine and headed to the second floor where there was plenty of parking.

The roads were still wet from the recent rain and downtown was quieter than the norm. There weren't a lot of people cluttering the wide sidewalks. Good, she didn't like downtown when it was busy. When it was busy on the weekends it got hard to walk around and not run into at least four people she used to know. She always ran into her college friends, and every now and then she ran into high school acquaintances. That was the worst. They never knew what to say. There would be awkward hellos and how are you's and then silence as everyone shifted their weight and then finally the, 'see you around.' No matter how much time had gone by, she was always the girl whose sister went missing.

She walked past the Ugly Mug on her way to McCann's and she peered in through the window. She always wished to be one of the few curled up in the corner in the big armchairs. To feel the heat from the fireplace while reading a good book; that was the dream. Mia was there by herself in a corner. She held a cup of coffee with both hands close to her face. She was breathing in the steam with her eyes closed. For the first time since Anderson had entered the girl's life, she had an expression of peace on her face. She had school books on the table in front of her but they were being ignored for the moment. Habits were hard to break, even if they were normally done with other people around. Anderson kept walking; she didn't want Mia thinking that she was being followed and spied on.

She turned in at the overhang that read McCann's and climbed the two flights of stairs to the restaurant and bar. The restaurant had about twenty-five tables total and the bar had nine bar stools. Behind the rows of alcohol bottles was a mirror that was not only smudged all on the bottom half but was also steaming up from the heat of so many bodies cramming the bar area. There weren't any stools available, but her stepmother would've had a conniption if they had sat there anyway. She turned to the hostess instead. The girl had bright blue eyes, and her smile was much too perky for Anderson's taste, especially since it was so quiet inside.

"There'll be three of us."

"Do you have a preference?" The girl gestured to the almost-empty dining room and Anderson took in the elaborate stained glass windows which cast emeralds and golds onto the tables and hardwood floor. It almost seemed like she was looking through a beer bottle.

"A window?"

She followed the blonde waif to a window booth in the far corner. She took a seat on the side that faced the front door. She barely even looked at the menu before a waitress with tattoos covering both of her arms traipsed over.

"Good evening," Her voice was low and sultry, but had an ashy tone to it as if she smoked often. "Can I get you something besides water while you wait for the rest of your party?"

"Yes, can I get an 805?"

"You got it."

The waitress left her alone again and she picked up the menu. It was dimly lit, which would be a problem for her parents, but she didn't need the light. She knew the menu well enough that she didn't need to look at it to know what she wanted. The low lighting would hide the red in her eyes anyway. She sat with her arms crossed and lazily drummed her fingers on her elbow. She didn't like waiting but she would rather be early than have Tracy lecture her for being late. Anything to avoid the lectures. She raised her eyes to the front area to watch her parents walk in. She waved them over. Her stepmother daintily picked her way between the tables and her father followed slowly in her wake. She stood to give them awkward hugs and then gestured for them to sit across from her.

Her stepmother had a tight-lipped smile on her face as she took her seat directly across from Emily. She looked out of place, perfectly groomed in the dark and dingy bar. Flawless, as always. Her father took his seat next to Tracy, he looked less out of place, but still uncomfortable in this setting. He probably hadn't stepped foot in a bar since he had married his second wife. He took her to one of his favorite bars when they were dating and she had not enjoyed the experience.

"Have you already ordered a drink?" asked her stepmother.

"Yes, I have. I didn't order for you though, I thought you would want to look at the wine list first."

She nodded in confirmation and silently perused the inadequate wine list. To her surprise though, her father picked up the beer list. She hadn't seen him drink a beer since her college days, which also coincidentally coincided with pre-Tracy days. He always stuck to wines.

"Eddy…" her stepmother scolded.

He shrugged his shoulders, "Why not? When in Rome, right?" He winked at Emily. He was in a pleasant mood. "What did you get, darling?"

"An 805."

He nodded in agreement. "That's a good choice."

A real smile crossed her face. At least he was trying to be a peacemaker. The waitress came back with her beer and placed it carefully on the table. Anderson watched Tracy give the waitress a sweeping look up and down, her lips in full pursed mode and her brows knitted together. Her eyes froze on the exposed arms with more colorful ink than the stained glass windows.

"I see the rest of the group has arrived. Can I get either of you something to drink?"

"I'll join the party and have an 805 as well." Anderson's dad shot the girl a pleasant smile while irritation flickered across Tracy's face.

"And for you ma'am?" Luckily, Tracy was able to fix her face into a smile before the waitress looked at her.

"How's your Malbec?"

The waitress frowned and tapped her pen on her pad in thought. "Well, personally I'm more of a lager gal, but I've heard the Malbec is preferred over our other reds. Although, I do enjoy the red blend."

The pursed lips came back. "Let's just stick with the Malbec, shall we?"

Emily always felt like an adolescent around her stepmother. Something about the woman just exasperated her. She could see why Caleb had turned to drugs after Emily had left for college and he no longer had her around to shield him from Tracy. Emily made eye contact with the waitress and tried to send reassuring vibes. When she pulled her gaze away from the girl she realized that her father was watching her. When she looked at him all she saw was sadness. Ashamed, she pretended to stare at her menu. It wasn't until the waitress had left them, her swagger intact, that Tracy spoke.

"Emily, what do you suggest to eat here?" Her stepmother had been squinting rather intently at the laminated page. It was too dark in here for her to read the menu.

"I usually just get a burger." She glanced at the menu for a second. "But you'll probably like the steak with the garlic mashed potatoes."

Tracy continued to stare at the menu with discontent. At this point, she had pulled her phone out and had opened the flashlight app to shine a light on the page. It glared off the lamination and Emily had to look away. It was too embarrassing to watch anyway. Anderson knew her stepmother would wind up ordering the steak. She was just being stubborn and wasting time continuing to look at the menu. Sure enough, when the poor waitress came back to take their orders her stepmother asked questions about three or four other dishes before finally ordering the steak, rare with another glass of Malbec. Her father was the last to order, a chicken pot pie.

"Now that that's done, how are you, dear?" She emphasized the first part as if ordering her meal had been such an ordeal for her.

Anderson took a sip of her beer, thank god the waitress had brought her a second one, trying to stall while she tried to think of something positive to say. A lot had been going on, but none of it was really news no was it good.

"Oh, you know… I'm the same as always..." Her voice trailed off as she lost traction.

"I can see that." Disapproval leaked into her stepmother's voice, "You look tired."

The low lighting didn't hide her red eyes as she had hoped.

"I work a lot. You are aware of this, aren't you?" Her dad shot her a look as sharp as her tone.

"Of course you do, dear." Tracy always found a way to sound belittling and as if she didn't really believe that Emily worked sixty hours a week, sometimes more.

"Don't you ever go out with your girlfriends anymore? What was that one girl's name?" She snapped her fingers for emphasis. "The one from college you used to go out with all the time."

"Sarah."

"Yes! Don't you ever go out with her anymore?"

"Not really, no."

"You know, she's worried about you, too. You really should take her up on those dates she tries to set up for you."

"How do you know about those?" Anderson didn't pose it as a question either, it was more of a growl that came from the back of her throat.

"Well, we talk about it sometimes."

"You talk to my friend Sarah about me?"

"Well, ever since Charlie left you've been such a mess…" Tracy kept talking, but she wasn't listening anymore. She refused to hear this tangent again. It was a never ending tirade that was brought up every time.

It had only taken her stepmother one glass of wine to bring up Charlie. That was a new record. Usually, it at least took until the food had been whisked from the kitchens and placed before them. Tracy bristled at the fact that Emily refused to talk about what happened, but then Anderson really didn't want them knowing about the fighting. So she sat through another session of Tracy picking her apart, trying to analyze what went wrong. In doing so, she did what she did best: telling Anderson all the reasons why she wasn't good enough. She tried hard to tune out the endless chatter but it was hard when her stepmother's criticism was so spot-on and, on occasion, something she agreed with. Her stepmother ended with, "Honestly, I'm amazed he stuck around as long as he did." Anderson was too. She spent many nights wondering the same thing.

Anderson was always amazed that her father just sat back and let this horrible woman talk shit to his only surviving daughter. However, his world revolved around his wife. If she had been Caleb, she would've left the house right after high school as well.

Tonight though, her father tried to step in to lessen the blow. "Well. No one is ever going to be good enough for our little girl." He gave a genuine smile that warmed Emily for a moment before she realized that he had said our, insinuating that she also belonged to Tracy.

Her stepmother turned her attention back to her food that had been delivered mid-lecture. Her father took the opportunity to ask about Emily's work.

"Well, I can't say much, but I'm working one case that has been giving me a bit of trouble, a missing girl actually."

"Her poor parents," he clucked his tongue and shook his head, "What else is going on?" He was clearly changing the subject. It saddened Emily that he couldn't even talk about it, especially since she could tell he was interested.

"Luke has been treating me more like an equal partner, more than he used to. Much more give and take now."

"Oh? Did he stop asking you to fetch him tea?" He made a classic dad face, the kind where he knew he was making a stupid joke but couldn't stop himself.

She let out a burst of laughter that startled Tracy into almost dropping her fork. "Yes! He stopped asking me to get him tea. I can't believe that you remember that. In fact, just the other day he brought *me* a cup of coffee."

"That's my girl!" He beamed at her and his wife.

Her stepmother finally spoke up, "Are you staying safe though?"

"As much as I can be in my line of work." Her voice went from expressive to cold and she couldn't stop herself from bringing a deadpan stare to Tracy's side of the table.

"What's that supposed to mean?"

"I catch criminals," she snapped, but then she saw her father's reproachful look and she tried to expand in a more pleasant tone. "I've, for the most part, been pretty lucky. Honestly, the girl that's missing sounds more dangerous than any of the other kids and parents I've talked to that knew her."

Tracy scoffed, "How scary can a young girl be?"

"You'd be surprised. This girl is the exact opposite of Jamie."

This was met with silence as it slowly sunk in that she had brought up the one topic that was off-limits in their family.

"I'm sorry, I didn't mean to bring her up. It just slipped out," she tried to backtrack.

"Let's not dwell on it," her father said as he lifted his half-empty beer glass to his lips.

"Sure, okay."

There was more silence as Anderson tried to think of something to say. She drew in her ketchup pile with one of her now-cold french fries.

Her dad slammed his glass down harder than he meant to, "Emily, stop playing with your food."

She fought the urge to tell her father she wasn't twelve but dropped the french fry anyway.

"Caleb stopped by the other night," she commented. She glanced up to see how they would react. Tracy tried to ignore it, but a serious look had crossed her father's face.

"And what did he want?"

"He was trying to detox again."

Her father shook his head and refused to say anything more. Anderson finished her beer before addressing Tracy again. "How's Mrs. Baum?"

"Oh honey, didn't you hear?" Her stepmother actually sounded concerned that Emily hadn't heard whatever interesting piece of gossip that was going around the neighborhood now. "She died a week ago."

Oof, that was actual news, not gossip. She felt guilty for a moment. Her stepmother prattled on about their neighbor, explaining about the heart attack and how stressed out she had been because of the kids being off doing god only knows what. This led to more gossip about the neighborhood women, which marriages were failing, which were flourishing, and who was cheating on who. Her guilt was gone after the first diversion. During all this, even her father had lost interest and busied himself by checking out the design in the stained glass behind him. "And the Randolphs' dog ran away. Anyway, if you're available, Mrs. Baum's memorial is this Saturday at nine am."

"Yes, of course, I'll be there."

She couldn't possibly say no to that without sounding like a hateful person, even though the last time she had had an interaction with Mrs. Baum was when she had been loading up her car when she was moving away to college. She was a grouchy old woman who was irritated because one of Emily's boxes was on her side of the property line and smothering one of her violet-colored petunias. The bill was placed in front of her father who quietly pulled out his wallet after checking the receipt.

"Wonderful. We can pick you up on the way there."

"Uh, I can just meet you there. There's no need for you to go out of your way to come to my part of town. It's not really a direct route for you." Emily rushed to pull a twenty out of her pocket, but he was too quick for her and handed his credit card off to the waitress.

Her stepmother looked offended for a moment but didn't push her luck. At least Emily was agreeing to go to an event with them outside of their monthly dinners. By the time they agreed on what time to meet, the waitress had brought back her dad's card. Once it was all signed for the three made their way down the stairs to street level in silence. The street was still as quiet as it had been before. They walked in the same direction, past the bookshop, the Ugly Mug, which Mia had left, and a myriad of little boutiques.

"Let's stop in here for a second," her father veered into the old-fashioned candy and pop shop.

She laughed, "I'm too old for this!"

"You are never too old for your old dad to buy you cookie dough ice cream on a waffle cone."

"I mean, I won't stop you."

Her stepmother sighed in exasperation, rolling her eyes to the sky, "You are both children," but she followed the two inside the shop and out of the wind.

They passed a glass case of truffles, a case of gummies, a case of taffy, and shelves of stuffed animals. In the back there was a mock bar area with high backless stools. Nineties pop music played lightly in the background. There were three workers behind the ice cream cabinet, chatting with each other about teachers and the classes they were taking. One of them broke away to help them. It took Emily a moment to recognize Tammi from the cheer squad. She wore a pale yellow long-sleeved shirt with dark overalls over the top. There were ice cream stains and chocolate sauce splattered on her overalls. Her jet black hair was pulled into a tight ponytail and she had flawless "barely there" makeup. Tammi was a beaute. The girl blinked back in surprise and then quickly masked her face.

Emily's stepmother nudged her, "You need to learn how to do that. See, her eyes don't look red."

"She's also sixteen, Tracy." Emily hissed. She tried to say this quietly, not wanting Tammi to overhear them talking about her.

Emily watched as the girl scooped her ice cream, her arm muscles tensing for just a moment, but not really showing any definition. She handed Emily the cone before lazily typing into the register the price of a cone for her and her father. Her dad paid before the girl started to scoop his chocolate peanut butter swirl. As they waited, her father wrapped one arm around her shoulders and leaned her into a sideways hug. Emily's heart swelled for a moment and everything that bothered her about their family dropped away. She half expected little Jamie to come running up behind her actual mother and Caleb trotting behind her, tagging along to his older sisters. Most likely, Jamie would've been holding a pink stuffed cat in her hands with huge eyes, begging to bring it home with them.

"Well, Tracy and I should get home."

Jamie's ghost vanished and Emily stood with her broken family. She stood awkwardly apart from them, torn between wanting to hug her father goodnight and distancing herself from Tracy.

She sat in her living room with the lights off. She had stopped by the liquor store on the way home and all she had managed was pouring a glass of whiskey. She lacked any motivation to do anything else. She didn't want to look at any files for once. She didn't want to go see Bea. She didn't even want to take a shower and go to bed. She just wanted to sit, and drink her whiskey. This happened every time she saw her parents. Her father really did try, but her stepmother didn't understand anything about her life. And she was left wondering what she and Jamie would be doing now if and what would be different if Jamie was still here. Anderson wouldn't have ever become a cop, she would've followed her dream of majoring in English. She had no idea what she would've done with that degree after school, but she knew that's what she would have pursued. She had a feeling that her sister would have gone after a fashion degree. She always had a knack for styles and colors for other people. Her stepmother wouldn't be so disapproving and cold all the time. She knew she and her sister would have talked about boys together. Things with Charlie wouldn't have fallen apart; they would've had a more playful relationship. But that wouldn't have worked anyway. It was her seriousness that drew him to her in the first place.

What would she do if Charlie ever asked for the ring back? She thought briefly about how the small sparkly ring had looked on her finger. If one phrase came to mind it was out of place. It was delicate, and she loved it, but it looked so wrong on her hand. She couldn't believe that Caleb had taken it, but she knew she shouldn't be surprised. This is what drug addicts did. She needed to stop treating him like someone she could trust.

When had she finished her glass? She poured another and pulled her jacket tighter around her torso. She fixed her brain to the ticking of the clock above her desk, letting the rhythm and the alcohol numb her mind.

2017, Day 12

Melissa was at her locker rummaging around for her Pre Calc and Early American History notebooks with Lauren at her side, chattering about something or other. All she had to do was nod and "mhmm" in the right spots to keep Lauren pleased. It was a pretty simple system; it made her seem social without her wasting her energy on the small things. Of course, she paid attention to the important stuff, but when it came to gossip about people she didn't really know and didn't interact with much, she just tuned it out. Lauren suddenly smacked Melissa's arm, one, two, three times.

"Oh my god. What is he doing staring you down?!"

Instinctively, Melissa swiveled her head around, looking up and down the hallway, "Who?" There were too many people crowding their lockers and the walkways for her to pinpoint who Lauren was referring to.

"No, don't look. God, don't you know anything?"

"Well then, who?" she turned back to her locker. It was typically organized, everything had its place, but this week had just been too hectic with her new friends and in her rush to grab and shove books in it was messier than the usual. "Gosh, why can't I find anything in here?"

"Cameron."

"Wait, who?"

"You know, Cameron. On the basketball team."

"Oh, I know who you're talking about. But what does he want with me? He's done a good job of ignoring me since…" she trailed off realizing what she was about to say. She didn't need to be the center of gossip. Just because she was part of the group now didn't mean she needed to be talked about by everyone else. Screw the notebooks. She shut her locker without finding them and blazed a path down the hall, Lauren at a trot in her wake.

"Since what?" Lauren sounded all too excited about the prospect of having new gossip in her clutches.

"Nothing. Just…forget it, would you?"

"Ummm. No. I don't think so. I knew there was something going on with you. There's no way you could fly under the radar as much as you *supposedly* do." Implying that Melissa had a wild streak she kept under wraps made Lauren smile wickedly. If they considered kissing Cameron and then bolting from a party a wild streak, then maybe she did have one.

Lauren trailed after Melissa even though she wasn't in the same Math class with her. She was still in Algebra I, with the rest of the girls. Instead, Melissa had the pleasure of sitting next to pimply Nick in this class, and he was a mouth breather. They passed Cameron and Melissa used every ounce of her self control to not look at him or any of his friends that were grouped around him as jocks always seemed to do.

"Ahhh! He's totally into you. He couldn't keep his eyes off you!" Lauren squealed in delight.

"Naw. There's no way. It's just me, ya know?"

"Girl, give yourself more credit," she said this as she raised an eyebrow at her.

"Whatever, see you after class."

She ducked into her classroom, cheeks flushed and running from the situation.

She was ambushed an hour later when class was let out. Not only was Lauren waiting for her, but she had called in reinforcements. Camille and Cass were there with her and the four of them walked to their next class together.

The other three were adamant about finding out what had happened and would not let it drop. Their persistence almost made her want to tell them about her night with Cameron. To be honest though, nothing really all that exciting happened.

"Just tell us!" Cass whined.

"Yeah, what's the big deal? We're your friends, aren't we?" asked Camille.

"Well yes, but…" she didn't know how to deflect the questions anymore.

"But what." It was more of a demand, as to be expected of Lauren. She was slowly turning into the new queen bee in Kate's absence.

Melissa sighed in frustration and stopped walking in the middle of the hallway. The others stopped with her and waited expectantly, their eyes shining with anticipation.

"Fine. Nothing happened. I just ran into him at that party and we hung out for a bit before I left."

"That's it? I mean, the guy has been drooling all over you all week."

"Well, I may have kissed him at the end of the night and then just left. It's really not a big deal though."

"What?!" they all shrieked in unison. The handyman to their left, who was working on fixing a door hinge, glanced up at the sound. She stared at her stark white Keds scuffing against the dirty linoleum floor and felt the color rise in her cheeks.

"No way. You totally didn't. No wonder he's been watching you. You totally left him wanting more." The shock in Camille's voice wasn't as offensive as it was reassuring. They didn't expect this type of behavior from her, and she appreciated that. Although, this one instance probably messed her image up.

"Yeah. I did actually. I was a little tipsy, I guess, and just thought why the hell not?"

"You were tipsy?"

She just nodded instead of using words since they were just digging her into a deeper hole.

"I told you guys she was cool."

Melissa lifted her head slowly to meet Lauren's steady gaze. She didn't seem to be joking. She seemed pretty sincere. Yet, she couldn't get out of her head how much Mia would hate this. She glanced around half-expecting for her to pop up on cue as she had a tendency to do, but she didn't. Melissa shook herself free of her thoughts and shot the other girls a dazzling smile.

"Shall we head to class?"

It was time for the new Melissa that debuted at the party to resurface. Old Melissa was gone for good and it was time to enjoy herself. She forced a small giggle, that's something one of the other girls would do, right? Then she led the girls into the classroom.

"Do you think we'll get our tests back today?"

She took her seat a few desks away from the rest and pulled out her notebook, ceremoniously lining up her pen exactly parallel to it. It was a habit; she couldn't stop herself. Mr. Rogers sat behind his desk and flipped through his notes, glancing at the clock, impatiently waiting for it to be time. Time for all of the students to find out how badly they'd done on the exam. For the first time in a long while, Melissa was actually bored waiting for class to start. She didn't look at her own notes and she didn't open her textbook for extra reading, nor did she pull out her fun reading book she always had waiting in her bag.

He stood, picked up a stack of papers, and started reading out names. As each name was called, its recipient would get up from their desk to receive their doom. She watched Camille and Lauren receive theirs and how their faces relaxed a little after looking at their scores. Lauren even gave her a thumbs up with a giant grin. It was then that she realized Mia was absent from class. Her desk sat empty and lonely. No backpack leaning against the chair to indicate that she was merely in the restroom. She just wasn't there.

2017, Day 12

"You look like crap, Emz."

She dragged her red eyes off the floor to glare at Luke. She didn't have the energy to tell him not to call her that. He was at his desk with an open file in front of him. How did he always get to work before her no matter how early she came in? The light above him flickered and she briefly thought about when they would get that fixed. It had been flickering the entire time she had worked here. It made the already dreary office seem even darker. At least the interview rooms where she had talked to the kids with their parents were a little brighter with their windows and artwork. She preferred to do her interviews in those rooms as opposed to her desk. She felt that it was depressing for victims to sit in front of a desk under a flickering light and talk about what went wrong with their lives. Luke was staring at her with an expectant expression on his deceptively young features. She realized that she had never actually responded to his comment.

"I couldn't sleep last night."

"Please tell me you at least showered." He was joking, possibly. She couldn't tell, she was too tired and she didn't have the energy to pretend to be offended. She slumped into her own chair and took a moment to just breathe. She needed to clear her mind. It was murky with thoughts of her personal life. It wasn't even a consistent stream of thoughts, just random ideas that were swimming around in her head at random. It was time to lock them away for the day. But they refused to stay in the drawers that she tried to tuck them into. The drawers kept opening and words were just floating out. Now her brain was a closet with a chest of drawers? What the hell was wrong with her today?

"Emz."

"Yeah?" She let her eyes remain lowered.

"You okay? You sure you don't need some time off? You seem a bit distracted and you have been since we started this case."

"I'm fine."

"I was looking at your sister's file last night."

She looked up at him finally and removed her fingers from where they were pressing into her temples, massaging, trying to get the headache to disappear. She wasn't hungover from the whiskey last night, but there was a persistent pounding in her head that refused to go away. Her brain was tired from the perpetual overuse.

"And?" she prompted him.

"Not only is the Caldwell case similar to it, but it happened during the same time of year. What, fifteen years ago now?" He glanced at the paper in front of him to verify the date. "If you need the time-"

She didn't let him finish.

"Just stop. Don't mind me, I can handle myself. The best thing for me is to keep working and keep busy. Honestly. Time off will just drive me crazy."

He looked skeptical, but let it go.

"Have you noticed at all how much Jamie looks like Kate and Melissa?"

She nodded slowly. "Yeah, struck me as odd the first time we saw a picture of her."

Luke hummed and tapped a finger on his desk. He was on to something and she didn't want to disrupt his thought process. She pulled up some photos from the Caldwell case on her computer. Her sister had been like these girls. Well-liked at school, smart, pretty… Then Luke was leaping out of his chair and dashing to Sanchez's office. Anderson followed in his wake, albeit at a much slower pace and with less enthusiasm. He knocked on the open door.

"Lieutenant, might I pick your brain for a moment?"

"Come in," he waved the two detectives in without looking up from his paperwork.

They hovered in front of his desk and Anderson looked to Luke to take the lead. They stood behind the chairs in front of his desk. Those chairs never saw any use, no one was ever in this office long enough to need them. Luke was deep in thought and didn't say anything until an impatient Sanchez put his pen down and gave them his undivided attention.

"Five years ago, you were a detective still, weren't you?"

"Yes."

"I know it wasn't your case, but do you remember when that teenage girl went missing? What was her name…" Luke snapped his fingers for emphasis. "She was about fifteen years old. From a middle-class neighborhood. We looked for weeks and never found anything."

Sanchez leaned forward and clasped his hands in front of him.

"Anna! Her name was Anna Clark." Luke practically shouted the name he was so excited to remember.

Recognition crossed the Lieutenant's face. Clearly, it was a name he knew well. Anderson had still been in college at the time and the name was unfamiliar to her. She had been too wrapped up in her own sorrows to pay attention to anything besides her schoolwork.

"Eerily similar to Kate's disappearance, and if I dare to mention, even Anderson's sister's disappearance."

"Three girls in fifteen years. What are you thinking?" Sanchez knew where Luke was going with this but needed him to say it.

"Is it possible that we have a serial on our hands?"

Anderson closed her eyes. If this was true then there was no hope that Jamie was still out there somewhere hoping to be saved. She could feel herself swaying back and forth unsteadily. Desperation clawed its way up her throat, she needed to know what happened to her sister, even if it destroyed her. With her eyes still shut, she flung a hand out in front of her, searching for the back of the chair that she knew was there. She needed to catch her balance. The ringing in her ears was throwing her off center.

"Anderson, if this is connected to your sister's case, then you will have to be relieved from this post. You cannot work this closely on your sister's case, you're too emotionally involved."

She opened her tired eyes. Both men were watching her.

"Please-"

She stopped when Sanchez held up a hand.

"Take some time off. That's an order. I don't want you anywhere near this. Do you understand?"

She nodded.

"Luke, I want you to work with Himura on this. He was the detective assigned to Anna's case. Do you have

Anderson's sister's file? Good. Find the detective who worked it. We need to pool all of our resources on this. Three girls in fifteen years. That's one girl every five years. This changes everything. Kate could still be out there waiting for us. This is your new priority. Go."

Anderson followed Luke to his desk. He flipped through papers looking at names and numbers and paused briefly when Anderson continued to hover.

"I know this is hard for you, Emz. But you need to go home."

"I can't. I need to be a part of this."

She refused to break eye contact. He needed to see how strong she was.

"I don't have time for this."

"Please."

"Officially, you can't be here." He glanced down for a moment thinking, "Unofficially, go talk to Himura and then report back to me. I'll handle everything to do with your sister's case. Got it?"

"Thank you." She couldn't stop the desperation in her voice. It was there and it was evident. She flicked out her phone and immediately scrolled through her contacts, looking for Detective Himura. She remembered him. He was an older guy who had retired last year. She held her phone up to her ear and listened to it ring on the other end a couple of times before someone picked up.

"Himura here." He still answered the phone the same way as when he was on the force.

"Hi, this is Detective Anderson." She paused, she wasn't really sure what for, but she felt that she needed to.

"What can I do for you?"

"I was wondering if I could come by and pick your brain on a case that you worked five years ago. It may be connected to a new case that we have right now."

"That shouldn't be a problem. I'm just cleaning up at home right now."

"Let me get your address."

"227 King St."

"I can be there in about fifteen minutes. Will that work for you?"

"Yes, see you soon, Detective."

She looked at Luke for a second before checking her pants pocket for her car keys. He was too busy to pay attention to her so off she went. They would talk later to exchange information anyway. With the possibility of a serial killer on their hands, there was no time to waste standing around.

Year Unknown, Day 112

She sat in the corner next to the door. Just to the right of the hinges. If the door were to open, she would remain hidden behind it. She had been preparing for weeks and finally, she was ready. Her muscles felt strong again and the anticipation was killing her. He hadn't been inside the room for a few days and she was due for a visit any time now. It felt as though she had been crouching by the door for hours. Her calves and quads were starting to cramp, but she didn't want to move from her position. She cracked her neck and wriggled her shoulders, trying to loosen the tension in her muscles. She was too high strung and she feared it would slow her reaction time. She twirled one of the shoelaces in her fingers. She had an end of it in each of her hands. She would attack from behind Him when He first entered.

The small sliding door opened and in dropped a tray with a hunk of dry bread, an orange, and a bottle of water.

The empty red tray that she had learned to leave by the door, was retrieved and the sliding door slammed shut once again. She sighed in frustration and ran a hand through her greasy, ratted hair. He had been visiting her several times a week, but of course, now that she was ready for Him, He refused to come inside her small world. She stood, relieving her leg muscles from their strain. She would take this new found time to stretch. It would be at least a couple of hours before He would come inside, now that she had her food. He never came inside right after leaving a meal. She tucked the shoelace back into her bra and then walked across the room and back to her food tray just to get her blood pumping again. The stillness was driving her nuts. She needed space to move around.

Instead, she sat cross-legged on the floor and started in on the orange. She wanted it in her system before it dried out in the room. Her body could use any vitamins it would provide. She had never liked oranges growing up. Something about their texture had always bothered her and she had always avoided them when possible. She didn't have a choice now. She ate whatever He deemed fit to bring her and whenever He thought to bring to it her. One time He had brought her a lemon. She had taken the peel off and squeezed the juice out of it onto her stale bread, it had made it wet enough to choke it down. She felt the orange was worse, merely because she actually had to eat it. Her teeth tore into a fourth bite and she forced herself to hold strong against her gag reflex. It wasn't easy.

She needed to shake it off. Nothing a repetition of jumping jacks and mountain climbers couldn't fix. She did four sets each before her throat felt like it could handle more of the orange. She switched to the bread just in case. She didn't want to push it. The last thing she needed was to make herself queasy when she was finally ready to take Him on. Her body still needed all the nutrition it could get. She had trouble with the hard crust on the bread. It was incredibly stale and the exterior was tough. When she had made it halfway through her water and food she stopped to do a workout, since she now had the time.

She cut the workout short, normally she would work for what felt like a few hours, but this time she kept it to the basics; jogging around the room for cardio and a few calisthenics for toning. She estimated maybe an hour or so in total. Then it was back to crouching next to the door. She had her food tray within reach so that she could slowly pick at it while she waited. She had a feeling that she would be here for a while and she was grateful for having something to keep her semi-busy. She pulled the shoelace out again and draped it across her knee for easy access, just in case.

2017, Day 12

Anderson was parked in front of 227 King Street. It was a middle class neighborhood, much like her own where she had grown up. The house was painted a cream color with a forest green trim, and it looked fresh. There were flowers lining the front walkway that looked well tended to and the lawn, which was recently mowed, was a vibrant green from all the recent rain. She almost felt bad pulling him back into the police world. He had just gotten out and it looked as if he was still adjusting to normal life at home. At least he was getting a lot done around the house it seemed. She made sure to grab the case file from the passenger seat before making her way up to the front door. She didn't want to look unprepared even though she hadn't really had the time to look through it yet. She brushed the wrinkles out of her pants and raised a fist to knock, but the door swung open before she was able to.

"I heard you drive up," he commented upon seeing the surprised look on her face. He looked to be in his late fifties with speckled grey hair. He had on a pair of old jeans and a crew neck brown sweater that had a few green and white splotches of paint. He had a steaming, half-empty mug of coffee in one hand. "Would you like a cup? I just brewed a new batch."

"Since you're offering, that would be great," she smiled at him, hoping he wouldn't see the twitch of awkwardness in her facial muscles.

"Us coppers really do have a caffeine problem," he chuckled while shaking his head.

He led her inside, past the living room and into the kitchen. There were dirty dishes piled up in the sink that looked as if they had been there for a while. The trash bin to the right of the countertop was overflowing and breakfast dishes were still on the kitchen table. Clearly, he had had cereal and coffee this morning. She tried not to judge the mess, but she had a feeling that the rest of the house looked the same as the kitchen. As if reading her mind, Himura quickly cleared the table off, casually piling the newly dirtied dishes in the sink. He pulled out a clean mug from the cupboard and poured her some fresh coffee.

"Cream or sugar?"

"No, thank you."

He placed the mug in front of her on the table and took a seat across from her.

"So tell me, what case do you want to talk about?"

"Well. As I mentioned before on the phone, it's from five years ago. I have the case file here in case you need to refresh your memory. It's extremely similar to a case that Luke and I are currently working on. We think there may be a connection between the two and that if we can learn everything we can about this one, that it may help with our current investigation."

He was nodding in agreement. Everything seemed pretty logical so far.

She placed the file on the table and hesitated for a moment before sliding it across to him.

"Do you remember Anna Clark?"

Himura sucked in his breath and pulled the file closer. He flipped it open and stared at her picture.

"Of course I remember Anna. She haunts me even now."

"She was fifteen years old, what would that make her? A sophomore in high school? Blonde, blue eyes."

Himura tore his eyes from the girl's picture to look at Anderson.

"She went missing one night when she went to a party. She was from the middle class, small family, with a younger brother. She was involved with the soccer team, friendly to other kids, but wasn't really one for going to parties, so it was a little out of character for her to be there. Her parents thought she had been finally breaking out of her shell and that's why they had said she could go to it. She was supposed to call them to get picked up, but she never called. Some of the other girls who had been there mentioned that she felt bad waking her parents up and said that she would walk home. She had a cell phone and thought she would be okay. That was the last anyone saw of her."

Anderson felt a wave of remorse hit her. She tried to push it aside. This wasn't her sister they were talking about. She could keep her composure. Kate's life depended on it.

"Our girl's name is Kate. She was taken almost two weeks ago now. Blonde, blue eyes. She had also been at a party when she went missing. She was walking with a group though when she was taken. No one noticed that she just wasn't there."

Himura nodded, taking in the information. "And you think the two cases are connected?"

"Yes. Well. There's a third girl who is also missing. About ten years ago now."

"Three girls?"

"Every five years."

"And she was also blonde, blue eyes, and on her way home from a party?"

"Yes, sir."

"I can see now why you think they might be connected."

"Is there anything else that you remember?" she was speaking in a quiet tone, not for his benefit, but for her own. She didn't want to be too harsh on herself.

"Well, we looked at the parents for a while, but ruled them out. There was nothing suspicious there. Other than that, there was really nothing to look into. She was just gone. Everyone remembers saying goodbye to her and then she just never made it home. She didn't seem to have any enemies at school. She was too quiet to make anyone mad."

"And there was nothing else?"

"Well, the dad was a drunk. But he was home that night."

"Really? Tell me more about that."

"To be honest, I always thought the dad beat the kids. I never had any proof though. I felt bad leaving the brother there alone. It was clear that he and Anna had been close and that she had been extremely protective of him."

"What was the brother's name? I only had a quick moment to go through the file, I must have skimmed over it."

Himura scanned through a few pages before finding it. "Jimmy. His name was Jimmy."

"Anything else that you can remember that might not be in that file?"

He flipped through it for a moment, trying to think if he had anything to add.

"I'm sorry, Detective. That's all that I can think of right now. Leave me your card though. If I think of anything else, I will give you a call."

She pulled a card from her pocket and handed it to him, he retrieved it with ink-stained fingers.

"Thank you for the coffee, and sorry to disturb your day."

"Not at all. It was kind of a nice distraction."

"Retirement not treating you well?" she laughed.

"No, it's fine. It's just…a little boring. And I miss being out on the streets."

"I'm sure the Lieutenant would be happy to have you as part of the volunteer group. If you get bored enough that is. Thank you again."

He walked her to the front door and she peeked into the living room as they passed. She had been right, it was just as messy as the kitchen. It hadn't been vacuumed in a long time, there were stains on the carpet, a single empty wine glass on the coffee table that was stained red. The coffee table was covered in newspapers, notebooks, and pencils. Clearly, the retired detective was having trouble giving up old habits. She remembered he would always show up early at the station with a newspaper in hand and would go through looking for any leaks of information. That would explain his ink stained hands.

She went back to the station and took a seat at her desk. Luke was nowhere in sight so she took that to mean that he was still interviewing the detective that had worked Jamie's case. She looked at Anna's picture and then at Kate's. There was something wrong with this profile. Kate didn't quite fit the description. Anna and Jamie seemed to be similar enough, but Kate didn't fit the mold.

"Anderson! I thought I told you to go home."

She swiveled her chair around to face Lieutenant Sanchez. She had forgotten all about him telling her to go home.

"Sir. I'm just finishing up some paperwork before I head out."

He looked like he didn't believe her, but he surprised her by letting it go. "I'm giving you an hour to finish up. I don't want to see you in here after that."

"Yes, sir."

He slammed his office door behind him, the blinds on the door snapping against the wood frame. Anderson quickly collected everything she thought she would need and immediately left the station. If she couldn't work here, she would work at the diner. She also sent a short text to Luke letting him know she had talked to Himura and where she would be so that he could find her when he was ready to trade information.

The lot behind the diner was mostly empty and Bea wasn't there when Anderson slid into her secreted booth. Bea normally worked the dinnertime crowd and it was only mid-afternoon, so it wasn't unexpected, but it was still disappointing to be missing the friendly face. The waitress that came to take her order was young and impatient. She had an expression of boredom plastered onto her sharply featured face and she pulled at her gauged earlobes with her right hand, possibly a nervous habit. She had her other hand tucked into the front pocket of her ripped jeans.

"What can I get you?"

"Cheeseburger and a water. Thanks."

She grunted in acknowledgment and disappeared from view. Anderson took a moment to look at the faces staring back at her from the laminated posters before opening Kate and Anna's case files side by side. She didn't need Jamie's file to compare all three, good thing since Luke still had her personal copy. What were these girls hiding? What did they have in common? Why didn't Kate fit the mold? Something just didn't seem right with the most recent girl. Anderson pulled her notebook out and made three columns, one for Anna, one for Jamie, and one for Kate. She started with listing things that all three girls had in common, such as age, and physical attributes. Then she started to write down the factors, like the neighborhoods they lived in and their family situations. She stared at the list for a moment and on a gut instinct decided that she was missing a column. Slowly, she wrote down

Melissa's name and started jotting down her info. When she was done, she sat back with her arms folded in front of her. What if Kate wasn't the target? What if the perp had made a mistake?

Her phone rattled on the table. She glanced at it. Unknown number. She answered without hesitation.

"Anderson here."

"Emz. Where are you?" There was panic in his voice.

"Caleb, are you okay?"

"Emz. I need you."

"Where are you?"

"At your apartment."

"Damn it, Caleb. You just had to pick today, didn't you? I'll be there as soon as I can."

She hung up on him before he could say anything else. She quickly hit her speed dial number two. It rang a few times before he picked up.

"Emily! What a surprise. What can I do for you?"

"Hey, Dad. I need a favor from you."

"Whatever you need, sweetie. You know that."

"I've had a huge break in the case I was telling you about and I need to jump on it. But I just got a call from

Caleb. He's at my apartment, waiting for me. I don't have the time to deal with him right now. Is there any way that you can swing by and take care of it for me?"

"Sweetie… I can't do that. I haven't spoken to Caleb in three years."

"Dad. This isn't a personal favor. I can't give you more details about the case, but this is important and time-sensitive. I've dealt with Caleb's addiction and helped him when he asked for it for the last several years. You have no idea what kind of position you've put me in by refusing to be his father. I need you to step up and do it just this once. Can you please do that?"

There was silence for a moment, then, "Give me your address. I'll do what I can."

"Thank you." She blinked in surprise, not sure how to handle the feeling of relief that was flooding through her.

Year Unknown, Day 117

She had been crouched here off and on for five days now. She feared her legs would become too numb and she would botch the job. Pins and needles danced up and down her calves and shins, even traveling and spinning through her ankles. She couldn't feel her toes anymore, between her blood circulation that had been cut off from her position and the chilly air seeping in through the gaping holes in her Chucks. She periodically rubbed her exposed toes with her hands and tried to warm them and restore some blood flow, but she didn't really notice a difference.

She had created a system of stretching and working out after her meals were delivered, it was the only safe time she had to herself. Exhaustion was beginning to take hold, but she refused to sleep. Every now and then she would nod off in her squatting position for short amounts of time. She always awoke with a start, terrified He would be there, standing over her, knowing her plan. He never was. Now her eyelids drooped and she struggled to keep them open. He had to be coming soon. It had been at least a week since she had seen Him. The isolation was unnerving and the silence from Him had her worried. The time she spent alone, unvisited from Him only doubled her aggression. Without an outlet for her anger, she felt as if her mind was unhinging all the while her muscles grew restless for action.

She missed her soccer team. She missed running the field on a sunny day and sucking in the fresh air by the lungful. She missed the way her cleats sounded when they collided with the black and white ball. She missed their warm-up drills and the constant competition the other girls provided. She always felt challenged to do better when they were around. When she did her workouts in this cage she kept these girls in mind and it's what kept her pushing so hard. Her memory of them and their workouts still challenged her. When she got out of here after finally taking Him down, she didn't want to be out of shape. Because she would get out of here.

She couldn't sit still any longer. She needed to stretch her limbs, so she stood and cracked some of her joints. She made her way to the left of the mattress before she kneeled to the floor. She lifted the mattress and pulled out her bobby pin. It felt scarily familiar and comforting in her fingers. There was no point in trying to hide her day count from Him anymore as they didn't even fit underneath the plastic cafeteria tray, so they remained exposed. She had briefly thought about hiding them underneath the mattress but had ultimately decided that it didn't really matter. Why would He even care if she was counting days?

That and it was too much effort to lift the mattress and hold it up while scratching into the cement. Now, she merely felt for them with a hand and started to etch in another line. Line number one ten. A hundred and ten days in this hole. Hopefully, she would leave this place and find herself among her teammates once more.

Once the new line was finished she hid the bobby pin once more and found her spot next to the door. She eased herself down with aching muscles to her squatting position and settled in to wait again.

2017, Day 12

The last bell for the day rang. Melissa and Camille walked to the locker room together. Camille was still obsessed with the thing about Cameron even though Lauren kept telling her to cool it. Mia yelled at them to shut the door as they entered, but they just rolled their eyes and ignored her. Everyone had noticed that Mia's temper was rising in the absence of Kate. Her fuse was getting shorter and she was prone to throwing tantrums. So they ignored her, figuring it wasn't personal. Without Kate there to promote Mia's status she was turning into a nobody. The only power she held was in cheer practice, and that didn't start for another ten minutes.

Cass yelled from across the room, "Hey Melissa, made out with Cameron yet?" she started laughing and winked at her.

Melissa's face flushed and she ducked her head, hiding from the stares she was receiving from the rest of the squad. Her small group had accepted her, but the rest of the squad was still wary.

Camille nudged her in the side with an elbow and flashed her a smug grin. "Oh come on. We're just kidding."

The girls quickly changed and headed to the gym. It was raining too much today and they couldn't hold practice outside. Their sneakers made squeaking sounds on the clean, reflective floor. The basketball team was doing their layup drills when the girls lined up with their own coach on the sidelines. She couldn't help herself, her eyes swept the room looking for him. He was already sweating through his light blue practice shirt. She tried to avert her eyes and pay attention to practice and Mia's criticisms, but she honestly didn't care what Mia had to say. In gaining anger, Mia was losing the respect of everyone around her. Anyway, Melissa still wanted to know where Mia had been when she had skipped school the other day.

Once a long, distracted practice was over, she took a longer shower than normal, hoping the other girls might have left without her by the time she got out. It was an unbiased hope since they had all started waiting for each other at the end of school. The girls were really too sweet to her. They even walked her to her brother's school every day now. The steam made her mascara run down her face so she washed off all of her make-up too. She wrapped herself in a towel and made her way to her locker. Lauren stood at her own locker, just two doors down, and was combing all the knots out of her hair. She glanced at Melissa as she spun her combo lock and swung the metal door open.

"Did you see how Cameron was watching you during practice today?"

Melissa shook her head and pulled out her street clothes. "No way."

"Definitely, isn't that right Cass?"

"Totally!" Cass called from across the room.

Mia was shooting daggers at them while she tied her shoelaces together. Melissa dressed quickly and pulled out her stained make-up bag. She sat on the floor in front of the full length mirror between Lauren and Cass.

"Hey guys, I have to take off early today, my mom needs help with baking. See ya!" Camille dashed off, basically running out the door to get away from Mia's glares.

"Hey, Mia?" Everyone turned to stare at Melissa. She was dabbing concealer underneath her eyes with a sponge as she addressed Mia. "Where were you the other day? You weren't in class when Mr. Rogers handed back our exams."

"None of your damn business." Snapped Mia. She snatched her backpack off the ground and raged out the door.

"Whoa," said Lauren, "What the hell was that?"

Melissa shrugged her shoulders and flicked on some mascara. "Whatever. That was weird."

"I heard she had a meltdown and her parents kept her home that day," offered one of the other girls.

Melissa raised her eyebrows. Mia having a meltdown didn't seem plausible, maybe a Kate-sized freakout though. A few of the others whispered they had heard something similar. She packed away her gym clothes and zipped up her backpack. "OK, I gotta go pick up my brother."

"I'll walk with you." Lauren shut her locker and followed Melissa out the door, they paused and glanced at Cass momentarily, but she was frowning and pawing through her backpack.

They both stopped short when the door swung shut behind them. Cameron was leaning on the wall next to the door with both hands in his pockets looking extremely relaxed. He pushed away from the wall at the sight of Melissa.

"Hey."

"Um, hi." She tucked a lock of hair behind one of her ears and looked at the floor. Lauren elbowed her sharply in the ribs. Melissa was sure she was trying to send some sort of girl signal, but she was still too new at this and didn't really get it. It really was like picking up another language.

"Can I talk to you for a second?" he asked.

She glanced at Lauren, who nodded and tried to mouth something to her. She had no idea what Lauren was trying to say. Exasperated, Lauren gave up and left the two of them alone, walking out the front doors of the school.

Cameron seemed to become nervous once they were alone in the hallway together.

"So uh. We haven't gotten a chance to talk since… well…you know. The party."

She continued to stare at the ground. She had no idea what to say. She wasn't used to talking to boys. That party was the one time that she allowed herself the liberty to explore outside her normal realm. She shifted her weight uncomfortably and slid her backpack further and more firmly onto her shoulder.

"You didn't even leave me your phone number."

He was trying really hard. She needed to do or say something. God, why was she so spazzy all the time?

"I guess, maybe, you didn't want to talk to me? Maybe you're aren't interested after all?" He sounded so sad that she had to respond.

"That's not it at all." She blurted out looking up at him. His blue eyes were full of curiosity. "I'm just still new at this. I'm not good at socializing."

He smiled. "Clearly."

She looked down again. "I have to go." She spun towards the main entrance and started to leave him there, keeping her eyes on the floor in front of her.

"Did I say something wrong?"

She glanced back at him. He was in loose-fitting jeans and his green cap-sleeved t-shirt was pulled taut around his pecs and shoulders. Why was he so good looking? This made it so much harder for her.

"No, I just have to pick up my brother from school. I'm already late."

"Let me walk with you."

Without waiting for her to decline him, he joined her by the door and started walking down the front steps. Lauren was at the base of the steps, impatiently texting with one hand and holding an umbrella in the other. She looked surprised that Cameron was joining them, but didn't say anything. Instead, she just shot Melissa a raised eyebrow. Again, she shrugged her shoulders, not really sure what to do or say. She had lost all control of the situation, but she was enjoying it. The three walked side by side in awkward silence for a while. Lauren was the only one with an umbrella and she only shared it with Melissa. Cameron was slowly getting more drenched by the second. The girls were both amused by this and wondered how long it would take him to get irritated and leave them to their girl talk. Melissa certainly was liking the view of his wet shirt sticking to his muscles. By the time they reached Danny's school, not a word had been said, but the girls were exchanging secretive glances and small smiles. This would surely be discussed later in detail.

Even in the rain, Danny was waiting by the gate like he always was. At this point, he knew who Lauren was and jumped up and down when he saw her, splashing water in every direction from the puddle he stood in.

"Lauren!" He ran to her and threw his arms around her, getting water all over her sweater.

"Hey, Danny." She grinned and wrapped her free arm around him in return.

He looked up at her. "Is your mom making a casserole soon?"

She glanced at Melissa before responding. "No, but she is getting my dad to make steak soon. You want me to save you some?"

"Yeah!" Danny then turned to Cameron and demanded, "Who are you?"

"Kiddo, this is Cameron. He's on our basketball team. Cameron, this is my brother, Danny."

Danny held his hand out and waited for Cameron to shake it. Cameron looked like a drowned cat with his hair plastered to the sides of his face and raindrops hanging from the tips of his eyelashes.

"Lissa! Did you hear what Lauren said? Her dad is making steak and we get to have some."

"I heard." She couldn't help but smile. He was just a bundle of joy and energy.

"Do you want to join us for dinner that night? I'm sure my mom won't mind. I was going to invite the other girls anyway."

"As long as Ma says OK."

Lauren's smile shone even brighter. "Great. I'll let my mom know and text you which day."

"So you do have a phone?" Cameron interjected.

"Of course she has a phone. Duh." Danny's voice seemed so high pitched compared to Cameron's.

Everyone started laughing.

"What's so funny? Stop laughing at me," pouted Danny.

They walked by Lauren's house and she broke off, waved at them, and disappeared inside. The rain was starting to let up, but since none of them had an umbrella now all three of them were dripping. Melissa was sure they would all get sick. She couldn't believe she had forgotten to grab an umbrella before she left this morning. She needed to make a note for herself and stick it next to her bedroom door so that she would see it on her way out tomorrow.

She couldn't tell if it was the cold from the rain or if it was her paranoia running rampant again, but the hairs on the back of her neck stood up. She glanced over her shoulder, panic lining her eyes but there was no one there.

"You okay?" asked Cameron.

"Yeah. I'm good. Sorry."

"Sorry for what?"

"Running off that night." She met his gaze and immediately dropped it.

They were standing in front of her house now and Danny was tugging at her hand.

"This is where you live?"

"Yeah."

She could tell he was trying to think of something nice to say and was failing miserably. She knew she would be too if she was in his position. Their house left a lot to be desired and not enough left to the imagination.

"You should see her room. It's great." Danny beamed at them.

Cameron let out another bark of laughter. "Oh yeah? Is it, kid?"

"Yeah. Lissa, you should show him."

She shook her head. "Another time. Maybe." She let the words hang in the air like a question. She was scared of the response that she would get.

Cameron rested a hand on one of her shoulders. She avoided his gaze, instead, she watched Danny as he played with some of the puddles, running and jumping in them. He was going to make a huge mess in the house that she would have to clean up.

"Alright kid, let's go inside." She pulled away from Cameron's hand and into the yard.

She didn't need to lead the way, Danny yanked his hand from hers and ran ahead of her to the side door. When she glanced over her shoulder Cameron was already gone. There was her answer.

Year Unknown, Day 118

She was slouched by the door, head hanging down in front of her chest, sleep had finally taken hold. She hadn't been remembering her dreams since she had been taken captive, but she was okay with that. She knew she was having nightmares because she always woke up even more tired. Sometimes she would wake up feeling terrified, but she didn't know from what. The lingering effects of a nightmare she presumed. She didn't want to remember any of these dreams; she was already living in constant a nightmare. She jolted upright, out of breath and eyes wide open. Nothing was there. He wasn't here. She was alone. She readjusted her position and pulled out the shoelace from where she had tucked it inside her bra. After her nap, she needed to prepare. He should be coming any time now.

She needed to get her mind off of her captivity. She closed her eyes and imagined Jimmy's chubby kid-like face. He was probably missing her right now, just as she was missing him. He would probably be in her bed trying to find some comfort there. That's what she would do if the roles were reversed. She envied him. At least he could draw comfort from someplace, even if it wasn't from their absentee parents. She hoped he had stopped taking his stuffed tiger with him to school. He loved dragging it by the tail everywhere he went. When he was nervous he would hug it so hard that it'd set off the button that would make it growl. She smiled to herself thinking about what he had named his furry friend. "Tiger, because he's a tiger!" He had always taken things too literally. She swore the kid was a genius of some sort—he was just so serious all the time. She dreamed of getting out of here so she could see him live up to his full potential. Their parents wouldn't be supportive, but she would. She would make sure he got to go to whichever school he wanted. During the last couple of years, she had taken summer jobs and been quietly saving all her money. She knew it would barely make a dent with his college tuition, but anything helped. She had a feeling he would go into engineering. He loved anything to do with computers and numbers.

The door swung open, pulling her out of her own mind. She silently rose from the floor, stretching her condensed quads and calves. The light from the outside room lit up the section of her prison where the mattress sat on the floor. The sliver of light showed that she was not asleep on it and as far as He could tell, nowhere else to be found. He stepped further into the room so that she was staring at the back of His head now. Just one more step and she would have the room she needed in order to attack. His eyes swept the left side of the room, looking, but not finding her. She rocked her weight onto the balls of her feet, ready to pounce. He took a step forward, exactly what she hoped for. He turned his head slightly so that he could see the right side of the room. She moved in sync with Him and remained in His blindspot as she finally sprung into action.

She had each end of the shoelace in either hand, twisted around her fingers so that she wouldn't lose her grip on it. She flung it around His neck, having to get unbearably close to Him. She had to fight her urges to put more space between them. She pulled the lace tight around His neck, pulling back as hard as she could with her arms. Her biceps bulged as she tugged. He immediately threw His hands to the lace, trying to loosen the hold she had. He was stronger than her and she struggled to maintain her foothold and leverage. Her fingers hurt; she felt as if she were cutting off her own circulation, but it was too late to stop now. She kicked Him in the back of His knees, forcing Him to drop to the floor. She was now taller than Him and pulled even harder on the lace and shoved a knee into his back, forcing Him closer to the floor so she stood above Him. He started to sputter and gasp. She waited a couple more heartbeats before dropping the lace, kicking Him in the back so that He hit the ground, and started running for the door. The shoelace fell from her hands as she ran and she left it where it lay in the doorway.

It was bright in the next room. She had to blink for a moment before she could focus on what she was seeing. She was aware of the time she was wasting just standing still. The room she found herself in was even smaller than her own room. There was a short stack of plastic trays by the open door, He must rotate between them every day. There was a single light bulb that hung from the middle of the ceiling with a string attached at its base to turn it on and off. The only way out was a staircase, and she had no idea where it would lead, not that she had a choice at this point. She made for the staircase, taking the stairs two at a time. She heard Him behind her, He had been able to compose Himself faster than she had anticipated. In a panic, she looked over her shoulder. He was at the doorway already, easily closing the little space she had managed to put between them.

Rage oozed from every one of His pores, but He didn't say a word, merely barreling after her, quickly reaching the stairs. She was halfway up the staircase and she could see the giant wooden door at the top. In a rush, she tripped on a step and crashed into the cement stairs. Her ribcage connected first, knocking the air out of her chest. Winded, she gasped for air, trying to fill her lungs. She clutched at her side while scrambling, trying desperately to get to her feet, but she was too slow. He was standing over her now and He reached down with one hand, grasping the back of her neck. His fingers and nails would leave a mark. She was so close to the door, she couldn't give up now. With His nails digging into her skin, He pulled her up to standing. She lashed out at the inside of His elbow, hoping to buckle His hold. He remained strong, not even flinching. He brought His face close to hers, she could feel His breath on her cheeks. She slashed at His face and managed to scratch Him across the cheekbone. As He clutched at His face with His free hand she put all her weight into stomping at His ankles. He stumbled backward on the staircase, letting go of her neck and falling backward. She took the opportunity and ran for the door.

She made it to the top of the stairs, ducked her head, and threw her dominant shoulder into the trap door above her. It wouldn't budge. Of course, it was locked. She pushed upwards with the palms of both her hands desperately. She couldn't even tell which edge had the hinges and she didn't have time to figure it out.

"No, no, no!" She screamed at it. "Damn it!"

She bent her knees in preparation to throw her entire body up at the trapdoor again. It didn't move, not even the slightest give, but the pain in her shoulder was searing through her entire body. She grabbed at her shoulder and panted. Her heart was beating faster than it ever had, it actually hurt. She didn't need to look to know that He was behind her. She slowly turned. His face was void of all emotion as she walked past him and started back down the stairs. Once she was in front of Him, He put a hand on her injured shoulder and squeezed hard. The pain shot up and down her arm. She bit her lower lip to refrain from yelling out.

"I will not forget this, Alice. I don't forgive easily." His voice was low and the control she could hear in His tone terrified her.

Even in His grasp, she tried to keep as much space between them as she could. He pushed her down the steps at a quick pace and followed her back into her cell. They stood there in silence, both refusing to say anything. Now He knew she wouldn't just sit around idly and twiddle her thumbs. Sure, she was scared of Him, but she had now proven that that wouldn't stop her from attempting to free herself. Her adrenaline was slowing down after the initial spike and she could feel the bruises on her ribs already forming. She tried not to favor them in any way, He didn't need to know that she was hurting more than what He could already see. She may have lost this time, but there was a strength in her eyes that He couldn't ignore. This would change their dynamic. He wouldn't ever trust that she was meek and wasn't planning something. It would be harder to attack in the future, He would be waiting for it. Just as she had been waiting for Him to visit, she would make Him wait for her next move. She needed to lull Him into a false sense of security before she could even begin to think about attacking again.

She broke eye contact first. He needed to still feel as if He was the dominant one, He was after all still in control of the situation.

"I'll be back tomorrow after I've thought of a suitable punishment. I will not tolerate this kind of disobedience." He left her then, but not before He reached down to retrieve the shoelace from the floor by the doorway.

The door shut and she was alone once more. She sat on the edge of the mattress allowing her legs to relax for the first time in about a week. She needed to think of a new plan. She wasn't sure if she was ready to attempt anything with the bobby pin yet, it was her last line of defense. She still had the second shoelace after all. But He may be expecting her to try this again, He would think of the second lace, just as she was right now. This meant she needed to be more creative this time. Creativity had never been her strong suit. Clearly, she had her work cut out for her, but she wasn't ready to give up. He hadn't killed her spirit yet.

2017, Day 12

"Damn it, Luke. Pick up, pick up, pick up." Anderson was muttering to herself anxiously. She had now called twice and he hadn't answered. She knew he was busy, but he needed the information that she had as well.

"You have reached the voicemail for—"

"Damn it." She hit the end call button and dialed again. She perched the phone between her ear and her shoulder so that she would have both hands free. As she listened to it ring once again, she packed up her files and left some cash on the table for her bill. The young waitress was quick to walk by and pick up the check from her. She got her keys out of her pocket and hung up at the voicemail message again. She needed to get back to the station, sure it would piss off Sanchez, but someone needed to hear her out before it was too late.

When she walked in the door Millie shook her head.

"What are you doing here, Detective? You are not supposed to be here."

"I know. This will only take a minute. Is Sanchez in his office?"

"Yes, but-"

Anderson ignored her and immediately headed for the office, blocking out the rest of what Millie had to say. Out of her peripherals, she could see Millie picking up the phone. Good, he'll be expecting her then. A few other faces watched as she passed by, everyone knew she had been given leave that morning. She tried to remain unaffected by the stares and kept her head held high. His office door flew open and he came storming out. He was not happy.

"Anderson." Sanchez was approaching her. "I thought I told you to go home."

"Yes sir, but I have something important to show you." She pulled out the chart she had made at the diner. "Another girl will go missing. I don't know when, but it will be soon."

Sanchez shook his head. "No, it's every five years."

"Sir, normally it is, but he took the wrong girl this time. Once he figures that out then he will want to correct his mistake. Something has been bothering me about Kate, I don't think she fits the pattern."

"Damn it."

She followed him into his office, Luke was there with a man she recognized from a long time ago, add ten years, and another man whom she didn't recognize. She nodded at the other two before addressing Luke.

"Luke, I called you three times." She didn't wait for him to respond. "This guy will try again, and soon."

"Anderson, we found a fourth case. One from before Anna and your sister."

She looked at her chart. "Let me guess, she's fifteen or sixteen, blonde with blue eyes. From mid to lower class, either a single parent or a broken home. She has a younger brother that she is close with. She has a small social life, if any, at school and she partakes in one after school program, something active."

Everyone looked at her, she had their attention.

"Yes. Her name was Megan. Lives in the same neighborhood as Melissa, actually, which shows that he has a regular hunting ground." Luke pointed at the open file on Sanchez's desk and gave Anderson a moment to read it over. This information only proved her point even more. She put her chart on the desk next to the file and added another column. She was quick to jot down the specs for Megan. Everyone in the office remained silent and motionless as she did so. When she was finished she looked around the room, making eye contact with each of the men.

"Do you see what I'm seeing here? There's a very clear pattern with the missing girls."

Luke tapped Melissa's name on her now wrinkled page, "But she wasn't taken."

"Right. But Kate was and she doesn't match the criteria. Both of those girls were at the same party that night. And we know that they were wearing the same exact thing. What if he made a mistake and took the wrong girl?"

It took a moment more of showing them that Kate's family life didn't fit, but that Melissa's did before the men were convinced. On top of that, Kate's social life was much more active and full than the other girls.

"Then Melissa is in danger. We need to go pick her up. She needs to have a protective detail." Luke looked at Sanchez who immediately granted them their wish.

They were quick to jump into action. It was after school hours, so Melissa should've been at home at this point in the day. Luke and Anderson quickly made for the parking lot, Sanchez let them go without voicing any qualms. Even if they had called and gotten a hold of her, they would want to make sure of her safety, so they sped through town at high speeds.

Luke raised an eyebrow at the house Anderson parked in front of. The yard seemed even more out of control than it had last time she had been here, especially with all the rain. The wind from the storm whipped the branches of the trees and bushes in every which direction. They both braved the downpour knowing it would be useless to try to wait it out. It wouldn't let up for hours. She led Luke around to the side door and knocked.

Through the door and over the wind she could hear that miserable woman yell, "Danny! Someone's at the door!"

They lingered patiently for a few moments, their clothes slowly becoming waterlogged while listening to the television play loudly. Some sort of drama, it sounded like the same show the mother had been watching when Anderson was stuck waiting for Melissa to come home. Luke was raising his fist to knock again when the door finally swung inward. They both looked down to see a toothy grin shining at them from under a mop of brown hair.

"I recognize you! You're the lady cop!"

She smiled at him, "That's right. Do you mind if we come inside and get out of the rain?"

The boy held open the door for them and they dripped onto the carpet just inside the door; they didn't want to track mud throughout the house. There was already a pile of muddy towels by the front doors. Clearly, someone else had already done that today.

"Danny, this is my partner Luke."

Luke held out his hand for a shake, "Hey there kid." Danny solemnly took Luke's hand and shook it vigorously.

They tried to address the mother, but she waved them off. They took this as permission to continue talking to Danny.

"Is your sister home?" asked Anderson.

"She just left."

"Can you tell us where she went?"

He looked like he wanted to tell them, but he remained silent. She glanced at Luke, maybe he would know what to do. She wasn't good with kids. He got the hint and took over.

"What are you worried about?"

The kid rubbed his toes on the dirty floor, with both arms behind his back. His head was hung low as he said, "Is Lissa in trouble?"

Luke chuckled, "No. Your sister is not in trouble. We just need to know where she is so we can make sure she's safe."

"Well, if she's with that guy then she's safe."

Filled with panic, Anderson jumped in, "What guy?"

"Cameron. From school. He's on the basketball team."

Anderson was soothed by this, not that she had expected a young bright girl like Melissa to wander off with a random older man. Clearly, if the guy was in high school then he was not old enough to be the guy they were after. "Is that her boyfriend?"

Danny shrugged his shoulders. "I don't think she has a boyfriend. At least, they didn't kiss at all when he walked us home today."

Anderson smiled, this kid was cute.

"So, if she's not with Cameron, then where do you think she went?" asked Luke.

"She went to Lauren's house. For dinner. Her mom always sends Lissa home with some for me."

"Do you know where Lauren lives?"

Danny shook his head.

"Miss Jameson." Luke approached the mother on the couch. She barely looked up. She was tuned in to her television show and not much could tear her away from it. "Miss Jameson." He said again.

She tore her eyes away, but only for a moment to look Luke up and down.

"Do you know who Lauren is and where she lives?"

"Ne'er heard of her."

Anderson was becoming impatient, the woman's incompetence irritated her. The way she treated her kids horrified Anderson. Danny tugged at her sleeve, trying to get her attention. She returned her eyes to him.

"Lauren is on the cheer team with Lissa."

"Thanks, Danny, that's very helpful."

He nodded and retreated to the kitchen table where his homework was laid out on the table. He immediately set about what looked like math equations. Luke came back to Anderson's side and they conferred for a moment.

"We can get Lauren's home address from Kate's cell phone," said Anderson.

"I can call Davis. He was at the station when we left. He can go through her contacts for us so we don't have to go back to the station. It should be in evidence."

"Let's get going then."

Anderson turned to Danny, "Thank you for your help," she glanced at the mother on the couch and then back at the kid. She pulled a business card out of her pocket and tucked it into his small hands. "If you ever need anything, don't hesitate to call me. Okay?"

He shot her a smile and waved, his chair tottering a little from his movement. By the time the detectives had shut the side door behind them, Luke was already on the phone and dialing Davis. They dashed through the storm again to the car, splashing water up their pant legs. She would need to get this suit dry cleaned. When they were inside the car, Luke tapped in an address to the GPS while still talking on the phone.

"We'll let you know if we need back up. I don't think there is immediate danger, just the potential for it… I'll keep you posted though."

He turned the key in the ignition and was speeding off as soon as he hung up. Lauren only lived about a ten minute drive away, something Melissa could've easily walked on her own. She probably had too. Anderson's stomach twisted. She pushed a hand on it, trying to calm her nerves. Luke glanced at her.

"You okay?"

"I'm fine. I just think we might need to give Child Protective Services a call soon." She ran her fingers through her silky hair, letting it glide down to the sides of her face and then seamlessly pulling it back up into a short ponytail. She needed her hair out of her face. There was so much going on, she needed to think.

Caleb. She had forgotten all about him. She pulled out her phone and quickly texted her dad asking for an update on the situation. He wasn't good with phones so he probably wouldn't respond for a while. She tucked it back into her pocket and looked out the window.

They pulled up in front of a two-story building that seemed similar to the Caldwell's. She almost couldn't believe that Melissa's home was just a few blocks away. It looked like a dollhouse with a perfectly manicured lawn in front. Luke took the lead this time, knocking on the door before Anderson had finished climbing the steps to the porch. She shook the water from her head and wrung out her hair.

A much shorter amount of time passed before the door opened. The woman who stood there looked fifties-esque with an apron tied around her waist. Her smile faltered when Luke and Anderson flashed their badges, but she managed to keep it plastered on her nearly wrinkle-less face.

"Are you Lauren's mother?" asked Luke.

"Yes, I'm Diane. How can I help you?"

"Is there a girl by the name of Melissa here?" asked Luke.

"Yes. She's inside. Come in and let me show you to her." She gestured the two of them inside. "Do you mind?" She pointed at their wet, muddy shoes.

Both quickly stripped to their socks before being escorted further into the house.

"Is she in some kind of trouble?"

The air temperature was much warmer than outside and Anderson was grateful for the comfort. The goosebumps on her arms from the wet clothes slowly disappeared as they wandered further into the house.

"No, she's not. We just have a few questions. We're so sorry to barge in on your fun dinner night."

This elicited a genuine smile from Diane. The woman was clearly proud of how she ran her household. It certainly was clean and well furnished. There were fresh vacuum lines in the carpeting throughout the hallway and photos of her children in dainty frames lining the walls. She ushered them into the kitchen where they found a group of four girls circled around a table and giggling. They recognized all of them from photos, but Melissa was the only one they could put a name to from memory. The four stared at the detectives, silently waiting for one of them to say something.

"We need to speak to Melissa." Luke's gruff voice sounded funny following the laughter that had previously filled the room.

She stood, slowly pushing her chair out behind her. She exchanged looks with her friends and then followed Luke and Anderson into the hallway. She appeared nervous, avoiding eye contact. Something was bothering her.

"What can I help you with?" she remained in control of her voice.

"I need you to be completely honest with us." Anderson waited for Melissa to nod, her blonde hair bouncing in her ponytail. "I think something else happened the night of the party that you aren't telling me about. Something small, a detail about the evening that you neglected to mention because you didn't think it was important. I want you to walk me through that evening one more time, in excruciating detail. Remember, you aren't in trouble for anything so you don't need to hide anything from us."

Melissa nodded again and paused for a moment, looking up at the detectives through her bangs. She took a deep breath before beginning. "I told you that I saw what she was wearing before I went and I copied her. I told you I

walked there-"

Luke cut in, "Do you remember anything weird

about the walk?"

She took a second to think. "Actually, yeah. I had a

weird feeling that I was being followed and watched. I had

that feeling for a couple of weeks honestly. But it really

freaked me out that night in particular. I kept looking

around, but no one was there. I just figured I was jittery

from walking by myself so late at night."

"Okay. What happened next?" Anderson steered her

further into her narrative.

"Well, I remember being cold, and I had forgotten

to wear a jacket. So the packed house was nice with all the

body heat. I went inside and talked to this guy, Cameron,

before I ran into Kate."

"Why didn't you mention him before?"

"I didn't think it was important." She shrugged her

shoulders. "Anyway. We had a really short conversation

before I went to the kitchen, which is where Kate was. She

flipped out. Like, she was cussing and everything. I thought

she was going to punch me, but Mia pulled her out of the

room. And then…well…" She trailed off and looked at the floor.

"This is where you also left out some details?" asked Anderson.

"Yeah. I didn't leave right away like I said I had."

"So, what did you do?"

"Well, Cameron wanted to hang out and I wanted to try beer for the first time. So I stuck around for a bit. Nothing too crazy. I think I was there for…maybe an hour? I didn't see Kate again that night. But she was there when I left. I know that for certain."

"And how do you know that?" asked Luke. He had his arms folded across his chest and he was leaning back on the cream painted wall, in the small space between the pictures.

"Well…" she shifted her weight. "When I was leaving I saw that Kate had left her things in the front hallway. I might have taken her jacket when I left." She glanced up from the floor sheepishly.

"So you were jacket-less when you arrived and you wore a jacket when you left. And for Kate, it was the opposite."

"Yeah. Pretty much."

"That fits perfectly with what we thought," Anderson said looking at Luke now.

Luke nodded slightly. "Okay, since the night of the party, have you experienced that weird feeling again?"

"It went away for a while. But I've been noticing it again this week. Anytime I walk anywhere, I feel like someone is watching me. And I look around, but never see anyone."

Luke rubbed a hand over his face. "You were right, Emz."

Melissa looked between the two of them. "Right about what?"

"We need you to stay calm. And know that we can offer protection, should you want it-"

"Protection from what? Am I in danger?" Melissa cut in, her voice squeaky.

"Kate wasn't the first girl to go missing. This guy has done it before and there is a clear pattern. What has thrown us off the scent is that Kate didn't fit the pattern. But you do. And since you took her jacket that night, he must have thought Kate was you. Thus taking her by accident—"

"Won't he know he has the wrong girl? What does that mean for me?" Panic filled her voice and her blue eyes darted between the two of them.

"We are worried that he will figure out he took the wrong one. That he will want to correct that mistake. As I have already said, we can offer you protection."

"I can't leave Danny." She didn't even have to think about it. Her first instinct was to think of her brother and how it would affect him. This came with years of raising him. Anderson briefly thought of her own sister and how Jamie always took care of Caleb.

"In that case, we would like to put a protective detail on you. You will have rides to school and your teachers will be keeping an eye on you while you are on school property. There will always be an officer near your location."

She was nodding along to all of this. "I can do that."

"Are you sure that's all you want?"

"Yes."

"We will need your mother's approval."

Melissa nodded. "That won't be hard, she won't even listen to what you have to say. She'll say okay as long you can let her watch her telly show."

"Okay. Do you want to stay for dinner? We can wait in the car." Offered Luke.

"I told Danny I would bring him leftovers."

"Okay, let us know when you are ready to leave. We will be right outside in our vehicle."

They walked her back into the kitchen where the family and friends were. The mother was working on the vegetables and garlic bread, and the dad was working on frying some chicken on a cast iron skillet. The girls were still at the table, talking in low voices and an older boy stood hovering at his mother's shoulder, trying to grab a slice off of the hot pan on the stove. Melissa found her place at the table again and was immediately accepted into the conversation. Diane looked up from her cooking and handed a spoon to the boy. She wiped her hands on her apron and came around the kitchen island towards the detectives.

"Would you like some dinner? I've made enough for quite a big group." She smiled warmly.

"We wouldn't want to intrude and make anyone uncomfortable," responded Anderson.

"You wouldn't be intruding! Honestly. The girls will probably break away to their own group anyway."

Anderson looked at Luke for help. "I always follow my stomach and it does smell wonderful in here. Better than this one's cooking," he chuckled and hiked a thumb in Anderson's direction.

"Hey, I used my good frozen pizza on you."

Diane smiled, "So you'll stay?"

"Since you are being gracious enough to invite us, we would be happy to stay and try whatever it is that smells so wonderful." Luke looked giddy with excitement and Anderson wondered why he was so excited at the prospect of a home cooked meal. Did Amy not cook for him?

"Brandon, could you set two more sets at the table?" She took over at the stove and the boy immediately set about his task. Three of the girls swiveled their heads to watch the boy walk past them. He pretended not to notice, but there was a slight grin plastered to his face.

Year Unknown, Day 119

She was laying on her left side, the side that hadn't gotten thrown into a door or the cement stairs outside of her cell. The entire right side of her body was swollen and ached constantly. She tried not to move at all. Even breathing sent twangs of pain throughout her torso. If she could see any better in this low light then she knew she would be able to see purple, nearly black marks covering her side. She almost felt as if she had cracked a rib, but she figured she would know if she had really hurt herself.

She remembered breaking her left arm when she was younger. It was before Jimmy was born and she actually hung out with another girl from down the street. She had been learning how to ride a bike. Her friend, Clara, was letting her use her new bike she had gotten for her seventh birthday. They thought it was so cool because it didn't have training wheels on it. The two girls were taking turns on it. She loved to move so fast, with the wind blowing her hair out behind her and the pink tassels on the handlebars tickling her wrists. It had been a sunny day, not a cloud was in the sky. Clara's mother watched from the kitchen window while she was washing dishes, carefully keeping an eye on the girls. Clara wasn't allowed to go very far from the house so they always made sure to stay within eyesight, only biking up and down the one street. They lived on a quiet street and there wasn't a lot of traffic, so when a car did turn onto their block, they were taken by surprise. She had looked over her shoulder at the oncoming sedan and hadn't been paying attention to where she was. The bike hit the curb and she was sent hurtling over the handlebars. She flung out an arm to brace herself from the fall, but she heard a sickening snap and plain flooded through her left arm. The driver had immediately pulled over and came running to her side. Clara's mother was only moments behind the driver. There had been a big fuss as they got her propped up in Clara's family van and she was shuttled off to the hospital. She remembered how anxious she felt when her mother had arrived at the hospital. Her anxiety had been unwarranted though. Besides the mild irritation from having to pick her up and leave the television, her mother barely said a word. When they returned home her father was nowhere to be found. It took him a few days to even notice the cast and sling and her mother just shrugged when he asked her about it. She blinked back the memory and the tears that had formed in her eyes.

The small sliding door slammed open and light came pouring in. She lifted her head from the mattress to watch as His hand appeared and dropped a tray on the floor. The door slid shut without any hesitation. She dropped her head again. As long as He didn't come inside the room again so soon she didn't really care. She lay there and just felt the throbbing sensation in her side. She was aware of her stretched and puffy skin, her blood pumping underneath the surface. She felt color rise in her cheeks and beads of sweat forming on her forehead. She uncurled her spine and cringed from the movement in her side. Breathing became difficult and laborious as she stretched.

Since she was moving anyway she decided to go investigate the tray while she had the momentum. She placed her palms flat on the mattress and pushed herself up to a sitting position. She had to stop once she was upright to catch her breath. She clutched at her ribs and gulped air into her lungs. She sat for a few minutes before the throbbing subsided and she was able to move again. When she did, she let herself onto the floor, the drop was only a few inches, and crawled across the room to the door. She propped herself up on one arm and let the other hand roam around, searching for the tray. She knew it when she felt it. It wasn't as cold as the cement on her skin and the material felt manufactured. She continued patting but couldn't find any food on the tray. There was no piece of fruit. There was no bread. There was only a bottle of water. Her stomach growled in response to this solemn news. She took the bottle and slowly made her way back to where she had started.

Once she was back beside the mattress she lifted a corner and found the bobby pin. She wanted to push it farther away from the edge, more towards the middle of the mattress. She didn't want it to be easy for him to find it from just picking up any corner and seeing it. She let out a growl from the effort of picking up the weight of the mattress. She pushed it up with one hand and lay down with her head tucked under it. Then with her free hand, she pushed the bobby pin as far as she could. She pulled herself out and let the mattress drop back into place. It landed with a thud. She wouldn't be pulling it out to make the marks in the floor anymore. Not while she was injured at least. It was simply too much effort. She wasn't sure how accurate her marks were anyway. Last time she counted them it had totaled to a hundred and thirteen days.

She pulled herself onto the mattress and lay back down on her left side, clutching the bottle to her chest. She wished the mattress was cushier, but it was firm and provided little comfort. She twisted the cap off the bottle and didn't stop to think why it hadn't been sealed. She lifted it to her lips and took a few gulps. Her throat felt dry and scratchy, but she needed to save some of it if it was going to last. She twisted the cap back on.

She went back to thinking about her friend Clara. She couldn't remember when they had stopped being friends. Possibly when she had joined the soccer team in junior high. Clara had been too much of a girly girl to enjoy sports. They had started hanging out with different groups and eventually stopped sitting together for lunch. Their friendship diminished. When they saw each other walking home from school they would lock eyes for a moment and nod to each other, but they never called out. Suddenly her eyes got droopy and heavy. She tried to shake it by thinking about more important things like planning her next attack. But she couldn't fight the urge. Her eyes shut and she let herself retreat into sleep.

2017, Day 12

Lauren was leaning across the table and her voice was low, the expression on her face was intense, "So what did the cops want?"

The other two nodded in unison, also wanting to know. The four girls were sitting around the circular kitchen table with their dinner plates. The detectives were at the dining room table with Lauren's parents and Brandon had retreated upstairs to his bedroom. The food was laid out on the kitchen counter, buffet-style so all could help themselves at their leisure. Melissa put her loaded fork down.

"They just had a few questions to ask about the party that night."

"Like what, though," persisted Camille.

"I don't know if I should say."

"Come on…please?" Cass batted her eyelashes at Melissa while making a pouty face at her. How could she say no to that? This is what friends were for right? To help each other during hard times.

Melissa sighed. "Fine. But this isn't gossip you can spread around, okay?" She waited for the three girls to nod. "Well, they wanted to know more details because they think the guy wasn't after Kate."

"Who was he after then?" Camille didn't want to let it go. She had also put her fork and knife down and was leaning forward now with her eyes wide, fingers gripping the edges of the table.

"I guess me." Melissa shrugged her shoulders and looked at her plate, not wanting to make eye contact with them anymore. All this attention was making her nervous, she didn't like it. She still had trouble keeping up with conversation all the time. She liked to just listen to the other girls talk.

"Why do they think that?" asked Camille.

"Apparently it's a serial killer and Kate didn't fit the profile or something."

"Oh my god. You guys wore the same thing that night." Leave it to Cass to point out the obvious. She was the simple-minded girl of the group.

"That's why they think it was possible for a mistake to have happened."

"How do you feel? Terrified?" Lauren took up with the questions now, her voice was still low as if she didn't want the grownups to hear. It's not like the detectives had told her not to tell anyone, but it didn't feel right for them to know that she was telling the others. This information seemed like something they would want to keep quiet until the guy was caught.

"I don't really know honestly." She picked up her fork again and finally took her bite of chicken, savoring the flavor as it hit her taste buds. She had never tasted meat this delicious before, certainly never at home. She glanced over her shoulder at the dining room where the detectives were. They were watching her while trying to maintain an awkward conversation with the couple across from them.

"Did they at least offer you protection?"

She snapped her attention back to Lauren. "Umm, yeah. They did. Can we please talk about something else now?"

"Like Cameron and that private chat you had earlier?" Cass's voice rose at the end of the sentence creating a giggling sound. They were back to teasing her, almost seamlessly.

Melissa whipped her head to stare at Lauren, "You told them about that?"

"Oh please, who do you think I was texting when you guys came outside?"

Melissa shoved her chair away from the table and stood, "Anyone want anything while I'm up?" She scurried to the countertop before anyone could respond and started loading up her plate with a second helping. As she crossed the room she saw the two detectives' heads swivel and follow her. Could she get no peace? As if on cue her phone buzzed in her back pocket. She pulled it out and glanced at the screen. It was a phone number she didn't recognize. She typed in her passcode to view it, 0-7-1-4, Danny's birthday.

Unfamiliar Number: Hey! I was wondering if I could see you this weekend. I felt bad about how we left things today. So I guess I will wait to hear back from you. Oh, this is Cameron btw.

She reread it two more times before shoving it in her pocket again and filling up her plate. She filled up her water cup and then took her place at the table again.

"So, would any of you know, by any chance, how Cameron got my number?" She calmly took a sip of her water before making any eye contact with the other girls.

Lauren had a devious smile on her face. "Why? Did he text you or something?"

Melissa nodded.

"Oooooh! What'd he say?" asked Camille, bouncing wildly in her seat.

"He wants to hang out this weekend. But seriously, how did he get my number? I didn't give it to him."

"Well, Brandon did me a favor," Lauren conceded. "See, Brandon texted Mark, who is on the football team with him, because Mark's younger brother is on the basketball team with Cameron. So they all just passed the message on for me."

"So all of them have my number? Lauren, what were you thinking?" exasperation seeped into Melissa's voice.

"I was thinking of how cute you and Cameron are together. You guys just need a little nudge to get there." Lauren winked at her.

Melissa shook her head. She wasn't really sure how mad she actually was, but she certainly wasn't happy about so many people having her number.

"Did you respond?" asked Cass quietly.

"Not yet, no."

"What are you going to say?"

She shrugged her shoulders. She honestly hadn't made up her mind yet about the situation. She liked him, that was certain. She always had butterflies in her stomach when he was around, but she had too many things going on.

She didn't need another distraction. She had to take care of Danny, and she needed to get good grades in order to get a scholarship for college. Plus, who knows what Ma would have to say about any of this.

2017, Day 12

Anderson glanced in the rearview mirror at Melissa, who was silent in the backseat. She was staring intently at her phone, a look of deep concentration on her young, but serious face. She was going to have worry lines etched into her face by the time she hit her early twenties. Luke was driving the three of them the short distance to Melissa's home from her friend's house. They could no longer risk letting her walk alone. The storm was letting up finally and the windshield wipers were on low, sweeping the small amount of water off to the sides. When they pulled upfront of the house, a uniform was already sitting in his car, watching the property. Anderson's pocket buzzed, startling all of them out of their silence. Melissa finally looked up from her phone, her blue eyes penetrating the back of

Anderson's headrest. Anderson pulled her own phone out and glanced at the screen, Dad.

"I need to take this." She looked at Luke and waited for him to nod before she answered. Luke and Melissa got out of the car, leaving Anderson alone to her call and the rain pounding the roof of the car.

"Hey, Dad. Now's not a great time."

"Emz, I know you said you're busy with work, but this will just take a second. I let Caleb into your apartment. He's coming down from a high and he's asleep right now on the couch. I was going to make him some food, but honey, your fridge is pretty empty. I can run to the store to get some groceries if you'd like."

"If you could stay put with Caleb, I would appreciate it. Last time he was alone in my apartment he stole something important to me. Just keep an eye on him. I'll be home soon. I can pick up some take-out on the way. What do you want?"

"What did he take?"

"Dad, it's not a big deal. Just leave it."

"Emz. What did he take from you?"

Anderson rubbed a hand over her tired face, rubbing off the last of her thinly-layered makeup. She hated arguing with him and she knew he would get upset and overreact somehow. "Just drop it. What kind of take-out do you want?"

"Whatever you want."

"Ok, see you soon, Dad."

She hung up and leaned her head back on the rest. She only had to wait a few minutes before Luke climbed back into the car, dripping water everywhere.

"Got permission from the mother. We're all set to go. Another uniform will switch out in about an hour. Ready to call it a day?"

She nodded. "Just get me back to my car."

They rode in silence again. Luke knew something was up from the look on her face and he didn't question her, just let her be alone in her thoughts. She was glad when they reached the station and she could be truly alone. She swung by a local Chinese restaurant a block away from her home. She frequented the tiny place once a week. The family that owned and ran the shop knew her by now. The short man behind the counter smiled at her through his wrinkled, leathery skin. She nodded back at him in greeting before ordering a little box of everything they had, who knew what Caleb would be hungry for. He moved like molasses as he gathered together the to-go boxes and for the first time she found herself becoming impatient with his slow movement. He always moved at this pace, but she had never before tonight been irritated by it. By the time she left, she had three full plastic bags of containers.

When she finally reached her apartment she opened the door to find Caleb still passed out on the couch and her dad looking over her bookshelves. He was inspecting each book spine like it was the first time he had ever seen them. She set her bags of food down on the coffee table before greeting him. He jumped even though the rustling of the bags was hard to miss.

"Has he woken up yet?" she asked.

"Not yet. He doesn't sleep well though."

She looked at her brother and noted how his eyes flickered in agitation underneath his eyelids. He was dreaming about something, and whatever it was, it wasn't good. His skin was pale and clammy from his cold sweat and he had dark bags under his eyes. Her dad had tucked a blanket all around Caleb's scrawny frame. He had never grown into his height, remaining tall and gangly long past his teenage years. On her tiny couch, his frame was squished together and his legs were tucked into his chest. It looked awkward and uncomfortable.

"You want some food, Dad?" She went to the kitchen to retrieve utensils for the three of them. She poured a water glass for Caleb but put the kettle on for herself. Since she refused to drink in front of her recovering brother, and since she was out of coffee grounds, she went to her next go-to drink. At least the tea would warm her body and maybe soothe her soul.

"I'd best be going, Emz."

"Dad. You did not come all the way out here to help me out, just to leave when I finally get to come home. Stay for a little while. Please." She was leaning backward, away from the countertop so that she could stare at her dad through the doorway. He had moved from the bookcase to the pictures that hung on the wall. He was studying the photographs intently. They were all from childhood and mostly of Caleb and Jamie. Eventually, he turned to face her. He looked just as tired as Caleb.

"I can stay for a short bit, but I am expected at home sometime soon. I couldn't exactly tell her that I was at your apartment taking care of Caleb."

"Great, what would you like to drink?"

"Just water." He took a seat on the floor next to the couch, by Caleb's head and ran his fingers through his son's sweaty brown hair. It was the first sign of affection that she had seen her dad give Caleb in years. She couldn't even remember the last time the three of them had been in the same room together. She wished she could enjoy this moment more.

She placed both water glasses on the cedar chest that doubled as her coffee table and returned to the kitchen to finish getting her tea. She grabbed one of her three mugs from the cupboard and got a chamomile tea bag ready. She got the small bottle of honey down from the cupboard next to the sugar and flour. She hesitated for a second before pulling down her bottle of honey Jack and pouring a small splash into the bottom of her mug. It would help her fall asleep. She stared at the kettle on the stove and listened to her dad take the containers out of the plastic bags. She smiled, glad that he was helping himself. He was always so reserved when Tracy was around, it was nice to see him be himself.

"So Emz, tell me. Have you been reading at all? Or are you too busy with work?"

This is what she missed. He may not actually have anything in common with her, but he always made an attempt. He wasn't much for reading, he preferred equations and numbers to words and syntax. The kettle on the stove began to whistle. She carefully lifted it and poured into her teal colored mug. She stirred in her honey and then took her seat beside her dad on the floor.

"Actually. I did try to do some reading last week. It didn't last long, I'd had a long day and couldn't get my eyes to focus." She let out a chuckle and took a sip of her tea.

Her dad smiled at her. "Which book?"

She reached across the small space and plucked the book off the shelf and handed it to him. She sat on the backs of her heels so she could see into all the food containers while he read the back. Teriyaki chicken and broccoli were calling her name. She reached for it and started eating right out of the box. Her dad laughed at her.

"You have always eaten out of the box. Even as a kid. We could never get you trained to grab a plate." He shook his head and laughed.

With her mouth still full, and with horrible manners she said, "Well, I never saw-," she paused to swallow, "-

saw the point of dirtying a perfectly clean plate. It's such a waste of energy to have to clean it later."

He chuckled and placed *The Beautiful and the Damned* carefully on the other side of the table. He pointed to it, "Sounds good."

"Dad." She almost dropped her fork and just gave him a look that she used to give him when she was taking AP English in High School and he pretended to know what she was talking about.

He froze with his own fork halfway between the container in his left hand and his mouth, "What?"

"Did you even understand the description on the back cover?"

He winked at her and took his bite. He definitely didn't understand what the book was about. She didn't mind, she was just happy to share it with him. She could never talk about these things with that horrible woman by his side. Caleb stirred on the couch and for a moment, she thought he was about to wake up. He rolled over onto his other side.

"Emz, what did he take from you?" Her dad stared at her unwaveringly. She knew he was trying to figure out what would be valuable enough in her apartment for Caleb to steal and pawn off.

"Dad, I told you to leave it. It's nothing I can't handle on my own."

"Honey, I know you can handle it, that doesn't mean that you should have to. You don't have to create an environment where he feels that he can come by whenever he needs someplace to recover. That's not fair for you. You have your own life and stresses to deal with, without him adding to them. That's not what brothers are for."

"Maybe I wouldn't have to take care of him if he felt like he could go to you. You are his dad after all. This is your job, and yet he comes to my doorstep. Every time."

"Emz…"

"No, Dad. I don't care what she thinks. You have two kids left out of three and yet you act like I'm the only one left. It's not right. I can't afford to send him to rehab." She felt awkward bringing up the subject of money, but she'd been meaning to do this for months. The moment was just never right to bring it up and now that she had him alone, she finally could.

"Oh, honey. I don't know how I feel about that."

"You mean, you don't know how she would feel about that. He's your kid and he needs help. You still have his college fund, don't you? Or did you let her spend that, too?"

"I think it's time I called it a night." He got to his feet and went to the coat rack. "How much was dinner?" He pulled his wallet out of his coat pocket and started counting out some bills.

"Don't worry about it." She didn't bother to look at him. She started closing up the food containers and cleaning up the utensils and cups when she heard the front door close. She glanced in the general direction of the door but was distracted by the wad of cash that was left in the open on her desk. She snatched it up on the way to the kitchen with the mugs. She tucked it into her jacket pocket. After cleaning up all the food, she went to her closet and dug into the back for a blanket. She tucked it in around Caleb, who didn't even flinch when she touched him. She took a blank sheet of paper from her desk and wrote a note in giant block letters for him, explaining that there was leftover food for him in the fridge and he could help himself. She left her shoes by the door and hung her jacket on the rack before heading to her room.

She lay in her bed staring at the ceiling for what felt like hours. Time was dragging by slowly. When she glanced at the clock on her nightstand, she found that only fifteen minutes had ticked by. Her eyes went back to the ceiling. She had no idea what to do about Caleb. Clearly talking to her dad wasn't an option considering how unreceptive he had been today to the topic of rehab. She shivered and pulled the comforter up to her chin. She listened to the wind whistle through the branches and leaves of the trees outside her window. She imagined the leaves breaking free from the branches and swirling around in the air, slowly sailing to the ground and finally settling on the minuscule lawn in front of the apartment building.

2017, Day 13

It was one a.m. and Melissa couldn't sleep. She hadn't realized how much everything was really weighing on her until she was in her room. After the detectives had dropped her off at home she had gone to Danny's room and helped him with some homework, trying to keep her mind busy. It was all just circling in her head and she was frightened. Being near Danny always soothed her though. He was an intuitive kid for his age and he knew something was wrong. When he was done with his homework, he asked if he could hang out with her in her room, sensing that she didn't want to be alone. He had sat in the middle of the floor and built a small fort out of her chair, some pillows, and the blanket that was always at the foot of her bed. He was hiding inside, reading one of the comic books that she had gotten him for his birthday last year. She was at her desk, leaning back in her chair while holding his blanket fort in place. She had been trying to work on an essay for Mr. Rogers' class, but she couldn't get her mind to focus on the task. All she had was her name, the title and half a sentence typed. The black cursor blinked at her expectantly. She had also been staring at her phone a lot, trying to figure out what to say to Cameron. It had been hours since he had sent the text and she still hadn't sent anything to him in response.

The blanket fort trembled as Danny moved around inside. It shook her from her thoughts and she picked up her phone again. It was time to respond. Old Melissa would let it go, but this was the new and improved version of her.

Even though this was the new her, it still needed to feel natural.

> Melissa: Hey! Sounds like fun, what
> do you think we should do?

There. That wasn't so scary, and she hoped that came off as interested but not over-the-top excited. She didn't want him to be scared off. Now that that was done she could focus on her paper. She glared at the blank white page in front of her, willing the words to come to her. If only that's how it worked. Danny poked his head out under the blanket.

"Hey, Lissa…"

"Yeah?"

"What did the cops want?"

She pulled the hair tie out with one hand and shook her hair down from the messy bun she had been rocking. She needed to be doing something with her hands, so she separated it into three sections and started braiding it. "Nothing. They were just checking in."

"But they gave you a ride home!"

"Yes, it was dark out and they wanted to make sure I got home okay."

He seemed placated by this and retreated into his tent. She could hear the rustle of paper as he flipped a page in his comic book. She could just picture him being careful to not put in any extra wrinkles into the edges of the paper.

"Hey, kid?"

"Yeah?"

"Which issue number are you on?"

"Forty-three."

She scribbled the number down on a post-it note. It was about time she got him a few more in the series. He was reading them so fast, she couldn't keep up. He liked the classics, Superman, Batman, and the Green Lantern. His all time favorite though, the Flash. He had been the Flash for Halloween this last year. He insisted that's what he would be again next Halloween, but he was growing so fast he would need a new costume. Maybe she would dress up with him this year and be Catwoman, or maybe Wonder Woman.

Her phone buzzed on the desk next to her wrist. She glanced at the screen, expecting it to be Lauren because the girls had been blowing up her phone since she got home.

Instead, she read "Cameron". Her heartbeat quickened immediately. She typed in her passcode and turned off the screen three or four times before she could muster the courage to actually read it.

> Cameron: Are you free now?
>
> Melissa: Sorta. I'm trying and failing to write this paper for Mr. Rogers' class :/
>
> Cameron: So that'd be a no to a moonlit stroll?

She stared at it for a second, making sure it really said what she was seeing. Could she? The butterflies in her stomach fluttered around making her uncomfortable and just a little queasy. Maybe she shouldn't. That crazy serial killer guy was still out there. On the other hand, she did have a cop keeping an eye on her. She should be safe, right?

> Melissa: Sure. When can you be here?
>
> Cameron: Twenty minutes
>
> Melissa: Meet me out front?

She sent a group text out to her friends. They would want to know. Her phone buzzed incessantly for a few seconds as her friends sent messages like rapid fire, congratulating her on her date if you could really call it that. She shut her laptop, the first time that she could ever recall leaving an assignment left unfinished.

"Danny?"

Danny poked his head out again.

"I'm going out for a little bit. You can stay in here with your fort if you'd like."

She bent over and slipped her shoes back onto her feet. Her jacket from earlier was still wet from the rain so she picked out a different one from her closet. Uncharacteristically, she checked her hair and makeup in the mirror. Her braid was tidy and her eyeliner was smudged underneath her eyes, but there was nothing she really needed to fix before she climbed into Danny's tent. He was laying on his stomach with his feet in the air, kicking back and forth. He didn't even look up from his comic. She reached over and ruffled his clean hair. He was such a good kid. She curved her spine so that she could gently brush her lips on his forehead.

"I'll be back in a little while, okay?"

He nodded but didn't remove his eyes from the brightly-colored graphics.

She hesitated, indecision and guilt piercing her. "Are you sure you'll be okay?"

She crawled out of the fort and slid open her window. She found the lantern in her closet, turned it on, and put it in the fort so that she could turn off her bedroom light. This way Ma would think both of them were asleep. The cherry blossom pink umbrella was tucked under one arm as she climbed out the window and slipped around to the front of the house to wait for Cameron.

Unknown Year, Day 121

She blinked, trying to clear her vision, but it didn't help. Everything was blurry and her head was pounding. How long had she been out for? She felt sick. The water bottle was still clutched to her chest, but it was empty. She must have woken up and finished drinking it at some point. She needed to get out of here, she couldn't waste any more time. The bobby pin was sharp enough to do some damage.

Maybe she could get close enough to go for His eyes, she had been able to get decently close to Him last time she had made an attempt. She blinked a couple more times before the room became discernible. She propped herself up on one elbow so that she had a view of the room. There was a new tray in front of the door that held another water bottle and, to her surprise, some food. She pushed herself up into a sitting position with her good arm. Her limbs didn't want to move, they felt heavy, like someone had tied weights to them and no matter how hard she tried to move them, the weights were just too much.

The door opened and she was sent back to blinking wildly. She was sensitive to everything. The light hurt her eyes, the creaking of the hinges seemed louder than usual, and even His footsteps inside the room seemed eerily loud. She struggled to really see Him. His brown hair, the round spectacles that were balanced on the brim of His nose, even the plaid shirt He wore with the wing-tipped shoes on His feet. She wanted to stand up so that she wasn't below Him, but her muscles weren't cooperating and she didn't want Him to know she was weak right now. He moved closer to the mattress and she had to tilt her face up so that she could maintain eye contact.

"Alice. You were a very bad girl the other day. What are we going to do about it?"

She remained silent and just stared at Him. He looked around the room, taking in the untouched tray by the door. He clucked His tongue and shook His head at her.

"Alice. Speak when I ask you a question." His voice was so sharp it bounced off the walls and attacked her.

Still, she remained silent. He looked disappointed and clasped His hands behind His back. He took a few steps closer and looked down at her, His glasses sliding down to the end of His nose.

"You're doing this to yourself, Alice. What did you really expect to accomplish?" He seemed so composed and calm.

This time she tried to respond. She opened her mouth, but the words wouldn't come. Her tongue felt thick and her lips were dry. She licked them and felt all the cracks and crevices in her bottom lip. Again, she tried to speak, but nothing came out.

"Alice, just tell me where you hid John. I know your mother was looking after him for a while. But she's sick and can't take care of him now. I am fully capable of looking after him. You know I would care for him like he is my own. Well, he is my own. I don't know why you insist on refusing to tell him who his father is."

"I'm not Alice," her voice cracked and she choked on her chalky tongue.

She didn't even see it coming, His fist collided with her jaw. Something was different this time. It felt cold. There was a metallic taste in her mouth, and she spat blood on the floor. When she looked back at Him, she saw that He had brass knuckles strapped to His hand. He came prepared this time. She wiped her mouth with the back of her wrist and looked at the red stain on her skin.

"You used to love me, Alice. What happened that made you want to leave? We were perfect for each other. Did I not please you?"

She couldn't meet his gaze this time and she braced herself for the impact. Even though she was waiting for it, the shock of the pain on the other side of her face made her double over. She clutched her head between her knees, hiding both sides of her face.

"Why did you stop loving me?"

His fist connected with her injured side and she cried out this time. The pain rippled up through her ribs and into her shoulder. Tears streamed down her face.

"Please stop," she begged.

The lines around his mouth and eyes deepened with disgust. There was something else there, He looked tired. This was wearing him down.

"Alice, if you had just behaved, this wouldn't be happening. You need to learn to live with the consequences of your actions."

With her head still tucked into her lap, she shook it, refusing to admit anything or to look at Him. He placed a hand on her right knee. Her skin was crawling and hairs all over her body stood on end. He had never touched her like this before. Something was about to happen. She still couldn't move, she was defenseless. His other hand found her chin and raised her face to look at Him. Her vision wavered, but this time it was because of the tears that were brimming and slowly flowing down her already purpling and swelling cheeks. The tears tickled her jawline as they dried there.

"You will love me again one day."

She cringed and couldn't stop the words that came to her. "No one will ever love such a monster." She tore her chin from His grasp and spat more blood from her mouth.

He flexed His fingers and enjoyed watching the expression of terror on her face. He had a smile on His face that made her want to vomit.

"You must get lonely down here. All alone in the dark."

He ran His pointer finger along her jawline. She shivered and tried to pull her face away, but He bent down to her eye level and held her face in place. He stared into her eyes. Panic spread throughout her as her heart rate quickened. She tried to control her breathing, but His face was close to hers and it was pointless. She scooted as far back on the mattress as she could get, the insides of her knees were pressing into the edges of the rough fabric she sat on. He bent closer still and brushed His lips to her cheek.

"You will love me." She could feel His breath warm on her skin. He dragged a finger up her thigh, His nail leaving a white line against her pale pink skin.

"Please, leave me alone," she whispered.

Her eyes were closed so that she didn't have to watch. She didn't need to see to know what was happening. Both sides of her face pulsed with the swelling and she tried to just focus on that one thing. Nothing else existed in that moment.

2017, Day 13

Melissa's phone glowed in the darkness, telling her it was three in the morning. She looked up at the stars and smiled. Cameron had taken her to the park nearby and they had strolled all the little winding dirt pathways, leaping around the quickly forming puddles. He had collected one blossom from each flower they passed. By the time they sat on a wooden bench, he had collected a myriad of flowers. He offered it to her now, and she shyly took the bouquet and held it to her nose. The wet stems coated her palms with rainwater. She breathed in the scent from between the petals before meeting his gaze. She couldn't stop smiling. Melissa snuggled closer to Cameron and he wrapped an arm around her shoulders.

"We should do this again."

She tilted her head backward to look at him. Strong, prominent cheekbones, cut jawline, and bright blue eyes. He gazed down at her, the edges of his lips curled upwards.

His body heat warmed her, and his smile melted her insides. She wanted nothing more than this right here. He squeezed her and she felt…special. She had never felt this way before.

"I agree," she smiled at him, showing him a sliver of her pearly whites. "I'm enjoying this. A lot." She retreated behind the bouquet again. Her cheeks flushed in embarrassment.

"So, you're enjoying walking on the wild side?"

"What counts as wild?" She raised an eyebrow.

He laughed and she felt his body shaking beside her. "Well, how about late night walks that technically turn into early morning hangouts."

"Then yes. I like the wild side."

"I thought you weren't interested." His voice was quiet.

"What gave you that idea?"

"Well, after that night I thought you were avoiding me at school."

"It's not like you really tried to talk to me either." He didn't respond so she continued. "That night, I wasn't myself. I don't know, or maybe I was finally coming into myself. I used to hold back a lot. I didn't have a lot of friends and I take care of Danny in my free time."

"So, what changed?"

"Honestly? Kate. With her gone some of the girls-"

"Like Lauren?"

"Yes, like Lauren. They began talking to me and, I guess, I'm just learning to be social?" She was having trouble forming her sentences properly, pausing to think of the right words to use.

"Well then, I like who you're becoming," he said definitively.

She examined the flowers, admiring the bold colors against the plain white blossoms and the green leaves. This was the first time anyone had given her flowers. It meant so much more since he had picked them himself, carefully choosing the prettiest one from each rain-beaten bush. She glanced at her phone again, three-thirty.

"We have school tomorrow. We really should call it a night." Her voice was carried away in the breeze.

"Let me walk you home."

She nodded and together they stood. She made sure to grab the handle of her umbrella. She had already almost forgotten it when she had set it down so she could ride on the slide. They walked by the playground again and she mindlessly grasped the chains on the tire swing, winding it up as she passed and letting go when she was an arms reach away. She looked back over her shoulder and watched it spin, the air current picked it up and tossed it around in every which direction. Her laugh filled the emptiness around them. When she looked at Cameron again he was watching her and grinning. He was loving every moment of being with her. And she was loving every moment with him, too.

They left the park behind them and wandered into the street. The lights cast glowing orbs into the night sky. The road was wet from the recent rain and they could hear water gushing through the rain gutters in the street. He laced his fingers between hers and tugged her closer, pulling her to a stop underneath one of the lights. She put her free hand on his chest and rubbed her thumb on the collar of his pale blue polo shirt. He brushed her tousled hair behind her ear and kissed her on her forehead. She looked up from his shirt to his face. She glanced at his eyes, but she couldn't stop herself from looking longingly at his lips. He curved his neck down and kissed her. It was soft and long. When they broke apart, she stumbled back, dazed. A permanent smile fixed itself on her round features.

"We should get going. It really is late." Her voice felt small.

He walked slightly ahead of her, pulling her by their connected fingers, in the general direction of her house. It was only a few blocks away and the cop car was still parked across the street. She had snuck by him earlier when she first met Cameron outside so she stayed behind the trees that lined the street, hoping he wouldn't see her sneaking back in. No one had to know that she had ever left the house.

"So, I'll see you at school tomorrow," she whispered, the wind carrying her voice to Cameron's ears.

He squeezed her hand and nodded. "Goodnight."

Then she was alone. She looked around at the oppressive blackness, surprised at the immediate fear that settled in from the lack of companionship. She slowly made her way to the side of the house, still staying out of sight, behind bushes and trees. Once she was in the side yard she figured she would be fine. It was a jungle in there and the cop wouldn't be able to see her climbing back in through her window anyway. She counted the windows, one, two, three, and then hers, the fourth. She could see a low glow through the glass, the lantern she had left Danny in his fort to read by. She assumed he was still in her room, although he had probably fallen asleep at this point. She propped the umbrella up against the wall in a spot that she could grab it once she had climbed inside. She put a hand on either side of the window sill and was about to hoist herself in when she heard a twig snap behind her. She whipped her head around to see who was there. Nothing. She squinted in the dark for a heartbeat, but when nothing moved she went back to her window. She bent her legs, preparing to give herself a little jump when she was grabbed from behind. A cloth was pressed to her face and she struggled for all of a few measly seconds before absolutely nothing.

2017, Day 13

Anderson barely slept at all that night. The fact that her little brother was sleeping fitfully on her couch disturbed her greatly. The light from the rising sun snuck into the room between the closed blinds, casting long shadows throughout the room. She heard a rustling sound and assumed it was the trees outside her windowsill. The rain had ceased to fall around two a.m., but the wind was still blowing fiercely. The clock on her dresser blinked five at her in blue lights. She threw the sheets off her body and planted both feet flat on the floor. If she couldn't descend into dreamland then she could at least stop pretending and get the day started. Her brain needed to be active, engaged in something to distract from anything Caleb-related. She slipped her frozen toes into her worn-through slippers that were waiting at the end of the bed. She slid open the closet door, pulled out an old sweatshirt that was still soft on the inside, and then paused, listening to the silence. She didn't want to wake him— he needed his sleep if he was going to recover. She didn't hear anything so she continued to dress before nudging open her bedroom door and trudging slowly to the kitchen to make a pot of coffee.

There were a few empty food cartons left on the countertop that had not been there when she had retired the night before, which meant that Caleb had gotten up in the middle of the night to eat. This was a good sign. There were only three containers left in the fridge and it looked like he had finished the last of her apple juice as well. She rinsed out her mug that still had a little coffee crud at the bottom and placed it beside the already warming up coffee pot. She got out another clean mug for when Caleb would wake up. He could do with a strong cup first thing.

She then went to her desk next to the front door, behind the couch Caleb was sleeping on, and pulled her phone off the charger. Luke had instructed the uniforms that were watching Melissa to send updates every two hours. She had four messages in total, all stating that everything at the girl's house was fine. She sent Luke a text letting him know that even though she was "on leave" she would still be working if he needed anything. She knew it was a bit early to be sending messages, but he would see it when he woke up. Hopefully, he would sleep through his phone going off. She herself was a light sleeper, which is why she always kept her phone in the living room at night.

She gathered her files, a notepad, and a pen, figuring she could work in her room so as not to disturb her brother. She dumped these supplies in her room before going back to the kitchen, where the pot was now full and steaming. She let the steam warm her face for a moment before adding a dash of cream. She retreated to her bedroom and left her door open so that she could keep an eye on the living room, just in case he got up again and needed something. She sat cross-legged with her materials spread around her in a semicircle. She took a sip of the swirling, steaming liquid of life and felt a jolt of energy instantaneously stir her brain.

Her hands went to the map of the city first. It had red X's where the girls had been taken. He had a hunting zone. He always took the girls from the same general vicinity which means he knows the area. She thought of the neighborhood map she had in the file she lent to Luke. Her sister wasn't taken by the field, but from inside the cul-de-sac. Had it been a neighbor? Someone they grew up next to possibly. Someone who worked at the school. She shook her head. She had thought about this a million times over the years and always came to the conclusion that she didn't know him. Almost all the girls had gone to the same high school. Out of the girls they knew about, only one of them had been in a different school district, but she lived in the same part of town as the rest. If it was a neighbor it would've been hard to hide a teenage girl from everyone. It wasn't the best neighborhood, but it also wasn't an area where people would turn a blind eye on something suspicious. He had to have a soundproof room, or a bunker of some sort if he was keeping them alive the whole five years, and she needed to believe that. He also needed to have a reliable mode of transportation. He couldn't have dragged an unconscious girl down a suburban street without drawing attention. Maybe he takes her to a location outside of the neighborhood? So then, he keeps her someplace he doesn't live and away from where he grew up. Or, only his hunting ground was where he grew up? There were too many possibilities to narrow it down right now.

Six a.m. She received another text, but this time everything wasn't okay. Melissa's younger brother had come out to the cop at five a.m.to say that Melissa had taken off during the night to see some friends and hadn't come home yet. Anderson immediately called Luke's cell as she cleaned up all her papers. It rang endlessly until it went to voicemail. She dialed again and put it on speakerphone so that she could put real clothes on simultaneously. She was buttoning her jeans when it went to voicemail for a second time. Shit. She dialed a third time while she was brushing her teeth, and then her hair, and was tying the laces on her Nikes. When it went to voicemail this time, she left a message.

"Hey, Luke. You can sleep through anything, can't you? Melissa is missing. I'm heading to her place right now to talk to the uniform. Call me when you get this."

She hurriedly sped through the kitchen filling up a travel mug with coffee, snatching her keys off the kitchen table and jacket off the coat rack. She glanced at the couch. Melissa wasn't the only person missing in action. Caleb was no longer there. She checked her jacket pocket and sure enough, the money she had stashed there from her dad was gone. This was an expensive habit.

2017, Day 13

Melissa drifted into consciousness. She stretched her tight muscles and looked around, trying to place where she was, all the while trying to keep her breathing under control. It was almost too dim to see anything around her, but she could see that it was just a bare room with a mattress pushed against one wall. She blinked a couple of times trying to clear her sight, which was still a little fuzzy. The air felt dry and her already irritated eyes itched.

There was someone on the mattress. Her pulse quickened. Oh god, what if it was a corpse? She pulled her knees to her chest and remained seated with her back pressed against the wall. She turned to make sure it really was a wall she was leaning on. It was, but there was a door right beside her. She must have been dumped just inside the room. It was a stupid hope, but she reached a shaking hand to the doorknob anyway. It didn't budge; she wasn't all that surprised.

What happened anyway? She had been out with Cameron at the park. She remembered he had walked her home when she saw the time and freaked. He had left her alone out front though. Alone, she had wandered around the side of her house to the window she had left open and had been trying to get the right leverage to pull herself in when- Her eyes widened. Someone had grabbed her from behind, putting something over her face, and then she assumed she had passed out. She probably watched too much tv, but she assumed it had to have been a chloroform-soaked rag. She stared at the figure that lay motionless on the mattress. It had to be Kate, right? Melissa forced herself to stand, trembling slightly from the effort, and slowly approached. Her breathing quickened to match her still-racing pulse.

She could feel her breath warming the air in front of her face before she passed through it. She squinted in the darkness, trying to see more of the figure from far away. Was she breathing? The figure had a ratted mess of blonde covering her face that was turned away from Melissa. She lay flat on her stomach, starfished across the small twin sized bed. It was definitely Kate, she was still wearing the same black mini skirt from the party and the purple halter top. Her bare back muscles were exposed now and looked odd motionless. Melissa was so used to seeing them in action at cheer practice. In fact, she didn't think she had ever seen Kate sit still before. She knelt down on the floor beside Kate's face, fighting the urge to shake her awake. Tentatively she held her hand underneath the girl's nose, fearing the worst. She waited a couple of heartbeats before she felt the breath on the back of her hand. Kate was still alive. Melissa tucked a lock of the blonde mess behind Kate's ear. The girl twitched upright, smacking Melissa's hand away.

"Fuck."

Melissa just blinked at Kate and waited for the girl to recognize her. Kate looked around the entire room before finally laying her eyes before her and squinting at Melissa.

"You?"

Melissa nodded quietly.

"Fuck. I'm trapped in here with you?"

"Just deal with it, would you?" Melissa snapped back. The new Melissa wouldn't be stifled just because she was here now. She certainly didn't want to be pushed around now that she was stuck alone with Kate.

Kate dragged her eyes up and down the length of Melissa's body as if she were still in competition. Maybe in here they still were, but she hoped to all hell that she was wrong.

"You grew a personality while I've been gone. " The air around Kate seemed to sizzle with animosity. "How long have I been here?"

"Almost two weeks."

Kate stood and meandered to a corner where Melissa had completely missed a tray of food. There were two water bottles, two chunks of bread with butter, and two apples. She brought it back to the bed with her and set it on the mattress in front of them while taking a seat beside Melissa, allowing plenty of space between them. No need to be getting friendly.

"Looks like He brought us both dinner."

"He?"

"Yeah. I think it's a he. He doesn't ever come inside here." She pointed at the base of the door, "There's a little trap door there that He delivers food by. Other than that I've never had any contact with Him."

Melissa stared at the door, trying to see the lines for the trap door. She would need to get up close to really see it. She returned to the food tray. She was starved and needed sustenance first before any exploring could be done. Kate was watching her intently.

"I was more freaked out than you are right now. Why is that?"

Melissa took a swig of her water. "Yeah, well. I was kind of expecting it. You weren't."

"How so?"

Melissa launched into describing what she knew of the investigation so far. The detectives interviewing her, stopping by cheer practice, even crashing the dinner party at Lauren's house.

"Wait… You went to Lauren's house for dinner?"

"That's what you're getting out of this? What's wrong with you?"

"No. What I'm getting is that you're the bitch that stole my jacket that night."

Melissa grinned momentarily. "Yeah. I did."

"You bitch. You're the reason why I'm here." Kate clearly had figured out that the missing jacket was the entire reason that she was taken in the first place. Didn't take her long to figure that out and Melissa had hoped it would be a while before that happened.

"So what now?" she asked.

Kate shrugged her shoulders. "Besides you staying away from me, there's not a lot to do in here."

"I can see that." She bit into her apple, the juice dribbling down her chin. Despite the setting, it was the most delicious thing she could have put in her mouth. They never had apples at home and she never had cash to get them from the cafeteria at school. It tasted fresh, but then again, she didn't really know what a fresh apple tasted like. She took another bite and savored the moment. When her eyes connected with Kate's again, the other girl had one eyebrow raised. "What? I've never had an apple."

"Like I care."

2017, Day 13

Anderson parked her car in front of the Jameson house and strode across the street to the two uniform cars that were parked there. Her footsteps on the wet road sounded loud to her ears. Three cops conferred amongst themselves and were blatantly waiting for someone to arrive and take charge of the situation. They made room for her in their small circle and all three sets of eyes blinked at her expectantly.

"Morning officers. Which one of you was on duty when Danny came outside?"

The youngest looking of the three let his medium build slouch.

"Right. Want to tell me how a fifteen-year-old girl snuck by you, officer….."

"Alvirez." He supplied his name, looking extremely uncomfortable as he did so. He tried to hold Anderson's gaze and she took his scratchy looking 5 o'clock shadow.

She stared at him, waiting. "Please, by all means, proceed."

"Oh, um. I took over watch around 12:15 a.m., I was watching the house, and I never saw her leave. Around five a.m. I saw her little brother leave by the side door and he walked right up to my car and knocked on the window. So of course I got out to talk to the kid. He said she had left the house at about one a.m. to meet up with a friend and she had told him that she would be back later. But it had been four hours and he was worried because she wasn't back yet."

"So, again, how did she sneak past you after only forty-five minutes of duty?"

Alvirez looked at his feet. Anderson shook her head in disgust.

"I've already called Detective Luke, he'll be here when he wakes up. Trust me, you're getting off easy because he's a heavy sleeper. Go back to the station. I want this report done now. Where's the little brother? And the mom?"

"Danny is here, the mom was out here initially, but she went back into the house an hour ago." Alvirez gestured at the backseat of his squad car. The kid was curled up with a blanket, but he wasn't asleep. His eyes were wide and he was watching the grownups talk. She made her way to the other side of the car, his head turned with her movement, and popped open the door next to him. She squatted down to his eye level so he wouldn't have to tilt his head up awkwardly.

"Hey, Danny. I know you've already talked to Officer Alvirez here, but do you mind just telling me again, what exactly happened?" It was cold enough that she could see her breath in the air. She was glad that Officer Alvirez had even thought to give the kid a blanket.

He nodded without blinking. The blanket was pulled up over his mouth and his voice was muffled, but she was still able to make out what he was saying. "Lissa was doing homework, and I was in my fort reading the Flash. Her phone kept buzzing, way more than it usually does. And she crawled inside my fort, gave me a light. She said was going out to meet a friend."

"You have a fort? That's so cool. Where is your fort?"

"In her room. She let me build it there." He stared at her with wide eyes, like he would be in trouble for building a fort there.

"That was nice of her. And she brought you a light to read by?"

"Yeah, a lantern. She keeps one in her closet for when Ma forgets to pay the electricity bill."

"Smart girl. And did she say who she was meeting with?"

Danny shook his head, his hair stuck up on one side from sleeping on it funny, it didn't even bounce.

"Do you have any idea who it might have been? Maybe a group of girls?"

"No. I don't think so. But I don't know."

"And you have no idea who?"

He shook his head again.

"Okay. So, what happened next?"

"She said I could stay in her room while she was gone, so I did. I stayed in the fort. And fell asleep.

"Did something wake you up? Why'd you come out here to tell Officer Alvirez that she's missing? Maybe she just hasn't come home yet."

His head shook vigorously, his hair still not moving. "I heard a sound, like a thump."

"A thump?"

"I was scared, but I came out of my fort to see."

"That was brave of you." She tried to smile encouragingly at him.

"She wasn't there. But the window was open. I looked out and there was nothing there."

"So you heard a thump, didn't see anything, but the window was open?"

He nodded.

"And you think she's missing because of this?"

He nodded again.

"Her window is on the left side of the house, right?"

He nodded and silently slid out of the car, still wrapped in the blanket, and led the way across the street. The blanket dragged across the cement, trailing behind him. She tapped one of the other uniforms on the shoulder as she passed and he fell into step behind her, pulling his flashlight from its holster. Upon reaching the side yard, Anderson stopped the group. There was no need to track extra sets of footprints through the dirt if they could avoid it. He pointed in a straight shot down the side of the house to an open window. She held out her hand to the cop behind her and he placed the already beaming flashlight into her palm. She pointed it in the dirt and immediately found one set of footprints, probably Melissa's. The ground was wet from the rain and she had already left a few of her own footprints. She tried to remain off the beaten track a little to preserve what was left. She pulled her phone from her pocket and started taking pictures of the ground in front of her. She followed the prints to the window where they were becoming deeper. Melissa must have stood here for a longer bit of time, trying to figure out how to get in through the window. There was a pale pink umbrella leaning against the side of the house. It was still dripping from recent use. And then she saw it. There was a second set of footprints, bigger too. Melissa's prints had small drag marks by the heels. Anderson's phone was by her ear in an instant. She hurried back to the sidewalk.

"I need that area roped off. No one can walk through here," she ordered the uniform beside her while waiting for Luke to pick up.

He nodded and set to work. She went back to Danny who was waiting quietly at the edge of the garden, watching the grownups work. Voicemail. Shit. She hung up and then crouched down in front of the kid. His eyes were puffy and red from sleepiness, but he never once yawned. He was managing to stay awake and alert.

"Is your mother home?"

He nodded, maintaining eye contact with her. The severity of the situation wasn't lost on the young kid. His expression could have been chiseled out of stone with how serious and unchanging it was. She was surprised he wasn't in tears, that would have been similar to Caleb's reaction when he first found out about Jamie.

"I need to talk to her. Can you take me to her?"

Again, he nodded without a single word.

"Okay. Give me just a minute and then we'll go inside."

She tried Luke's cell one more time. Danny watched with his red, unblinking eyes. It was unnerving. She almost wished for more of a reaction from him. At least she could handle that, but this, she didn't know what to do with it. He was just so silent. How do you comfort silent? Finally, and thankfully, Luke picked up.

His raspy morning voice croaked, "Anderson. What?"

"Melissa's missing. There's a sign of an attacker. I'm about to talk to the mother. How soon can you be here and do you want me to wait for you?"

The grogginess was gone in an instant and he was completely alert. "Give me fifteen minutes." The line went dead.

"Alvirez. Get in touch with Child Protective Services. We're not leaving Danny here alone tonight. I want you to stay here with him until they get here." Alvirez nodded and immediately got his phone out. She took Danny's outstretched hand and let him lead her into the house. The change in temperature inside the house was welcome, although slight. They didn't have to wander very far inside to find her, she was fast asleep on the couch with an empty bottle of Burnett's London Dry Gin lying on the floor by her outstretched hand. She was about to sit Danny down at the kitchen table when he launched himself onto the couch. He shook his mother with both of his small hands.

"Ma. Ma. Ma."

She grunted and mumbled something under her breath and turned away from him. He didn't let this deter him and kept shaking her and calling to her. Anderson stepped forward and pulled him away from her. She pointed at the kitchen and Danny retreated, having to hop up in order to get himself tall enough to get situated in the wooden chair at the table. She placed a calm hand on the woman's shoulder and softly shook it.

"Ma'am. I need you to wake up." She forced her voice to be firm and sharp.

The distinct difference between a child's voice and Anderson's mature tone was enough to stir the slumbering woman. She took in Anderson's badge, which she had produced from her coat pocket, and frowned.

"What did the little brat do now?"

Anderson shook her head. "She hasn't done anything wrong. Can I make you some coffee?"

The woman didn't really respond with a positive or a negative, but Anderson took that to mean that she would need some caffeine and encouragement to have an actual conversation. She went back to the kitchen, leaving Melissa's mother alone on the couch. Danny's head swiveled as Anderson walked past him to the small L-shaped countertop. She opened a few of the cupboards before she found coffee filters and mugs. The filter in the coffee machine looked like it hadn't been changed in ages. Her nose crinkled to the stench of old coffee grounds as she dumped it in the trash. She wiped it clean before putting in a new filter. She looked around the countertops. Now, where were the coffee grounds? She glanced at Danny and he silently pointed at the cupboard to her left. She nodded in thanks and finished prepping the pot.

"Cream and sugar?" she asked the mother while she waited for the coffee brew.

The mother just gave her a blank stare. She glanced at Danny again. He slid off the chair and pulled a tupperware container that had little creamer cups, like the ones at the diner she frequented, out of the nearly empty fridge, and carefully placed it on the countertop next to the mug with coffee stains rimming the inside. He let his eyes connect with Anderson's for a lingering moment before averting his eyes to the floor. He was used to the role of being silent and invisible, it was clear this was the way his mother preferred things. The aroma of fresh coffee filled the room, overpowering the stench of the rotting food in the trash can. There was a knock at the door that startled her from her thoughts. She went to the door to let Luke in.

"That was fast," she commented as she stepped aside to let him inside the house.

She led him into the kitchen where two more mugs had appeared and all three had been filled with steaming coffee. One of the cups already had cream mixed in, clearly made the way the mother liked it. Danny was perched on his chair again.

"Thanks, Danny. Why don't you go to your room for a little bit?"

He stared at her, his disapproval of the idea was written all over his face. Luke was already sitting beside Ms. Jameson on the couch and was handing her the mug that her son had prepared when Anderson joined him.

"When was the last time you saw your daughter?" Luke took the lead in asking questions.

"I guess when she got home from school."

"And what time do you recall that being?"

Ms. Jameson shrugged her shoulders. "Around five. It woulda been after her cheer practice got out."

"Did she go straight to her room? Did she go back out later?" He tried prompting her, but the mother wasn't very forthcoming. That, or she really didn't know anything useful. "Walk me through your evening."

"She came home and went to her room right away. I was watchin' the telly all evenin' and I don't remember seeing her come out here again."

Anderson grimaced. It was like pulling nails trying to get information out of this extremely irritating woman.

Luke watched impassively as the large woman drained her coffee cup and then felt around for her gin bottle, shifting around on the couch and amongst the discarded wrappers.

"Ma'am, you do understand what's happening here, correct?"

She didn't even look up from what she was doing.

"Their father isn't around anymore?"

That got her attention. "Nah, he left us a long time ago. Danny was still just a babe, he doesn't even have memories of his Pa. He left us and never looked back. Not once did he reach out for the kids. It's just us three." She looked down at the bottle that her fingers had finally found between the cushions. When she looked back up there were tears in her eyes. "Is my girl goin' to be ok?"

Anderson jumped in, "We're going to do everything we can to get her back. In the meantime, Danny needs you. If you can't step up and take care of him we'll bring someone in who can."

The mother nodded dejectedly. "I'm worthless, Melissa is a better caretaker for him than I ever was. I wasn't always like this. After he left, I got laid off. The last few years have been a struggle. Thank goodness for unemployment. I just let Melissa pick out what she and

Danny absolutely need from the grocery store and hope it's enough. I keep an eye on them enough to know they are in school." She paused for a moment and let out a half-hearted belch. "What happens now?"

"Unless you have any helpful information for us, then we'll get back out there and won't stop looking until we find her."

She shook her head. "I'm sorry. I don't know anything. I slept through the whole evening."

Anderson and Luke stood, she didn't know about him, but she was glad to not be sitting on the dirty furniture anymore. "Ms. Jameson, we'll be leaving an officer outside for you if you need anything or if you think of anything else." She crossed the room and put the collection of three mugs on the counter. One was empty and two were still half full.

"Well, that was useless," commented Luke once they were outside.

The rain had picked up and they had to dash across the street to their cars. Anderson still wound up drenched by the time she got into her vehicle. The storm clouds made the already dark night sky appear completely black. It wasn't particularly helpful for driving back to the station in the rain. It was hard to see, even with the headlights on and her windshield wipers going at maximum speed. It was eerie and ominous how the weather seemed to mirror the events of the night. He had both girls now.

Anderson and Luke stood in Sanchez's office. He had not been pleased when he had arrived at the station that morning to be immediately thrown into this briefing. His brow was furrowed as he listened to Anderson's account of the morning. When she finished he shook his head in disgust.

"How could we lose a teenage girl in less than eight hours?" He didn't wait for either of the detectives to respond. "Luke, I want you on the ground for this. Follow any leads that come from the scene at the house." He paused here and nodded at Luke, signaling his release from the meeting.

Luke awkwardly nodded back and then bowed out of the room. Anderson shifted weight several times.

"Now. Technically you're still on leave. And I can't have you out in the field working on this. Stay out of our way Anderson, I don't want this getting messy because you can't stay away. Go home and get some sleep."

"Yes, sir."

She found Luke waiting for her halfway between the office and her desk. "Did he tell you to go home?"

"Yes."

"And are you?"

"What do you think?"

She found herself making a beeline for the parking lot away from the station, away from Luke, and away from the pressure. She needed to be in her safe place. The diner was the only place she could really think in. If she went home she would just be distracted by all the silence and emptiness. She checked her phone as she climbed into her car. 8:27a.m. Her dad was probably awake now and headed to work, a decent time of the morning to send him a message.

Caleb was gone when I got up this morning. I think you should reconsider helping me send him to rehab. He needs help.

She shoved her phone back in her pocket and made a mental note to ignore it unless it was Sanchez or Luke calling. Her dad knew how she felt about the situation and she had nothing more to say on the matter. She wasn't sure if there was anything that she could say to convince her dad to agree with her.

The diner was in its mid-morning rush when she pushed open the front door. Her usual booth was taken for once and she had to make do with a big six-person booth next to one of the front windows. It would be difficult to not be distracted by all the pedestrians. She spread out her paperwork as much as possible. She wanted to be able to see as many of the details as she could simultaneously. The more of the pieces she could see at once the more she would be able to fit them together.

This guy had to be somewhere between thirty-five and forty-five. That's assuming that the four girls she knew about were the only girls that had been taken. Four girls equaled about twenty years and he must have been in his late teens or early twenties when he started. He grew up in this town, he knew it like the back of his hand. He was partial to the area with Marina High School, he had probably attended there. She scanned the pages about the missing girls. All blondes, blue eyes, active-

"Hi, what can I get you?"

Startled, she glanced up to find the same girl as last time. Fantastic. She was chewing a very loud stick of gum this time.

"Hi. Coffee, and a Belgian waffle combo."

"How do you want your eggs?" The girl started to blow a bubble.

"Fried, please." *Pop.* Anderson cringed. She had never liked that habit.

"Sausage or bacon?"

"Sausage."

The girl turned on her heel and stalked off. Anderson blinked and shook her head, trying to clear her brain and focus herself again on the case. She stared at the pages spread out before her. Where was she? She had just been on to something when she had been interrupted. Her phone buzzed, rattling the tabletop. She was destined to be interrupted. It was a text from Luke.

Found cigarette butts. Our guy smokes.

She sent back a quick little note.

Not the mom?

He responded immediately, she had barely even placed the phone back down when it had rung again.

Okay, so the guy smoked, that narrowed it down to roughly forty percent of the town's population. She pulled her pad of paper closer and started jotting down ideas. Local, smokes, somewhere between 35 and 45 years old, probably lives alone, potentially didn't go to college. He was too obsessed with the girls to focus on schooling. She put "finish HS?" at the end. Something traumatic had happened in his life and it was possible he hadn't finished high school. He didn't have many friends, so that ruled out anyone who would have been active in any clubs or on any teams. She dug out the school's phone number from her notes. She glanced around her table, there wasn't anyone nearby to disturb so she hit the call button.

"Marina High School. Ms. Thompson speaking."

"Hello, this is Detective Anderson calling."

"What can I do for you?"

"Can you send me the school's records of all the senior level boys between the years of 1987 and 1997?"

"That's going to be a lot of names. Are you looking for something particular?"

"Someone who wasn't on any teams or part of any clubs or part of student government. There may have been something tragic that happened while he was there. He may not have finished school."

"That will still be a lot of names. I'll see what I can do."

"One more thing, can you also send a list, if there are any names, of girls that either went missing or was in an accident during those same years?" She would have called the station and had them look it up, but she wasn't supposed to be working on the case anymore.

Anderson gave Ms. Thompson her email address before hanging up. She was jittery from all the caffeine she had consumed this morning. This must be about her third or fourth cup so far. She waited for her email app to ding letting her know that she had new incoming emails. She quickly pulled it up and went directly to the girls' names. There were five. Three of which had merely dropped out of school. Then there was Tammi Michelson. She was a

brunette who had gone missing in the middle of her senior

year in 1988. Anderson Googled the girl's name. She had

been a misfit who had run away from home and had been a

few counties over when she was arrested for drug

possession. The last name on the list was Alice Milne. She

had been on the soccer team her entire high school career.

She had blonde hair and blue eyes. Again, Anderson just

typed the name into Google. Several articles popped up.

Turns out Alice had gotten pregnant in her junior year. She

had a baby boy, John, in May of 1992. They both died in a

car crash that summer. The circumstances of the crash were

suspicious. Alice had been in the passenger seat and John in

the back in his car seat, but the driver's seat had been

vacant. According to the news articles, they had never

found the driver. Who got her pregnant? None of the

articles mentioned a father or a boyfriend. At least this

narrowed the year down.

Thankfully, Ms. Thompson had organized the boy's

names by year. Anderson scrolled through until she got to

1992. There were quite a few names. She started looking up

each one and making her own list of the names, with the

dates they either dropped out or had to take a leave of

absence. She wasn't really sure what she was looking for but figured she would know it when she saw it. At the top of the page, she had the information about Alice hastily jotted down.

Her phone vibrated again. It was her dad this time, informing her that he would be talking to Tracy that night about Caleb's situation. She could feel her shoulders droop, weighed down. That wouldn't do anything. Talking to her about spending money on someone else—she would never go for it, it was pointless. She placed her phone back on the table, screen down.

She looked at the names again. He would've had trouble or dropped out roughly around the same time Alice either announced her pregnancy or Alice's accident. Realizing this, she focused on the dates and began putting lines through the ones that didn't coincide with Alice. Her left hand smeared the wet ink and made all the words look fuzzy like they were out of focus.

Two plates clattered to the table in front of her, powdered sugar spraying sideways and dusting the pages that were still visible. Anderson glanced up at the teen who was cracking her gum. "Need anything else?" She wanted a refill on her coffee, but she needed the sound to go away even more. Maybe the gum snapping was bothering her because she was over-caffeinated. She waited for the girl's shadow to disappear before looking back to the page with all the names while she took a bite of the slightly burnt sausage. It tasted ashy and it crunched louder than it should have.

Her phone buzzed, not a text, but a phone call type of buzzing. She flipped it over, Luke calling.

"Hey. Find anything?" she asked.

"Yeah. Ms. Jameson agreed to let us have access to Melissa's phone records. They just came through in an email."

"Anything pertinent?"

"Yes. She was out with a boy last night. A date of sorts. His name is Cameron, he goes to her school. They met at one-thirty in the morning."

Her lips twisted as she bit her lower lip, thinking. "So, we still don't know what time she actually went missing. We need to talk to that boy."

"I can handle that, Emz. I'm on my way to the school already. You got anything to add?"

"Don't call me that," she said dismissively as her eyes skimmed the page of names. "Actually. I'll meet you there."

She ignored Luke's protests that she was supposed to stay out of this and scarfed down the waffle combo. She hung up on Luke and left a twenty on the table before gathering all her materials and heading to her car.

Unknown Year, Day 271

She was curled in a ball on her side next to the door. She had fallen asleep after scratching a line into the floor. There was a small part of her brain that screamed at her, telling her that she had lost count a long time ago. But she couldn't break the habit. Her fingers weren't swollen anymore, but merely callused and rough. She peeled her flattened face off the cement and wiped the slim trail of drool with the back of her hand.

She was numb and had lost interest in doing anything besides being immobile. There wasn't any point in trying. She could barely move her arms or legs. It took all of her energy to crawl from one side of her concrete prison to the other. She wanted nothing more than for all of this to be over, at any cost. Even thinking of her brother, Jimmy, couldn't make her smile anymore. Those memories were the last thing she had held onto, but now it was time to let go. She tried to breathe deeply. She sucked in thick, dusty air into her nose and lungs, and violently began coughing. Images from His last visit flitted through her mind. She coughed a few more times and then scrunched her eyes and nose, trying to clear her head. She didn't want to see this, she tried to dream up the scent of a freshly cut soccer field or the picture of the sun's rays bouncing off a deep blue reflective ocean. None of it came to her. She couldn't conjure these things at will anymore. Sometimes they just came while she sat in the corners or while she slept, but never when she needed them. Instead, she was stuck with Him and His tiring questions.

Her limbs twitched as she tried to stretch them out. They barely moved and ached from the lack of action. She feared she would rot here. Maybe that would be her escape from this place. A few tears from her mostly dried ducts streaked down her cheeks, but she was too exhausted to properly cry. The blood pounding through her head was entirely distracting, luckily. The silence echoed, bouncing off the walls and encompassing her. The reverberations folded around the edges of her body.

Again, His face flashed through her mind, and how close it had been to hers only yesterday. Moments she wished weren't memories. She dragged her fingers over the etches in the floor and dreamed to cease existing.

2017, Day 13

Anderson had barely shut the car door when Luke began berating her about how she was supposed to be at home. Her brown eyes flicked to his unshaven face, he stopped mid-sentence and shut his gaping jaw. She led the way to the Principal's office, greeting Ms. Thompson with a curt nod.

"Detectives. What more can I do for you? I hope the information I sent over earlier this morning was helpful."

Luke raised an eyebrow at his partner, but didn't say a word.

"Yes, actually, do you mind getting me a more detailed account of—" Anderson paused and dug out her paper, one finger guiding her gaze until she found it. "Richard Dachs. He attended here from 1989 to 1992."

The receptionist nodded, "I can certainly get you a past record of him. But I can also get you his employee. He's one of our handymen."

Anderson froze. "He is?"

"Actually, he called out today."

"Do you have a current address for him?"

"Of course, I can include it in the print outs for you."

"Also," interrupted Luke. He waited for Ms. Thompson to pause and look up from her computer screen. "We need to speak to a Cameron Eckleson. I believe he's a senior here."

The woman nodded again, her huge gold pendent-esque earrings swinging back and forth, emphasizing her movement.

"Looks like Cameron is in study hall right now, let me check with Mr. Murphy to make sure I can call him here."

Anderson couldn't stop herself, she was staring at the bright pink lipstick smudge on Ms. Thompson's teeth. Last time she had been here, the receptionist's cardigan had been mis-buttoned. She was just one of those people who was always a little jumbled.

"Great, thanks." Luke drummed his fingers on the countertop while they watched her disappear into the office. As soon as she was out of earshot Luke hissed to Anderson. "You've already called here today? What have you not told me?"

"I'll fill you in after we talk to Cameron. One thing at a time."

Before he could respond, the receptionist and the principal approached.

"Principal Murphy will take you to Mr. Eckleson. When you return I will have a print out ready for you."

"Thank you."

Ms. Thompson folded herself back into her swivel chair behind her desk and the clacking of her keyboard resumed. Principal Murphy ushered them into the familiar hallways. This time it wasn't quiet. Every time they passed a classroom door they could hear teachers calling out instructions and lecturing and students chattering discreetly and answering questions. The overhead speaker crackled and then Ms. Thompson's voice called Cameron to the office. Principal Murphy cleared his throat. "How's the investigation proceeding?"

"We're hopeful." It was all Luke would say.

"Good." Principal Murphy's voice was gruff. He stopped in front of room 148. He peered in through the small window in the door. A roomful of pubescent eyes turned and watched as Cameron, a blonde-haired boy near the back, looking uncertain about the whole thing, gathered his school books from his desk and untangled himself from the chair. He was tall and would've been gangly if not for the arm muscles jutting out of the plain black t-shirt. A sidelong glance was exchanged with a buddy to his left and then he weaved between the desks and outstretched legs, walking directly towards them. Principal Murphy held the door open for the kid and they all stepped back out into the hall. Cameron readjusted the strap off of his backpack, keeping his gaze low.

"Am I in trouble for something?" He said it quietly, it was almost a murmur.

Luke used his reassuring tone of voice that he used during witness interviews. "No, you're not in trouble. We're not interviewing you. We just have a few questions. Do you want your parents here?"

Cameron finally drew his eyes from the floor to look at the three adults. He shook his head. "No, I'm fine without them."

Principal Murphy led them down the hall and back into his office for privacy.

"Alright then. First, we have some news. A girl by the name of Melissa Jameson went missing earlier this morning."

"What?" A twinge of pain went through Anderson's stomach as she watched the raw shock cross the boy's face. It was all so familiar. She had only been a year older than him when her own sister had gone missing. The three adults gave him a moment to recover before continuing.

"We can see from your phone records that you saw her last night. Can you tell us about that?"

"Y-yes," he stammered, his eyes were still wide, processing the information as fast as he could, but he still was struggling to keep up with their pace.

"Take your time, please. We know this is difficult for you." She didn't know how to comfort him Luke made no moves to say or do anything, either. Cameron nodded, and let his head bob for a while.

Finally, he sucked in a large gulp of air. "For the record, I texted her at dinnertime, maybe around seven. She's the one who responded at one in the morning. We met a half an hour later. Out front of her house. She didn't want me knocking on the door. I got the feeling she was sneaking out to see me."

Anderson glanced at Luke. So much for the lookout. He hadn't seen either of the kids that morning, coming or going. "And what did the two of you do?"

"We went to the park a couple of blocks away. I think it's Highland Park. We wandered around mostly, I pushed her on the swings for a short bit." He shrugged his shoulders. "Nothing crazy."

"And what time did she head home?" asked Luke.

"At three I walked her home. I remember because she checked her phone and freaked out when she saw the time. I left her standing in front of the house. I thought she'd be okay from there. I should have stayed and watched her go inside or walked her up to the door." Remorse flooded his eyes.

"It's not your fault." Anderson attempted to be soothing.

"Can you tell me, do you remember anything else in those moments before you went home?" Luke took up the questioning again.

He shook his head, "No. Nothing. I'm so sorry."

Anderson and Luke glanced at each other. Cameron fidgeted with the belt loops on his jeans. They waited a few more beats, but it became evident that he had nothing else to add.

"Thank you, Mr. Eckleson. You can go back to class," Principal Murphy dismissed him.

"Let me know if there's anything that I can do to help bring her home." The boy turned and trudged back towards his classroom. They waited for the door to shut behind him before turning back towards the direction they had come from. The principal kept glancing at them, trying to glean anything he could from the expressions on the detectives' faces. When they arrived back at the office though, he remained as out of the loop as he had been at the start of their visit.

Ms. Thompson's eyes wavered between the detectives and her computer screen as they entered her domain. Anderson thought there was irritation there for a moment, but then it was gone in a flash. Her lips parted as she began to speak. Anderson was distracted by the lipstick smudge that was still on the woman's teeth. Luckily, she didn't need to be listening to what the woman was saying to understand that she was supposed to take the pages that were being held out to her.

"Thank you very much." Luke thanked both the receptionist and the principal.

Before they had even left the room, the doors to his office had clicked shut and the clacking of Ms. Thompson's keyboard had resumed as if they had never been there and interrupted their day. After the glow of fluorescent lighting, the natural sunlight felt harsh on her eyes, even Luke was shading his face with a hand held up to his brow line. They paused beside his car, not sure what their next move was.

"Do you want coffee? I could go for some tea." Luke said finally.

"Sure. I'll meet you at the Ugly Mug?"

He nodded and then they were both off, climbing into their separate cars. Her car sputtered a couple of times before actually starting and she caught Luke watching, waiting to make sure her car wasn't dead. She thought she could see irritation flickering across his face and then he was pulling out of the lot and heading eastward down the street.

Unknown Year, Day 354

She was drenched in sweat, and her chest was heaving as she filled her lungs with air as fast as she could. It wasn't that she was working out a lot or even at all, it was that the little work she could manage expended all of her energy. She still hadn't figured out what had changed. It had been like a switch had flipped. After she had attacked Him, which felt like ages ago, she had suddenly lost her energy and motivation to move or do anything. She spent most of the day laying on her back and staring at the ceiling. There were no thoughts that circled through her mind anymore. Nothing exciting ever happened. She had lost all hope of getting out of here and returning home. She knew she would never see Jimmy again. Or the view of the skyline from the roof of her house. She no longer dreamed of freedom, or wind on her face. She wished for it all to just end. She remained completely still on the floor, thinking of nothing. She was scared of what her brain would come up with if she let it wander. She was in tune with her motionless muscles—they didn't even twitch. She wished to be as static as the air around her. Maybe if she laid as still as possible, she would become one with her surroundings and simply disappear, her skin and bones melting into the cement beneath her, her dust particles floating through the air vents and finally settling outside in the real world. At least, if this was the case, her final resting place would be in the open. She didn't know where in the city this bunker was, but maybe the wind would catch her and carry her to the ocean. She would like that; to go swimming one last time.

He visited a lot now, more frequently than He used to. He used to only come once a week, if that, but now He was showing up three times a week. He was always angry with her. She wasn't ready to give in yet. She couldn't claim to be someone that she wasn't, but He was slowly beating down her resolve. Now she just remained silent when He came to see her. She couldn't tell if this made Him angrier, or if His anger had just plateaued at this point. At least it took less energy to just not respond to His questions. She didn't have the energy to make responses anyway. She just stared at Him blankly whenever He was in the room.

She heaved a heavy sigh and felt her esophagus and vocal cords rattle. The air pressed through her lips as her lungs collapsed and she felt empty for a brief moment. Her vacant expression mirrored her insides. When she felt like her lungs were on fire she finally inhaled, sucking in as much air as she could manage. She noticed each muscle as every now and then one of them would twitch as her brain checked each of them to make sure they were functioning. Eventually, her eyes closed and she fell into a fitful slumber.

2017, Day 13

By the time Luke walked inside the dimly lit building, Anderson had already gotten them both drinks and had pitched camp in a quiet corner near the back of the room. It took a moment for him to spot her, she could see him blinking, trying to adjust his eyes from the brightness outside. He sat across from her, the small round table between them with the small stack of paper that Ms.

Thompson had handed them earlier placed carefully in the middle with a yellow highlighter uncapped in her hand.

"So, explain what this is all about." He indicated to the papers with a small flick of his wrist.

She briefly explained her line of reasoning from that morning that had led her to the name Richard Dachs.

"This is all based on the assumption that you've guessed his age correctly, and that is based on the assumption that we know about all of the missing girls. What if there's another one out there that we don't know about? Or what if there's two?"

She nodded, realizing how crazy it sounded, so she launched into telling him about Alice. This time he nodded along with her. He agreed that it did sound plausible that Alice was the first and it had to be someone close in age to her, thus a classmate and making Richard Dachs a viable suspect. Now they just needed to prove it and uncover his moves since the night of the car accident. Where had he disappeared to?

"Alright, this is your find, you take the lead here. What are we looking for?"

She took a deep breath and tried to center herself before diving in. "Well, I thought it would be good to see if he has any records from the school of odd social behavior, or what they thought his home was like. He dropped out of school shortly after the car accident, so obviously, that was a catalyst of sorts. He snapped at some point. But we need to prove that he was unstable to begin with. And to top things off, Ms. Thompson said he works at the school as a handyman. All of the girls so far have gone to Marina High. He must be picking them out there, and then stalking them would be fairly easy since he would have so much access to their lives already."

He nodded. He picked up the papers and flipped through, dividing them into two stacks and placing one in front of her. He fished his own pen out of the inside pocket of his jacket. "So we possibly found his hunting ground, if this is our guy. You take the school-related papers and I'll sort through the home life."

She nodded, but before she could even begin her phone rattled in her pocket. She dug her hand in her pants pocket and pulled out her small phone. The screen had the name "Caleb" flashing across it. "I have to take this. Excuse me."

He nodded and then took the highlighter as she pushed back from the table and went outside. She refused to be one of those people who answered their phone in a restaurant.

"Caleb! I was worried. You were gone when I got up this morning."

She was greeted with silence from the other side, and a few murmurs that were indistinct. Did he butt dial her by accident?

"Caleb?"

She could hear muffled voices, but couldn't make out the words. He was talking to someone and was completely unaware that he had accidentally called her. She was about to hang up on him when she heard a woman's voice that she thought she recognized. She tried turning the volume up on her phone, but it was already turned up all the way.

"—more money." It was muffled, but of course, that's what Caleb was saying. What else would he be talking to another human being about? He always let his addiction get the best of him. She strained her ears to hear more.

"I can't keep doing this. He'll start to notice it's missing."

Who was that?

"I know. I just…" His whiney voice trailed off. There was nothing to excuse his behavior and even in his drugged up state he knew this.

"No. I can't anymore." The voice was louder and sharper now. She knew who the woman was. Anderson clicked the end call button and immediately dialed her dad. He didn't pick up, so she left him a message that they needed to talk as soon as possible. Some new information had come to light and she needed to speak to him, urgently.

She returned to the table to find that Luke had gone through both stacks in the time she had been outside.

"Everything okay, Emz?"

"Yeah. Just family drama. Don't call me that."

He smirked a little at the last bit and then turned his attention to the papers. "He was a troubled kid from the start. It was mild at first, small things, and then the accident with Alice happened. I already called the station and had Officer Williams run the name through the system. I'm waiting to hear back right now. His grades were poor, his teachers wrote that he had zero desire to learn."

"What about home life?"

"Raised by a single mother, who died about a year after he dropped out of school."

"What from?"

"Cancer. It looks like there's a note here from the mother to the principal requesting that none of the teachers talk about it in front of him or make any reference to it."

"I wonder why that is." That certainly was an odd request. Maybe she hadn't told him that she was sick yet. If she had died before she had the chance to tell him then her death would have come as a surprise, further pushing him into his instability. "Do you know if he still lives in the same house?"

She took a sip of her coffee that was now barely warm at all and waited for Luke to flip through the pages, scanning for highlighted sections.

"It's the one that's still on file with the school."

She tapped her pointer finger on the side of her coffee cup, feigning to be deep in thought, a slight smile pulling at her mouth. "I have a hunch we'll find something there."

"Of course you do. Let's go." He calmly got lids for both of their cups while she gathered all the paper together, organizing them into their original order.

Anderson couldn't help but notice all the things that were happening around her while she waited. There was a group of teenage girls posing for a picture with their coffee cups while a boyfriend, who had mistakenly tagged along for the day, took a photo with one of their phones. There was a couple that sat near the front door, but not in the window seat, who looked to be in the midst of a breakup. Another couple near the front window sat side by side, coffees ignored on the table in front of them, and awkwardly making out. Lastly, there was a guy, who looked to be in his twenties, that wore a plaid flannel shirt and had let his beard grow out to an unruly length. He stood at the counter waiting for his drink. He was trying to have a deep discussion with a clearly agitated barista about the type of coffee beans that were used in the brew.

Luke pushed the door outward and held it open for her as he pulled his car keys from his pocket. A small cloud had appeared out of nowhere and was covering part of the sun. She tilted her face upward to look at it. It was a dark cloud and there were more on the horizon. Another storm was coming.

2017, Day 13

Melissa was sitting on the floor while Kate was on the mattress. Kate still strived to be above her somehow; it was the natural order of things. Melissa didn't mind, she didn't want to sit on the mattress, the stains that covered almost every inch of it freaked her out, but she didn't say this out loud. She would let Kate have this small victory.

Once all of the food had been consumed, which was fairly quickly, Melissa had placed the plastic cafeteria tray near the door and pushed it up against a wall so that it would be out of the way. Kate had already demanded an update on the cheer squad and her group of followers. Melissa had indulged this request. After all, Kate had been in this hell hole for two weeks, all alone, and needed something to hold on to in order to get out of here with some resemblance of sanity.

"Do you think he has some weird twin obsession?" Kate had asked at some point. "I mean, we do look like we could be twins."

Melissa had just nodded and agreed with her even though she didn't believe this theory. Melissa still believed that the detectives were right. Whoever had taken them only wanted one of them, the other…well. She hoped her imagination was wrong about whoever was unwanted or unneeded.

Whatever the room next door to them was had a light flipped on, they could tell because the square sliding door at the bottom of the main door was outlined in light. Someone was in the other room right this second. Melissa made eye contact with Kate, who merely shrugged and stated, "That's never happened before. I have no idea what to expect." They heard a loud clunking sound as if something heavy had been slid into place. The door swung open, into the room and both girls were blinded for a moment by the intense light of the outer room. Then the door slammed shut once more and they were cast into darkness again. It took Melissa a few blinks before she was able to make out the outline of a third figure. He was tall. He may have been skinny and gangly as a teenager but then put on some weight in his older years and filled out his frame. He looked familiar to her, but she couldn't quite place it.

"So tell me." His voice was gruff and scratchy. "Which one of you is Alice?" Despite the gruffness, the girl's name escaped his mouth in a hiss.

Melissa and Kate glanced at each other. Melissa was just confused, but Kate, the rage had built up for a couple of weeks and couldn't be contained anymore. "Who the fuck is Alice?" she demanded to know. He cocked his head and just looked at her. His eyes were unblinking and consistent, they didn't waver for a moment and he never glanced at Melissa. In one movement he closed the gap between himself and Kate and took a charged swing at her. His fist connected with her face with a cracking sound. Kate emitted a sound that could only be identified as a shriek. Melissa didn't recognize it as the shrieks that erupted during cheer practice when a football was tossed into the group of girls. It couldn't even compare to the sound that now filled the small room.

"What the hell?!" she screamed at him as she pushed herself off the mattress to stand. He towered over her and Melissa noticed when Kate shrunk away from him a little. He would surely notice it, too.

"If you're not Alice, then she is," he said and pummeled her again with a tightly clenched fist.

She almost lost her balance and started to tumble to the ground, but she caught herself and remained upright. Melissa flung herself at the man, trying to scratch at his face. She remembered vaguely hearing somewhere that you were supposed to aim for the eyes. She missed those and only managed to get a couple of scratches on his left cheek before he gripped her wrists and then tossed her to the side as if she weighed nothing. She hit the floor and felt all the bones in her right side collide with the cement, knocking the air from her chest. He returned his attention to Kate.

"Please stop," whimpered Melissa.

"I will not let this imposter continue to walk about the streets."

He lunged at her and she staggered backward, tripping on the mattress and falling onto her back. He fell on top of her. Melissa felt useless as she watched him get a hand on the other girl's throat and hold her down as he pummeled her face with his free fist. Blood bubbled from Kate's mouth as she screamed for him to stop. Melissa crawled over to his side and reached one hand up to grab the arm that he was punching with. He was much stronger than her and it did nothing to hold him back.

"Stop it!" She screamed it louder this time, hoping that the commanding tone she heard in her head would seep through into the words that escaped her lips.

He didn't even look away from Kate. There was blood on his hands now, but Kate's legs were still kicking, she was still struggling. Melissa tried harder this time to grab his arm, she threw her whole body weight at it. He turned his attention to her now. He used both hands this time to toss her backward. She smacked the back of her head on the cement as she tumbled away from the two. Dark splotches flashed before her eyes. By the time she had recovered, sweeping her hair away from her face with one hand and sat up again, Kate was silent and motionless on the mattress and he was standing, staring down at Kate's body.

"That's better, isn't it, Alice?" he said.

She just stared at him, quivering from fear. She had never felt so terrified and powerless in her life. He didn't vocalize the message here, but she understood it loud and clear. Do not cross him. So she nodded in response. "Yes. Much better."

He smiled at her, it probably wasn't meant in the creepy way that it came off in. She was sure it was supposed to be reassuring. He left her then, alone in the room with Kate's lifeless body on the mattress. She slowly forced herself to go to the body. Her eyes were still open.

Melissa did what she had seen in movies and television shows, she reached over with one hand and gently closed Kate's eyes with two fingers. Her skin was still warm. Of course it was, she had just died. Melissa hadn't liked Kate, but that didn't stop her from shedding tears over the girl and giving her one last hug. When she finally pulled away from Kate, she didn't bother with wiping away the mascara stains she left on the girl's neck. She left them there as a symbol that she would be missed by someone somewhere, even if it wasn't true. It was better than the reality that everyone back home had already moved on.

2017, Day 13

Luke let Anderson drive this time. She drove faster anyway with her lead foot, it seemed like she just dropped a brick on the gas pedal. The house was in the same neighborhood as Melissa's home, as well as Sarah's and Alice's. Anderson's childhood home wasn't too far from here, but it wasn't really considered part of this neighborhood. This bode well for them being on the right track. This was definitely his hunting ground. They parked a couple of houses down and across the street to avoid looking conspicuous even though the house looked abandoned, strange if this was his current address. If it was at all possible, the yard looked even less tended to than the yard at Melissa's home. It was certainly the eyesore of the street. Every street has a fixer upper, this was that house.

"Shall we take a walk?" asked Anderson.

Luke checked his phone, no missed calls. He made a noncommittal grunt, but opened his door and started to climb out. Anderson followed suit. In this part of town, the storm clouds completely blocked out the mid-afternoon sun, providing them with zero light to work with. They tried to casually stroll down the street to get the lay of the land, but they looked out of place in their pantsuits. The house's backyard opened up in the field. It was the same field Jamie was by when she had been taken. The same field that Jamie's phone had been found in. This was no mere coincidence.

"This is the place," Anderson murmured, her eyes wandering the length of the house and alighting on the fact that there was no fence separating the field from the back yard.

Luke glanced at her. "How can you be so sure?"

She shook her head, her lips pressed together in a grimace. "I just know."

Luke glanced around to make sure none of the neighbors were watching and then walked up to a window. His nose pressed into the glass, one hand shielding any of the light that might have been reflecting through the clouds from his eyes. Anderson picked her way up the front pathway, which was more like a hiking trail now, and to the front door. Twigs snapped underneath her feet and bushes pulled at her pants as she ascended the steps to the porch and she was reminded of the last time she had gone hiking in the mountains. It had been with Jamie at the beginning of their last school year together. They had driven the hour drive up to the summit pass and parked at one of those turn-offs marked "summit pass viewing station." They found a small trail that led away from the parking lot. Anderson didn't think it was actually a trail since there were no signs marking it as one, but it was there so the sisters had taken it. They had walked for what seemed like hours. Eventually, they came out near the top of one of the ridges and the view had been breathtaking. They could see the coastline, the metropolitan skyline, and where the city met the base of the mountain. Anderson wished she had savored the moment more, but she had never been particularly good at living in the present.

She reached the door and glanced up at the porch light above her. It was missing a light bulb. The window to the left of the front door was open just a sliver, it was such a small space that she almost missed it. She froze in place. Luke looked her way and she held a finger up to her lips. He nodded and quietly pulled himself away from his window and joined her at the door. She pointed at the open window. He nodded in her direction, indicating that he would follow her lead. She moved forward with one hand outstretched, grasping the doorknob gently and twisting as slowly as she could. It wasn't locked and swung open silently. Someone kept these door hinges well-oiled so they wouldn't creak. Luke raised his eyebrows at her, prompting her to keep moving. He covered her back as she inched into the house, taking in the layers of dust covering all the surfaces. It looked as if it hadn't been lived in for several years. It eased her mind a little, but they needed to make sure. They both had their guns drawn and ready. They quietly moved through every room, clearing them before finally holstering their weapons.

"False alarm. With the window open, I assumed someone was here or had been here recently."

Luke nodded in agreement. "A realtor wouldn't have left it open. Maybe a squatter left it open in case the door got locked. But it doesn't look like anyone has been living here. At least not for a long time."

"Let's just canvas the place anyway. You take the living room and kitchen. I'll take the bedrooms. Meet you in the hall."

Again, Luke gave her a quick nod and then headed back to the front of the house. Anderson started in the master bedroom and figured she'd work her way through the back part of the house. This was Dachs's mother's room when he was a kid. In the far corner, by the window that perfectly framed the backyard, there was still a bed frame with an old mattress on it. It was complete with sheets and pillows, but it looked dusty and unused. Beside it was a short bedside table with a small lamp on it. This was also light bulb-less and dusty. Directly to her right and just inside the doorway was an old, small armoire pushed up against the wall. On one side it had a door that swung open and had shelves. Beside this was the chest of drawers, four of them, and a tarnished mirror sat on top. There was a small wooden jewelry box placed in front of the mirror. Beside this was a framed photo of a young boy. Anderson presumed this was Dachs as a kid. The wall across from the bed was the closet with sliding doors, but no full length mirrors. That was it as far as furniture went. Anderson checked out the floor before she entered, there were no footprints or tracks in the dust. If this house was used, then this room had been left alone. She flicked the light switch beside the doorway. Nothing happened. No lights came to life. She wasn't sure what she was expecting, but she was slightly disappointed by the lack of action. Clearly, there was no electricity in the house.

Anderson cleared the doorway of spiderwebs before finally letting herself move inside, stirring the stagnant dust in the sleepy room. She opened drawers and slid open the closet doors, checking anything she could think of. Under the mattress, in the stacks of clothes on the shelves, in the nightstand's drawer. Nothing of importance seemed to present itself to her. Eventually, she chalked up the master bedroom as a miss and decided to move to the next room. The next room was much smaller than the first. It was painted a navy blue color and the bedsheets on the twin sized bed were black, really solidifying the darkness of the room. To save space, the dresser was housed inside the closet. She flicked the light switch up. Nothing happened. She did the same as before and checked the dustiness of the floor before entering. It looked undisturbed, the same as the rest of the house. Something was off and she couldn't place her finger on it. She shook her head, trying to erase her unease.

The room itself was bland, the opposite of the mothers. There were no framed pictures. No band or movie posters. No sports memorabilia. The small bookshelf in the corner by the closet only contained school textbooks. A desktop computer sat atop the desk, coated in dust and grime. The keyboard looked to be in similar shape. She took a moment to realize the lack of electricity meant she couldn't take a look at the contents of the computer. She glanced around the room blankly, there had to be something else here. Where would a high school-aged boy hide things he didn't want his mother to find? She paced in the small room. She had already dug through the dresser and desk drawers and checked under the mattress as she had in the mother's room. No valuables could be found, no notebooks

with his secrets filling the pages, no hidden photos of love
interests. Old school work filled the drawers with basic
office supplies and his dresser had only clothing. Anderson
was struck by how utterly personality-less Dachs seemed to
have been in high school.

"Are you having any luck?" she called out into the
hallway.

"Not so much. You?" Luke's voice sounded distant
and barely trailed its way into Richard's room.

"Not yet." She stood in the doorway, just on the
brink of giving up. She glanced back into the room over her
shoulder for one last look, just for good measure. She was
still disappointed that the computer was of no use to them
right now. Then she was moving on and into the shared
bathroom. Her sense of unease vanished as she left the
bedroom. She crossed the small hallway and passed into the
bathroom, walking through a small cobweb. She rubbed her
face trying to get the small strings off.

The tile in the bathroom screamed '80s remodel at
her. There was a pedestal sink, a medicine cabinet above
that, a toilet, and a shower/tub combination. There was a
framed cross-stitch on one wall that had been embroidered
with, "The greatest act of faith some days is to simply get

up and face another day." The bathtub had a dark brown ring staining the inside that made Anderson's nose wrinkle. She let her eyes glaze over the mold-coated toilet and opened the medicine cabinet. It was pretty standard, hidden behind a mirror were three shelves. There were two toothbrushes in travel cases, old toothpaste tubes, and travel-sized floss. An expired Aspirin bottle sat on the middle shelf next to a medicine bottle. Both items Anderson took a picture of, assuming she would look at the labels later. She'd look up the prescription and doctor's name later. On the top shelf sat a contacts case and saline solution for cleaning contacts. Anderson closed the dust-covered mirror and stared at her makeup-less face for a moment before taking the edge of her jacket sleeve and rubbing off her fingerprints from the mirror. The bags under her eyes from the lack of sleep pulled at her skin and weighed her eyes down.

Luke appeared in the doorway, hands pressed into either side of the door frame. His dark clothes were a stark contrast to the off-white walls. He looked like a shadow in her peripheral vision.

"I didn't see anything out of place in the living room or the kitchen. Nothing that made it seem like someone has been living here. The kitchen cabinets and fridge are empty."

She nodded in agreement to his statement and followed him into the hallway. Something pulled at the back of her mind and she took another look into Dachs's bedroom as she passed by it. Maybe it was the distance from the room that made her notice it. Or maybe it's because she wasn't standing over it. Either way, as she glanced in again, she noticed one floorboard didn't quite sit evenly with the rest of the floor.

"Hold on a sec." She reached out and grabbed Luke's elbow, gently pulling him back.

She led the way back into the bedroom and to the window next to the small bed. She kneeled down and pushed down on the floorboard. It gave a little and bounced back up when she let up on the pressure. She glanced up at Luke.

"Here, let me pry it up." He kneeled down beside her and felt where the edges stuck up naturally. He eased it up slowly and pulled it up just high enough that Anderson could sneak a hand inside and feel around. She pulled her hand back out holding a small stack of papers. Luke dropped the board back into place. They crouched on the floor together, neither one of them wanting to fully sit on the filthy floor, in order to flip through the papers together.

"Why don't we just take these with us?" asked Luke.

"Because someone has been here." Anderson surprised herself with the comment. All of the evidence so far indicated that the house had been left undisturbed for a long time now.

"How do you figure?"

"Were there cobwebs in the kitchen and the living room? Possibly in the doorways?"

"Yes."

"As there were to the mother's bedroom and the bathroom. However, Richard's bedroom doorway had no cobwebs, nor do I see any inside the room."

"So you're saying he doesn't live here, but he comes to the house purely to see his room."

"Yes." She let her answer hang in the air for a moment before continuing. "We should take pictures of these and put them back. If he's been visiting this room, this is the only thing I've found in here worth coming back for."

They crouched in silence. Although she would never admit it to him, her legs were on fire from the prolonged position. She tore her eyes away from the wrinkled papers in her hands to look at Luke. Her eyes made contact with his brown ones. Did she see something like approval in his eyes?

"That's quite a reach you know. Assuming he's been here based on the missing cobwebs. I'm not sure I would've caught that." Luke pulled his phone out of his jacket pocket and pulled up the camera app.

Anderson held each page out individually and Luke took a picture of each one. Then he pried up the board again and she deposited the papers back where she had found them. She stood up, stretching her tight hamstrings and shaking the blood flow back into her legs. Then she led the way back out to the car.

"There weren't any cobwebs in the front doorway either," she commented as they closed the door behind them.

Unknown Year, Day 571

She was losing herself to this place. It was just a little bit every day, but over time it was adding up. She couldn't dream up Jimmy's face anymore. She couldn't remember what a home-cooked meal smelled like. She couldn't picture what the front yard of her old home looked like. She couldn't remember what it felt like to run on the field and feel the wind pulling her hair behind her. She guessed she wouldn't be able to pass any of her exams in school if she tried. Her new activity to keep herself occupied was to recall her favorite books and running through the scenes in her mind. She gave faces to the characters, imagined the settings, and sometimes dreamed alternate endings to their stories. Always, every time, she wished she was one of these characters that had a happy ending, but now she knew the reality that not everyone gets one.

She had finally begun responding to the name Alice even though she had promised herself long ago that she never would. She just couldn't take the abuse that came from refusing, not anymore. She was kneeling on the mattress, her palms pressed flat on either side of her knees. She just wanted it all the end. She didn't care about getting out and going home. They probably had stopped looking for her a long time ago anyway. Her mother probably hadn't even cared to look in the first place. She was assuming that the only person who truly missed her was Jimmy.

The veins in her neck throbbed. Instinctively, one hand left the mattress and pressed into her bruise. She winced a little, but let her fingers explore the swollen tissue that surrounded her throat. This was misery. It needed to end. She let her mind wander to her sharpened bobby pin that still remained underneath the mattress, untouched for months now. She had never made another attempt to escape. After the first botched try, she had given up entirely. The punishment that had come afterward had been excruciating and she didn't want to repeat it. However, she could use the bobby pin to end things for herself. He still came sporadically to visit her. Sometimes He just wanted to chat and sometimes He wanted physical companionship. Sometimes He came to ask her about John. At this point, she had figured out that John was the child of Him and Alice, but she still didn't know what had happened to either of them. She shook her head, trying to clear her mind of these thoughts. This was crazy. Still, she found herself rolling off the bed to the floor. She landed with a small, light thump. Was she really doing this? She lifted the mattress off the floor and reached one hand underneath to retrieve the bobby pin. When her fingers touched the cold metal, goosebumps covered her body. She licked her cracked and dry lips, they ached all the time now. She was sure they were permanently raw. She crawled back up onto the mattress and sat silently. The bobby pin was sitting in front of her now and she couldn't tear her gaze from it. It was demanding all of her attention. Now that it was out of its hiding spot she needed to get up the courage to use it. Her logic was telling her it was the only way out, but her instincts were telling her to put it away again. She still wanted a life after all, just preferably not this one. She would never get out of here and she knew that now. She ducked her head and stared at her knees, blowing out a deep, slow breath. She needed to do this, to getaway. This was still a form of escape, right? He couldn't win if she refused to play His game entirely and the only way to leave the game was to end it once and for all.

Slowly, with determination, one hand grasped the sharp metal tool and held it, hovering above the other wrist. She was frozen like this for a while, her hands shaking, while she tried to steady her breathing. Her heart pounded crazily in her chest and panic was seeping into her brain. She needed to gain control. She focused on her breathing. In, out, in, out, in—before she could stop herself, she brought the sharp edge down to her wrist and slashed as hard as she could at her skin—out. A sob erupted from her small, malnourished frame. Her wrist felt like it was on fire as blood gushed out. She quickly grasped the bobby pin with her injured hand and did the same thing to the other side before she lost her nerve completely. She couldn't stop halfway through the job or she'd never finish it. The cut wasn't as deep the second time, but it bled all the same. Now all she had to do was sit and wait and hope He didn't come to visit anytime soon. Hopefully, she could bleed out before He arrived. She lay on her side and let her cuts bleed into the mattress, creating new stains to add to the already stained fabric. Tears slid down her face and she tried to think of Jimmy once more. Her poor little brother. She'd never see him again and she couldn't even recall the shape of his nose.

Melissa sat next to Kate's still body. She hadn't been able to bring herself to move away from the other girl yet. Kate's blood saturated the bed, mixing with the old stains, creating deeper, darker reddish-brown colors. What was she supposed to do now? How was she supposed to move forward? Her own tears had stopped falling already, but the streaks on her face left dry ticklish trails in her skin. She needed to get off this bed at some point and explore the room. Kate wasn't the most observant person around, maybe she had missed something. It was doubtful, but she at least needed to try. Melissa gave Kate's cold hand one more squeeze before pushing herself into a standing position.

She walked a quick perimeter of the room, just to see how big it actually was. She let her fingers trail along the cold cement walls. When she reached the door that he had come and gone by her fingers fell in and out of ridges carved into the door. She knelt down to look at them better, exploring them intently with her fingers. Fingernail scratches. Someone had clawed at the door. She reeled back in disgust. Kate's fingers hadn't been raw from scratching, at least not that Melissa had noticed. This had to mean that

Kate wasn't the first girl to be held captive here. She stood and stared at the door. The detectives had been right. There was a serial out there hunting girls like herself. Her throat choked up and her eyes watered instinctively. She forced herself to breathe deeply until she had regained her composure. If a multitude of girls had been imprisoned here, then the likelihood of her finding a way out that the previous prisoners hadn't was incredibly low. This moved her to the next question. How long would she be held here before he tired of her and ended her the way he had Kate?

Her eyes shut as she focused on not completely losing it mentally. She bounced up and down on the balls of her feet, feeling her loose hair bounce a fraction of a second after her heels hit the ground. Kate would never feel her ponytail spinning around while she was flipping in the air before landing in the grass and picking up her pom-poms. This thought didn't help with regaining her composure. She sat cross-legged on the floor beside the door. She didn't want to sit next to Kate's corpse again. She didn't think she could. She had never thought of herself as particularly squeamish since she didn't have any problems with dissecting things in Biology. But now that she was presented with the dead body of someone she had known, she was torn between hopelessness, fear, and nausea. A chill ran down her spine as she recalled watching him pull back his arm and then letting his fists fly. He had been unstoppable in his resolve. He had tunnel vision and couldn't stop until his single task had been completed. Melissa shuddered. If Kate hadn't said anything, it could have been her who had been killed instead of Kate.

Melissa recognized what was happening; despair and panic had finally settled in. She couldn't keep it at bay any longer. The rush of emotions took over and she began to shake violently. Kate had been wrong. Melissa wasn't handling this well, she wasn't calm. Things had just started to go well for her at home. She had made friends. There was a boy interested in her. She had finally made flyer on the cheer squad, even though it was clear Mia still hated her. Things were finally falling into place and she was building a life. Now she could kiss all that goodbye. She had once thought that if she disappeared only her brother would miss her. That was all different now. She knew for a fact that people would notice and miss her. She rocked side to side, hoping the movement would help disperse her thoughts.

She placed her hands on the floor, hoping to steady herself. Instead, her fingers found even more scratches. But as she felt them, she realized they weren't random. They were tally marks. But what were they counting? What was there to count besides the days? Her eyes widened in fear as she let her fingers cruise over them all, feeling how many sets of five there were. They were a count of how many days someone had spent here. She pulled her arms back and wrapped them tight around her torso, hugging herself. The tears flowed freely now down her cheeks.

What did he do to the girls while he had them held captive here? Kate said he had left her alone. She didn't think this was the norm though because he also had known he had taken the wrong girl this time. It was possible he left Kate alone because he knew she wasn't the girl he wanted. Melissa shuddered, letting her mind go to the gutter thinking of all the possible things he could do to her.

With renewed vigor, she pushed herself off the floor and paced the room again, taking a better look at her surroundings. She immediately spotted the air vent and dismissed it just as quickly. There was no way she could reach it, even with the bucket turned upside down underneath it. She was too short at 5'3". The door was of course locked. Besides that, there was literally no way to the outside world. There was no light switch or lightbulb hanging from the ceiling. She wondered if there was even any electricity in the building. If there wasn't any electricity then she debated where in city limits she was being kept. It couldn't be too far from home she thought. She hadn't thought she had been unconscious for that long. Maybe she was wrong though, maybe she had been out for a lengthy amount of time.

2017, Day 13

Anderson and Luke found themselves at the Ugly Mug again, claiming the back corner table as their own. They sat in cushy, forest green armchairs with a standup lamp behind Luke's, casting light onto the table at an angle. Luke had, surprisingly, jumped at the chance for coffee when Anderson had mentioned needing more caffeine before looking at the pictures on his phone. She had a suspicion they needed to walk through the field. Her gut was telling her that what they were looking for would be there, somewhere. Luke plopped down in the chair across from her and sipped his two-sugars-no-cream-coffee and let out a sigh of happiness.

"It's the little things, you know," he said contentedly.

"I thought you didn't drink coffee."

"I don't usually, but sometimes, you just need the caffeine."

She gave him a small smile. It wasn't necessarily an agreement, but she also wasn't disagreeing. She wished she could find happiness in the small things like he could. That had always been Charlie's role in the relationship. She was always the naysayer and he had always cast her doubts and pessimism to the side with his positivity.

Luke pulled his phone out and pulled up the camera roll. The first snapshot of the group was of a photograph that Dachs had. Even on the phone screen, they could tell that the picture had been looked at often over the years, it was covered in wrinkles and fingerprints graced both the left and right sides where it had been held. It was a picture of a girl in sweatpants and a loose t-shirt sitting on a couch. She tenderly held a bundle close to her chest. From behind a curtain of blonde hair, a pair of blue eyes and a huge grin beamed up at whoever was taking the picture. The cloth of the bundle fell in just a way that you could see a sweet, bright pink baby face peeking out. Alice and John. It was an intimate photo, taken from the privacy of her home with a smile reserved for someone special. Alice looked so similar to Kate and Melissa. Even Jamie.

"Do you think he took this? Or did she give it to him?" asked Anderson.

"I think it doesn't matter. Either way, this proves they were together. Or that he was obsessed with her." Luke thumbed over to the next picture.

It was a handwritten letter with splotches sprinkling the page, wet spots that had made the ink bleed and hard to read in places. Tear stains? Anderson glanced up at Luke for permission before zooming in so that she could read it. It was wrought with raw emotion. Alice was being forced to end things with Dachs. Her mother thought he was unstable. When Alice had initially refused the order, her mother had given her an ultimatum. Either end things with Dachs and receive financial support for John or stay with Dachs and receive no help. She went on to explain that even though she wished to stay with him and that it broke her heart, she could not. She needed to think of the child's future. She couldn't raise him on her own, she needed the help and security that her mother could provide.

Could he have been in the car when she had crashed? The report had only mentioned Alice and John being in the car. Could they have been arguing about this? If Dachs was as unstable as Alice's mother thought and his school file said, then he was quick to anger. With all of these factors, it was no surprise that there had been an accident.

Anderson and Luke were looking at the catalyst of it all. This one letter, moment, argument, had catapulted an already volatile teen into completely losing his mind and grasp on reality. And now he was a serial killer with two teen girls held captive somewhere in their city. Anderson zoomed out from the photo and leaned back in her chair, taking a long sip from her coffee. She tried to think of nothing but the warmth of the liquid spreading through her body. Neither of them spoke for a minute, they merely sat in silence. The stillness of the moment swept over Anderson. She was suddenly exhausted, despite the copious amounts of caffeine. She chided herself, only half the job was done, and it was the easy part. They still had to catch him and bring the girls home, hopefully, alive and well.

Luke cleared his throat, drawing her attention back to the real world outside of her mind. She raised her eyebrows at him, indicating that she was listening.

"You were right. I'm sorry I didn't believe you at the beginning. I'm glad that you didn't let me dissuade you from pursuing this. I know I was pushing looking into Mia and boys a lot."

She didn't respond, she didn't think she needed to. The shrill tone of Luke's phone ringing pierced the silence, breaking whatever bonding moment it was that they were having.

"It's Williams," he said to Anderson before standing and walking outside with it. While she waited for him to return, she shot off another text to her dad asking him to call her when he had a minute, that it was really quite important and needed to be discussed today. Then, on her phone, she pulled up a map of the neighborhood that included the field. She zoomed in on the details of the field. It was fairly common knowledge that if you hiked long enough through it, you would eventually run into the woods.

Luke plopped back down into his chair, startling her. She hadn't noticed him come back inside. He picked up his coffee and let her stew for a few seconds until she finally had to prompt him.

"So? What did Williams have to say?"

"Well. It sounds like our boy Dachs spent his mother's savings on commissioning the building of a shack next to Miller's Pond."

"In Miller's Woods?"

"That's the one."

"She had enough money saved up?"

"Well, as it happens, she is the last of the actual members of the Miller family. So firstly, she owns the land, or she did when she was alive. The main strain of the family died off, losing the Miller name. Because of all the female descendants and married names, the Miller name was lost."

"This has got to be the craziest case." She sat stunned, not sure what else to say, and turned her attention back to her phone. She zoomed in on the woods and easily found the pond. The photo must have been old though because there was no shack on the map. She glanced back up at him, "How in the world did he get permits to build there?"

Luke shrugged his shoulders. "Miller's Will left the property to the nearest descendent. And she, in turn, left everything to Dachs when she died."

"Why didn't Dachs's mother make use of it?"

"That part is unclear. But what we do know is that after the mother's death, Dachs spent a lot of time at the library looking at local historical documents. I called Alvirez and had him track all his cards and there was a lot of use of his library cards. He could have easily pieced it all together. Then all he would have had to do when getting permits is prove his rights to the land. As long as the shack was built within certain dimensions he wouldn't even have to be taxed, because it wouldn't be considered a house."

Anderson nodded. "So what are we waiting for? Let's go."

"I already asked Williams and Alvirez to bring back up and meet us at the field."

The two downed the rest of their coffees and rushed out the door. They wanted to be the first ones on the scene so they could take charge of the search as soon as everyone arrived. They needed to search not only the shack but the immediate surrounding area. Clearly, Dachs had chosen this area for a reason and he had the upper hand with years of intimate knowledge of the area. Add to this that evening was quickly closing in and the dark was approaching. They would need flashlights and all the manpower they could get. Anderson let herself smile. The end was in sight.

Unknown Year, Day 572

Her wrists felt like they were on fire. There were stiff bandages wrapped tightly around them, almost tight enough to be considered a tourniquet. She lay on the mattress staring at the ceiling. She had not succeeded in her escape. She didn't remember what had happened. All she knew was that she had eventually passed out from the blood loss and she had awoken with her wrists bandaged. He must have found her right after she passed out, just in time to save her. Maybe she had lost enough blood that she could still fall asleep and not wake up again. She highly doubted it though.

She was angry with herself. She should have tried sooner and she should have cut deeper. It was too late now to think about it. She hadn't moved yet to see if He had found her bobby pin and removed it from the room, but she assumed that He had. She was effectively weaponless from here on out. She continued to stare at the ceiling unblinkingly. To say that she had no fight left in her was an understatement. Maybe if she refused to eat and drink water she would just starve and thirst to death. It seemed more pleasant than the alternative. She lifted her head off the mattress and surveyed the room. A tray of food was beside the bed, within reach so that she wouldn't have to go fetch it. How considerate of Him. With little energy, she slowly picked up her arm and pushed the tray away, out of reach. Her stomach grumbled in protest, but she ignored it and rolled over on her side, away from the tray so that she couldn't even look at it. If she couldn't see it, then she could pretend it wasn't there at all. If she could just make it through the first day or two then it wouldn't be so bad. She must have been unconscious for a long time because she couldn't remember being this hungry in a while. She had been behaving herself so well that He hadn't felt the need to skip giving her a meal. Her stomach panged with hunger. Of course, now that she was thinking about it, it was more noticeable.

To distract herself, she examined the bandages. They were nowhere near professionally done. He didn't know what He was doing. At least she could assume that He wasn't a doctor of some sort. Slowly, she began unwrapping her left wrist. She wanted to see how He had saved her. The gauzy wrap was stiff with dried blood and looked gross with the brown stains. She reminded herself that it was her own blood when she caught herself trying to grip the gauze on the white, stain-free edges. Finally, the last stretch fell off of her wrist and she stared at her botched up skin. He had tried to stitch her skin back together, but because He had no experience, and she assumed none of the necessary tools, it was sloppily done. He had used thread, and none of the stitch lengths were the same. The thread zig-zagged across her wrist, barely holding her skin together. It was trying to scab over, but the cut was deep. The skin all around it was red and puffy, showing signs of infection. She poked at the tender skin and winced briefly. She became hopeful at the thought of dying from an infection. She rapidly took off the bandage on her other wrist and inspected the cut. It also looked infected. She left the bandages off and hoped that whatever dust was in the air would imbed itself into her wounds.

She forced the smile off her face. Hope was a dangerous thing. It had let her down now for five hundred and seventy-two days. It was possible that her bad luck streak was about to end.

2107, Day 13

They stood at the edge of the field. Their backup had just arrived and for the first time, Anderson felt more than a little daunted by the case. She had only really dealt with crimes of passion, breaking and entering, and the like. She had never come face to face with a perp who had not only planned the kidnapping and murder of not only one, but many people.

The sun was working its way down the cloud-filled sky, casting pinks and oranges in all directions. The lit-up clouds silhouetted the tree line in the distance. They needed to get a move on. She turned back to look at the gathered group of officers that Luke was already briefing. The seriousness of the situation wasn't lost on any one of the officers in front of her. At Luke's final word they paired off and entered the field. The shack wasn't notated on any maps, but they had tracked a Miller's Pond hashtag on Instagram and a general idea of where to look had emerged.

Once they found the shack, all the officers were instructed to radio out the location. Anderson and Luke wanted to be the first ones to enter the building.

The tall, wet grass made swooshing sounds against their pant legs, the sound put her on edge. She worried that the sun would disappear by the time they reached the forest. She wasn't fond of the idea of stumbling around in the forest blind. She flicked on the flashlight she had snatched from the trunk of Luke's car. She held it so that it lit up only the area in which Luke and her were about to walk through. He used the beam of his own flashlight to comb the surrounding area. It took them a shorter amount of time than expected to reach the forest edge.

No one had found anything in the field. The silence echoed in her ears, and she jumped when the radio sparked into life. She was only slightly disappointed when they were radioed by one of the boys that the shack had been found. A small piece of her wanted to be the one who found it.

The two picked their way without a trail to the southeast corner of the pond. Only a few of the officers had arrived at the location so far. Luke took the lead stepping toward the unpainted shelter. The lone window on one side was covered with a curtain, but a small glow peeked through around the edges. Someone was home. He grasped the doorknob silently and slowly pushed the door inward. Anderson was close behind, following him into the small shelter. The walls were undecorated, much like his bedroom in his childhood home. There was a lone chair with a table beside it. The lantern on the table was lit, the flame being the only source of light in the room.

"Detectives." The man in the chair greeted them as if he had been expecting them for a while now.

"Richard Dachs." Luke approached the chair.

The man nodded. He wore beige slacks and a white button-down shirt. His brown hair was held back from his face by the reading glasses that had been hastily shoved to the top of his head. Anderson was captivated by how huge his hands were, and that his knuckles were bruised and caked with dried blood. His shirt had matching splatters.

"I need you to put your hands above your head and get out of the chair," instructed Luke.

"You'll never find her." Dachs smiled tauntingly, but he followed orders. He was tall once he had unfolded himself from the wooden chair. He was roughly a head taller than Luke.

"Who won't we find Richard?" asked Anderson.

For the first time since they had entered, Dachs swiveled his head to look at her. He held her in his gaze, his eyes piercing right through her.

"Alice, of course." His lips curled into a devilish smile.

He was insane. He had completely cracked. She knew that he actually believed that he had Alice somewhere. Luke was cuffing him now. Anderson glanced around the room. There was nothing here. No other rooms to explore, no rugs to check under for trapdoors. Nothing to suggest another room where he held the girls. They were nowhere closer to finding Melissa and Kate. She hoped that by the sight of his beaten hands, that they weren't already too late.

"Where are they? We know you have two girls." She stated. She didn't expect to get any real sort of answer from him. He was too delusional for that.

"They?"

Anderson didn't respond. She was going to wait this out. He seemed to be enjoying this too much. This was a game to him. She glanced at Luke to see if he had picked up the same thing. He was frowning at the back of Dachs's head. He had at least picked up that something was wrong with him mentally, that the man was unstable. The smile was fading from Dachs' face.

"One of them wasn't Alice."

"What did you do to the imposter?" If she played his game, maybe he would reveal too much.

The smile came back. "I took care of the imposter. There is only one Alice."

"And after that?"

He shook his head.

"Luke, get him in a squad car. I think the girls are nearby."

The smile completely slipped from his face. He wouldn't want them to be too far away. He needed them to be nearby so that he could mess with them when he felt the urge. Luke took two officers with him to escort Dachs to a squad car. The remaining officers were to stay and help Anderson comb the immediate area surrounding the shack for anything out of place, something that might indicate where the girls were being kept. Anderson had another one of her hunches and stuck to the bushes, anything off the trail and heavily overgrown.

2017, Day 13

This had to be the longest day ever. She was huddled in a corner now, her knees pulled to her chest. She was shaking violently from the cold. The cement did nothing to provide any heat. She was glad that unlike Kate, she had at least been snatched when she had been wearing a jacket. It was zipped all the way up, providing a tiny layer of protection around her neck as well. She had both arms wrapped tightly around her legs. Her fingers were numb, but she gripped at her calves as hard as she could. The sleeves of the jacket weren't quite long enough to pull down over her hands, leaving them exposed to the cold of the room. She had her face tucked between her knees, hiding from the reality of what she was surrounded by. She couldn't bear to look at it. She couldn't look at Kate anymore. The lifeless body was just a sack of skin and bones now and was a constant reminder of what would probably happen to her as well. It had hardly been a day in here alone and she was already losing it. How did Kate last two weeks? Melissa's eyes flicked back to the corpse on the other side of the room. Kate didn't have to deal with that.

She shook her head, violently tossing blonde curls everywhere, blurring her vision. No matter how much she shook, she couldn't dislodge the voices in her head. She couldn't understand what they were saying, they were just mumblings with indistinguishable syllables.

Confused, she lifted her head and surveyed the room. No one was there. She rested her chin on the tops of her knees and tried to listen. There were several voices, one female and two male. One of the male voices was gruff and low, the other was deep and resonant; the kind of voice that if you were standing beside the man, you would feel it vibrating your bones. Melissa let out a sharp Ha. She was giving character to the voices in her head now. She was going to go seriously crazy in here. It would become a necessity to have distractions.

Forcing herself into movement, her body lurched forward to standing. Physical activity could help her mindset. She glanced at Kate's unmoving body again.

"So, Kate; which warm-up do you want to do today?" Melissa pretended she was back in cheer practice and Kate was still captain. From across the room, mid jumping jack is when she noticed the air vent near the ceiling. It took her a minute to really register what she was seeing and what it meant. Maybe those voices weren't in her head after all. If she could hear people through the vent then she couldn't be too far away from them, or the surface.

2017, Day 13

After taking Dachs, the group had split. Three officers had stayed in the shack to search it and catalog everything there. The rest of the group was helping to search the woods. Anderson was standing at the edge of Miller's Pond, staring into the abyss. The sun had set and the blackness of the sky blended with the emptiness of the water. The view before her was empty, a black void. It held nothing of substance. She doubted they would find the girls tonight. They would need to regroup at daybreak. She could feel the stress in her face, tightening the muscles, and weighing her down. She stifled a yawn. It had been twenty hours since she had awoken that morning. It wasn't like she was really getting much sleep these days, not with this case on her mind, or everything with Caleb going on. Her dad still hadn't called her back. Did she not sound urgent enough in her voicemail? She glanced at the glowing phone screen, showing that she had no missed calls or messages. She angrily pocketed the useless device and ran her free hand through her cropped locks with a long sigh. Today's victory felt pointless without the girls. She met Luke's gaze. He was waiting for her before moving on to a different pond edge, he didn't want to leave her alone in the dark. She trudged through the mossy underbrush away from the water.

2017, Day 13

Melissa listened to the voices fade. Whatever hope had bubbled up slowly dissipated and she was left even more broken and empty than before. She dropped to the floor beside the mattress and lost all control. The sobs erupted from her chest, scratching her throat up. She couldn't catch her breath as the tears pulled down her cheeks, salty wet trails carving into her skin. She wasn't sure how loud she was actually being, but the noise bounced off the walls and echoed around, taunting her. Her own weeping, laughing at her.

Unknown Year, Day 792

She had finally stopped counting the days. It didn't matter anymore. She was sure she had lost count at some point. And it wasn't as if she was getting out of here. She was trapped for her eternity, and she was certain that to Him she was just a fleeting moment. She wouldn't be the last. She longed for the day that He tired of her, the day it would all end. She wanted it, craved it, needed it. She supposed that if she wasn't such a wuss that she could end it all by smashing her head into the walls. She didn't have the nerve, the thought put a metallic taste in her mouth. Instead, she sat in self-loathing and stared at the door. Every time it opened she hoped it would be the day. He didn't seem to be in any hurry though. She had a feeling that she had to wait for a while yet. She slammed both fists into the floor, screaming from the jolt of pain that shot up through her wrists and arms. Anything was better than the ever-present numbness.

2017, Day 14

The clock had finally struck midnight. A layer of fog sat on top of the pond, preventing the starlight from reflecting off the water. The cold air wrapped itself around Anderson's small frame and squeezed, leaving her slightly breathless. She watched her breath take shape in front of her, floating away and mixing with the mist that was seeping through the forest.

"Emz, we have him. He can't hurt the girls tonight. Let's get a few hours of shut eye and reconvene here when our brains are clear."

She dragged her eyes from the pond and to the shadow that was his figure. She didn't agree, but she let him lead her back to the field where the rest of the offices were starting to gather. She was disappointed. She had been so sure they would end this tonight. They made plans to meet in the a.m. with troops, fresh-eyed. Luke dropped her at her car not much later. She started to climb out when he stopped her.

"Emz, we'll find them. This isn't defeat."

She was too tired to tell him not to call her that. She merely nodded and continued on her way.

2017, Day 14

"No!" she screamed. Melissa could hear the voices getting more distant. "I'm here! Please!" The voices were gone. She sank to the floor and broke down sobbing. How could they not hear her? She could hear them. Shouldn't it go both ways?

The silence was oppressive, pressing on her from all sides, suffocating her. It was worse than the cold. She was next to Kate again.

"We were so close, Kate," she told the still girl. "We're going home soon. I promise. The voices will be back. I know it." She had to bring Kate home to her parents. It was only fair. It was her fault the dead girl had been taken in the first place. Exhaustion consumed her, whisking her away to dreams of a better place, a better time.

2017, Day 14

Anderson slept, but she felt unrested when she woke. She got the pot of coffee started and jumped in the shower, turning the water knob as cold as she could stand, hoping it would shock the sleepiness from her body. When she was done, the air in her bedroom caressed her skin, stealing the goosebumps from her flesh. She dressed and trudged to the kitchen to pour herself a mug. Anderson inhaled deeply, closing her eyes. This was one of her favorite scents. When she was finally ready she sent Luke a message to meet her at the field when he could. Her phone glowed, showing the time as six a.m. Who needs sleep? There were two girls still missing—they were more important.

The sun was just rising over the meadow as, alone, Emily picked her way through the tall, untended grass. She was dressed for the hiking, this time in jeans that were tucked into all-weather boots. The treads on the bottoms of her shoes helped her keep her balance as she traversed the uneven earth with all the gopher holes. The sun's warmth fought for control of the sky after the night's chill. She watched the steam rise off the grass as the rays from the sun melted the morning dew. Emily choked back the hopeful feeling that began to bubble in the back of her mind. Hope was for suckers, she needed to stay rational and logical. The tree line loomed before her, dark and as uninviting as ever.

It seemed to her that Dachs would keep the girls someplace close to him, someplace easy to keep an eye on. His cabin was in the woods, thus the girls would also be somewhere in the woods, preferably a place he had access to that others would not. They had already conducted a search of the cabin that had resulted in nothing, no hidden trapdoors, or rooms, or passageways. A second look through wouldn't hurt though. She pushed her way through the branch and bushes, mud trying to suck her shoes further down into the earth. She stopped a few yards back and gazed at the small, three room building. The wood was weather-worn and looked as if it was beginning to rot. Moss grew up the sides, blending the shack in with the rest of its surroundings. The shutters of the windows were firmly closed, solidifying the desolate feel of the place. A shiver ran through her and she tried to shake it off. The full trees blocked the light of the rising sun as well as its warmth. She noticed now, without all her comrades around her filling the space, how still and silent it was. There were no birds chirping, and no squirrels rustling in the trees, everything was still. She didn't like this place, no one did. It felt unnatural. She found herself rushing forward, towards the little shack, wanting to get away from the odd silence outside.

The door slammed shut behind her, making her jump. For the second time in twelve hours, she surveyed the room. One armchair in the back right corner, a fireplace in the middle of the back wall. A small bunk was pushed against the wall to her right, sheets untucked and loose. Two doors to the left beside each other led to a tiny lavatory and a small, bare-minimum cooking space. Besides the stack of a change of clothes at the end of the bed, the room was bare. It reminded her of his teenage room at his mother's house: no books, photos, or unnecessary sentiment. There had to be a secret place, like his old bedroom, where he hid away his valuables.

She started with the obvious, checking underneath and behind anything movable, meaning the scant furniture and the stack of clothes. Next, she investigated the bathroom. There was a large basin in which to bathe in, a bucket beside it, which she assumed he retrieved water from the pond since the shack had no running water. There was a small mirror tacked to the wall, just large enough to see one's face in a shelf just below this held a cup with a toothbrush, and a bar of soap. A sink with no faucets or knobs, but a drain that on further inspection led to the outhouse style toilet.

She gently pushed every floorboard with the toes of her left foot, nothing was loose. She tried moving the basin, and checked under the bucket, behind the mirror. Nothing presented itself to her. Her phone buzzed, she tried to ignore it, this early it must be Luke, but it continued to vibrate in her pocket. She didn't even look at the caller ID, merely slid the answer button across the screen to unlock it while she continued to rummage around the room.

"Anderson speaking."

"Hi, honey. Sorry I couldn't call you yesterday."

"Dad. Hi. You caught me off guard, I wasn't expecting you to call this early."

"I can call you back later—"

"No, Dad, now is fine. This is important." She paused, not sure how to begin.

"What's going on, sweetie?"

"Well, I know last time I saw you we talked about getting Caleb help. And I've been wondering how he affords his habit, besides the bits and baubles that he takes from me when he visits. But, I've got it figured out finally."

"Okay," he sounded hesitant as if knowing and being forced to deal with the situation was such a bad thing.

She needed fresh air, it was too closed off in here, she could feel her throat closing up. The sun was up and shone through the foliage in the little spurts.

"Dad, I don't know how to put this. Tracy's funding it."

Silence.

"Dad?"

"Why would she do a thing like that?"

"I don't know. I just know that she is. Haven't you noticed any chunks of cash missing?"

He made a noncommittal grunt. So he had noticed and just hadn't asked where the money was going. A twig snapped somewhere behind her, breaking the stillness. She twirled around, eyes darting everywhere until they settled on Luke. He had both hands up and a guilty expression on his face. How much had he heard?

"Dad, I really gotta go. My partner just got here and we're trying to wrap this case up. This is in your hands now. Let me know when you make a decision on what you want to do.”

She shoved her phone back in her pocket after hanging up and sent Luke a reproachful look. “Took you long enough to get here.” She grumbled, leading the way inside.

2017, Day 14

Her muscles were stiff and hurt from sleeping on the floor. Kate’s body seemed to emanate a chill, Melissa shivered and wrapped her arms around her torso. A yawn slipped out. How long had she been asleep and why had she woken up? The voices were back. She leapt to her feet and bounded across the room to place herself under the air vent, and began shrieking. The voices stopped. Were they gone already or had they heard her?

She yelled again. “I’m here! Please!”

She heard…something. It wasn’t clear enough to understand, but it seemed they heard her. She sat underneath the vent just in case, by some miracle, they figured out a way to communicate. As she waited, her stomach began to grumble and her throat felt parched. When was the last time he had come with food? She dropped her forehead to her knees and settled in to wait.

2017, Day 14

They had barely reached the door when they heard a muffled shout. No one was in the clearing with them. Distant muffling of some sort.

"Emz, here." Luke had pulled back a few bushes and was pointing at an air vent covered in rust and moss, on the side of the shack.

"There has to be a basement to this place," she said. "But I couldn't find an entrance inside."

"So, maybe it's outside. If the vent is here, then the door has got to be nearby."

It took them about an hour to find the small trapdoor with the rusted handle tucked under a cedar tree with low-hanging branches. Once the door was dropped open Anderson stepped back a few paces. Even with the door open, it was hidden by a low-growing Dutchman's Breeches. Poison oak lined the other side of the door and the two detectives hugged the left side to avoid the branches that stretched out. Once they had ducked inside and had begun to descend the steps, Luke found a light switch on the wall. A single bulb at the bottom of the staircase flickered momentarily before creating a solid yellow glow in the confined space. Anderson led the way down. She paused briefly at the bottom when they were face to face with a dead bolted door.

"We should probably call the medics. Who knows what we'll find behind this door." Luke said this as he pulled his phone out and began to dial. She barely even registered his words, the sound of her heart beating drowned out everything else. Time slowed and her eyes zeroed in on the door as if it was the only thing that existed. She couldn't hear anything from the other side of it. Luke gently brushed her aside and unbolted it. The heavy door swung inward, letting light into the next room like a tunnel, illuminating just a sliver of the floor. Anderson's eyes followed Luke's back as he entered the room. Her breathing shortened and quickened. Why couldn't she move her feet?

2017, Day 14

She was curled in a ball with her head resting on her knees still when the door opened. Slowly, she lifted her red eyes to see him. Her eyes ached and were dried out from all the crying she had done. He looked young, maybe early thirties, with chocolate brown hair. Her stomach banged at the thought of food. He was hesitant as moved closer and she saw him glance at Kate.

"She's dead." Her voice sounded emotionless. She hoped he didn't hold it against her, she was just emotionally drained and tired. It was over. Relief flooded through her and she dropped her head again. It was too heavy to hold up any longer and now she didn't need to hold herself up.

"Melissa?"

"Yes." She croaked, her voice cracking at the end.

"I'm detective Luke Zappone. We've met before, but I don't know if you remember me. We've been looking for you. Your brother has been very worried."

"Is he okay?"

"He's at home with your mother."

Her head snapped up. "Alone?" She had a desperate need to get home. He had never been home alone with their mother before.

"Right now you just need to focus on getting out of here and getting some food into your system."

"What about her?" Melissa directed her gaze to Kate. She didn't want to leave the other girl.

"Let me worry about that. Come on." He held out a hand to her, letting her be the one to initiate contact if she wanted it. She reached out her hand and let him pull her to her feet. She looked back at Kate again, the sense of dread and betrayal for leaving her behind grew in her chest. He supported most of her weight. She was too weak from the lack of food. Once they were in the outer room they walked past another woman. She looked disheveled and tired. Her pants were covered in small twigs and leaves and there were coffee stains on her shirt. She seemed to be frozen in place, staring into the room.

Melissa looked at Luke, "What's wrong with her?"

He shook his head and didn't say anything.

2017, Day 14

"Emz."

There was a hand on her shoulder, shaking her out of her trance.

"My sister used to call me that." Anderson finally turned to look at Luke.

Understanding passed over his face, he finally knew why she was opposed to the nickname. He held up both hands in an apologetic gesture.

She shrugged noncommittally. "So tell me."

"Melissa was locked in that room. We've already gotten her to the hospital to be looked at by a doctor. Officer Williams is with her."

"And Kate?"

He hesitated for a moment before responding. "She was already dead when we got here."

"Melissa was locked in a room with a dead girl?"

"Yeah. It looked brutal, too. She was beaten to death. Poor Melissa didn't want to leave her behind."

Anderson closed her eyes and shuddered.

"I'm sorry, -. I know this isn't how we hoped it would pan out. But we need to move on. Come on."

2017, Day 17

Emily sat in one of the cozy chairs in the back of the room and kept an eye on the door at the front. He was late. He was never late. It was making her nervous. She was supposed to be the late one, not him. He had always been the one to rush her to get her out of the house on time. Her mocha grew cold on the table in front of her, untouched and full. She glanced at the clock behind the barista bar. Five minutes past the hour. The bells above the door jangled and she sat up straighter, expectantly staring at the door. It wasn't him. She leaned back into her chair again. Where the hell was he? She checked her phone, no new messages.

"Hey."

She looked up from her phone. "Damn it, Luke. What are you doing here?"

"They have the best herbal tea choices here. Mind if I sit?"

"I'm kind of waiting for someone." She glanced around. Hell. He wasn't coming. If he was, he would've been here ten minutes ago. "You know what. Sure. Sit."

Luke raised an eyebrow at her but sat across from her with his steaming tea. "Your drink looks cold."

"It is cold."

"Wow. You let perfectly good coffee get cold. What are you nervous about?"

"I'm meeting Charlie." She choked the words out.

"Did you get your ring back from your brother?"

She shook her head. "No, it's gone."

"I'm sorry, Emily. So why are you guys meeting?"

She raised an eyebrow. "No more nickname? You're easy to train."

"Only when I know the reason why."

She checked her phone again. Fifteen minutes late. She cleared her throat. "So uh, I don't know. He called yesterday and asked to meet. I guess to chat? I don't know."

"Well, I can leave if you want." Luke offered, but he made no move to stand and leave her on her own. She found that she didn't want to be left alone either.

"Anything new with your brother?'

"Actually, Dad stuck him in a rehabilitation facility up north. Hopefully, things will be looking up soon. He and Tracy have decided to go to marriage counseling." She found this ironic since what landed them in therapy was her striving to have the perfect family.

"Good. I'm glad." He swirled his tea, watching the steam rise before he took a small sip.

"So how are you and Amy doing? You haven't mentioned her in a while."

He glanced down at the table. "Actually. We're not together anymore."

Anderson reached across the table and took his hand with hers. "I'm so sorry. I know you really liked her."

He shrugged nonchalantly. "It's alright. When it came down to it she couldn't hang with the lifestyle that came with dating a cop. The hours were tearing us apart."

"Yeah, I can understand."

"How are you really doing?" He watched her face as she thought about the question.

"I'm okay. I'm still mulling things over. Mostly I'm mad that the only thing we can actually pin him on is Kate and Melissa. It's not like we found a mass grave or his trophies or anything like that."

"That reminds me, I have your sister's file at my desk. I brought it back from home. Figured I was done with it since we have him."

"We don't have him until he's been charged and convicted of everything he's done. I know he did it to Jamie and Anna. And I will find proof." She stared intently at Luke as she said this. His lips spread into a thin line. He didn't say it, she knew what he was thinking. They sipped their drinks in silence.

A shadow fell over the table. She was too scared to look. Instead, she disentangled one hand from her hair and folded both of them neatly in her lap, trying not to fidget. Luke relinquished his plush armchair. "I'll see you at the station later."

The other figure seated himself across from her. "Are you going to look at me?"

So, she did. She took in the sandy blonde hair, and how his t-shirt pulled nicely across his chest. "Charlie," she breathed, trying not to flinch beneath his gaze. He always had a weird way of looking at her and knowing what she was thinking, and she didn't want him to know what was running through her mind right now. He was the first to break the silence.

"So. How've you been? You look rested for once."

"I'm good. We just closed a big case."

"The one on the news? That was yours?"

"Yeah. Well. It started off as mine. But it got personal so it was given to Luke."

"Personal?"

"Jamie."

"Oh, wow. That's gotta be a huge relief. Finally having the answers."

She shrugged. "I don't know. I feel kinda empty now. I'm not sure what to do next. Anyway, there's still a lot to do before it's over."

Silence again. She picked at the edge of the plastic lid on her to-go cup. His eyes went straight to it. He quietly placed a gentle hand on her fidgeting one.

"Charlie. Why are we here?"

He never took his eyes off their hands. "I want to come home, Emz."

She had dreamed of this moment. Hoped for it, and wished for it. But she had never expected it. She had always thought that she would be the one to break down and call him.

"Emz?"

"Huh?"

"What do you think?" He was finally holding her gaze, and she really saw him this time. The bags under his eyes, the redness to his pupils. His skin was pale next to his blonde hair. He didn't look good. His hair was greasy and disheveled.

"Well…" she stuttered, unsure of what to say. "I honestly don't know." She was surprised by her own words. "I don't know if I can be with someone who can walk away from a relationship so easily. I needed you and you left me. I'm still a mess." She didn't even know she had felt that way. "I'm sorry, Charlie."

She pushed back from the table, picked up her purse and cold coffee, and walked out of the Ugly Mug without a glance back or a second's worth of hesitation.

9 780578 713847